# PRETEND
# YOU *Want* ME

New York Times & USA Today Bestselling Author

# CYNTHIA
# EDEN

# CHAPTER ONE

"You're in great hands, Aspen," Ben Wilde assured her as the elevator doors opened, and he turned to flash her a quick smile. "My brother's protection firm is the best in the business. You don't need to worry any longer."

If only. But she'd been busy worrying for quite some time. Not that Aspen Gray let her worry or her growing nervousness show. She never did. She'd learned long ago that in order to succeed in this world, you always had to project an air of confidence and poise, even when you were so nervous that your knees wanted to knock and it felt as if you might vomit at any moment.

She'd been that nervous the first time she met Ben Wilde. She'd walked into the law school class, surrounded by so many people who were worlds away from the rough life she'd grown up living, and she'd been sure they would realize she was a fraud. The seats in the class had been full...well, except for one chair. The one next to Ben. He'd offered it to her with a wide grin—his trademark smile—and then he'd offered her his friendship.

She was counting on that unwavering friendship to seriously help her out of the rather terrifying situation that she'd found herself facing.

"Complete discretion," Ben assured her as he held the elevator door. His gold wedding ring gleamed. She'd danced at his wedding. Been thrilled for him and his bride. She and Ben had always *only* been friends. It was a rule she had. She never wanted sex to get in the way of a good friendship, and Ben *was* a good friend...so good, in fact, that he'd been willing to help her out, to give her the VIP treatment at his brother's business, after she'd called him out of the blue.

"Discretion is of the utmost importance," she agreed, pleased that her voice came out all cool and steady as she and Ben began walking down the lushly carpeted hallway. The main Wilde office was located in Atlanta, in one of the big skyscrapers, and when her gaze darted to the left—to the line of windows there—she could see the killer view. "That's why, you, ah, mentioned my requirements to your brother?" Aspen asked delicately.

"Don't worry. You're certainly not the first client to want undercover protection. The agents here know the drill. They are all about making a good cover story."

She released a quick breath of relief. *Excellent.* Because the agent she was hiring today—that individual would need to accompany her back to her home in Pensacola, Florida. And then things would get...tricky.

*Be careful what you reveal. Play this game wisely.*

Ben walked them past an assistant and straight to a heavy, wooden door. He didn't pause, just swung it right open with a typical Ben flourish. Her shoulders stiffened, her chin notched up just a bit, and Aspen marched inside to meet the man who would—

*No.*

She stopped. Her eyes were locked on the man behind the desk. A man who wore a black t-shirt that stretched over the muscled arms that were crossed over his chest. A man who wore ragged jeans and dark boots that he currently had propped up on the edge of the gleaming desk. A man who had green eyes that seemed to blaze with electric energy as they pinned her. His face was all hard angles and planes, and he probably *shouldn't* have been handsome. Maybe he wasn't, technically, but he *was* sexy. The kind of rough and hard and hot sexy that just poured naturally from men that you knew were going to be trouble.

And he was currently sweeping that hot stare of his slowly over her body.

"I think there is a mistake," Aspen said immediately. She'd been promised a former soldier. One of those true-blue types who would protect and defend at all costs. She'd specifically requested such a man. Not a guy who seemed like he could easily spend his days hanging at her friend Ramsey's old bar, a place frequented by some of the most dangerous criminals out there.

*I don't need more trouble in my life.* She'd like less, please.

"Yeah, the mistake is that Eric is going to kick your ass for sitting in his chair," Ben fired as he closed in on the other man. "Gideon, you know better. Eric gets oddly territorial about shit like this."

*Gideon* just shrugged his massive shoulders. "Eric got held up. Told me to start the meeting without him." He uncrossed his arms. Pointed one rather large hand toward Aspen. "She the client?"

No, she was just the woman who'd randomly wandered in from the street. Her eyes narrowed on him. Of course, she was the client. But he was *not* the man she'd requested. "I think we need to review my requirements." She sounded prim. Not her intention, but he was throwing her off her game, and when she got thrown off...she tended to get extra icy.

When Ben's gaze cut her way, she realized that he'd noticed her little, ah, tell. He'd figured it out back in their mock courtroom days.

"Requirements, huh?" Gideon nodded. Then he carefully lowered his feet. Slowly rose. And he was a big one. Maybe six-foot-three. All muscle. All power. If she was looking for someone high on the physical intimidation scale, then he'd be a great fit. But she wasn't looking for that so much. She needed...

"Blending," Aspen blurted. "The agent I hire today has to be able to blend into my life. It is imperative that none of my friends or work associates realize that I have hired a Wilde agent." Because the agent's job wasn't just to watch her ass—though that was certainly a bonus. She needed someone to help her find out who the hell was messing with her life. Aspen winced as her stare held Gideon's. "Sorry, but I don't think you are going to blend so well."

His lips hitched into what *could* have been a smile. "You'd be surprised."

Doubtful. Few things surprised her these days. Except, perhaps, the not-so-little matter of *being stalked by a dead man.*

Before she could speak, Aspen heard the door open behind her and fast footsteps entered the office.

"Sorry I'm late," Eric Wilde began in his deep and rumbling voice. "Minor emergency."

She turned toward him, wondering what counted as "minor" in his mind.

Eric grinned at her. He'd always been a bigger, rougher, slightly scarier version of Ben. "Aspen! Great to see you again."

She hurried into his embrace. The Wilde brothers had always been good to her. Maybe too good. If they knew all of her secrets, would they still treat her the same way?

Would anyone?

His arms closed around her. For a moment, she felt safe. Yes, this was what she craved. *Safety.* Wasn't that why she'd turned to Ben? Why she'd used her connection to get in and have this meeting with Eric? She was desperate, and safety was what she needed.

"*Ahem.*" A loud throat cleared. Gideon. "This reunion is touching as hell..." He did not sound as if he meant those words. In fact, he sounded rather annoyed. "But could we get along to the business at hand?"

She backed away from Eric, but held his gaze. "I don't think he is going to do at all." Again, she was prim. *Dammit.*

Eric's eyebrows rose. "Why not? Gideon checks off all your boxes." He walked around her and headed for his desk. He frowned at the chair, then cut a suspicious glance toward Gideon.

Gideon smiled. Almost angelically.

Her stomach did what *had* to be a nervous dip. Because of the situation she was in. *Not* because of that smile. *It had better not be because of that smile.* The last thing she needed was to suddenly develop an attraction to this—this—

Eric lowered into the chair and raised one finger. "You want someone who is former military."

Yes, because she'd been looking for the clean-cut, true-blue—

Another finger. "Someone who is skilled at undercover operations."

Again, yes, because she wanted this guy to *blend* in her life, and big, bad Gideon hardly looked like—

Another finger. "Someone with a track record of success regarding investigation cases."

"Great success," Gideon cut in to say with a roll of one shoulder. "Though, you know, I don't like to brag."

"Since when?" Ben muttered.

Gideon winked at him.

Ben laughed.

Wonderful. So they were all friends. Good for them. But she wasn't looking for a friend or a buddy or—or someone who made her stomach do weird twists. She was looking for a man who could help save her ass *and* keep her secrets.

But, apparently, Eric wasn't done lifting his fingers because now he had a fourth finger up in the air. "You wanted someone who could move to your home and stay there for an indefinite period of time."

Gideon's eyes were on hers. "I think a beach trip sounds great."

She would *not* growl at him.

A fifth finger was up in the air. Eric might as well be waving at her. "You also wanted someone who was not afraid to get his hands dirty."

"I like being dirty," came from Gideon.

She swallowed. "I just bet you do."

He flashed that *angelic* grin, and she blushed. *Blushed*. What in the hell?

"Were there other criteria that I missed?" Eric wanted to know. "Because if so..."

"He has to play my lover," she said with her spine as straight as could be and her chin still up. "He has to be comfortable acting like we're romantically involved. *Other* people have to buy that we are together. I can't have anyone in my life back home knowing what is happening." Because then there would be too many questions. Questions that she could not—would not— answer.

"Don't worry." Gideon stalked toward her. "I know the drill." *Closer. Closer.* His scent—crisp, masculine, and oddly compelling—wrapped around her. "Not my first time at bat."

Fabulous to know.

He stopped right in front of her. His green gaze seemed to burn. "I've done this gig before."

Good for him. Why was it so hot in there?

"I play your boyfriend. I stare at you like you're the only person in the world."

Um, his stare was pretty intense.

"I get pissy as hell when other men get close because I'm possessive, and I want everyone to know you're mine."

Okay...

"I stay close to you because I can't stand the idea of you being separated from me."

His voice had gone all growly and...hot. And she had to admit... "Fine," Aspen snapped. "You can act like you want me. Got it." *Someone give this man a cookie.*

His long lashes—why were his lashes so thick, damn him—lowered. "Right. I can act like I want you." He backed up a step.

She sucked in a breath. "It's just..." *Find a way to explain this!* "My associates know the type of man I am usually with. It's not—"

"Me?" he finished. His lips quirked, and Gideon jerked a thumb toward Ben. "Let me guess...you're usually with someone like him. Fancy suit."

"Thanks for noticing it," Ben replied with a pleased smile. "I bought it last week."

"Perfectly styled hair. Pretty boy face."

"Hey!" Now Ben was annoyed. "I like the phrase 'classically handsome' if you don't mind."

Gideon grunted. She took that to mean he did mind. Or maybe he just didn't give a fuck. Fair enough. He continued, "I can be anyone. Not an issue. You want me in a suit, I'll wear a suit. You want me to cut my hair. I'll cut the hair. Doesn't matter how I look, though, what matters is that I do the job." His gaze still held hers. Still burned. "And trust me, anyone who sees us together will believe that I want you more than anything else. I will sell that we're lovers, and then I'll do the important part of my job." His eyes narrowed. "I'll protect you. I'll make sure you can sleep well at night. And I'll find whoever the hell it is that has you running to Wilde because you're so scared." A brief pause. "Even though you do a damn good job at hiding your fear."

"You have a very good sales pitch," Aspen allowed as she smoothed her hands over the front of her black pants.

"Thanks for noticing."

She knew he'd deliberately thrown out the same words Ben had used. Her breath rushed out. "Are you really good or are you just being cocky?"

"I'm not good. I'm fucking fantastic."

Her heart surged in her chest, and Aspen slanted a glance toward Eric.

He'd lowered his hand. Eric's expression was serious as he inclined his head. "I was lucky to have Gideon join my team. He's former Delta Force, and one of the toughest badasses I know."

"Now you're just flattering me."

When she glanced back at Gideon, she found his eyes were still on her.

"He's got a case closure rate that can't be beat, and I can give you a list of his previous clients who will all vouch for him. He's protected rock stars, tech CEOs, and several heads of state. If you want low profile, he can give you that. If you want safety, he will provide it. I trust him completely or I would not be recommending him to someone I consider a friend." A pause. "You're important, Aspen. Ben and I aren't screwing around with your safety."

"Damn straight," Ben chimed in to say.

Aw, they were so sweet to her. She blinked quickly. Didn't cry. Never cried. But Ben and Eric had no idea just how rattled she really was. Mostly because they didn't know her, not down deep where she kept all of her dark secrets. "Thank you." Okay, time for a reevaluation. She *did* trust Eric. His reputation was first-class, and he'd always been wonderful to her. If he said Gideon was the agent for her then... Aspen held out her hand. "I'm Aspen Gray, and I guess I'm now your girlfriend."

His hand swallowed hers. She could feel the calluses on his fingertips, but his hold was surprisingly gentle. "I'm Gideon Ranier, and I'm the man who'll walk through hell for you."

She licked her lower lip. "Hopefully, that won't be necessary."

His gaze was on her mouth. "You never know..."

\*\*\*

"Kid gloves," Eric Wilde announced flatly.

Gideon watched as the door closed behind his new client. Ben had just taken her out for coffee. An unnecessary move—coffee could have been brought into the boss's office, but Eric had been the one to suggest that Aspen be taken down to the break room...which had been code for...*I want to talk with Gideon alone.*

"You understand me, Gideon?"

He could still smell her. He could have sworn she actually smelled like candy apples. Crazy, right? But at Eric's question, Gideon's head turned, and he met the boss's stare. "I understand. I'll be sure to give her the deluxe treatment."

Eric shook his head. "I'm not screwing around here. Aspen is important to me and my brother."

Yeah, he'd gotten that—her importance had been clear in the way-too-long hug that Eric had given her and the protective pose of Ben's body when he'd been near Aspen. For some reason, both actions had made Gideon feel twitchy. "What's the story there?" He sauntered closer to Eric, acting as if he didn't care but...

*Fuck it. I do.* And that was going to be problematic.

"The story is that she's a client. A true VIP. You'll be on your best behavior with her, and you will damn well make sure that she is safe at all times." Eric looked down at his laptop. Tapped quickly. "I'm assigning Elijah as your backup. He'll stay close for whenever you need him."

It was standard practice at Wilde to send out two agents. But... "Not sure Elijah will go so well with the cover story we have going on."

"He'll be in the background. No exposure. Elijah knows how to stick to the shadows."

Sure, he did. And Eric was trying to distract him. Because just saying that the gorgeous Aspen was a VIP didn't cut it. They had plenty of VIPs. None of those VIPs had ever warranted Gideon being pulled *off* another case and flown in during the middle of the night so that he could be reassigned. Obviously, Aspen was special. "Your brother involved with her?"

Eric glanced up. "Ben is married. Happily."

"But...before. I read her file. She's a lawyer, too. What did they do, hook up in law school?" And *why* was he tensing as he waited for a reply?

Eric shut his laptop. "They are friends. Just as I am *friends* with Aspen. She has been in our lives for a long time, and we value her. Understand?"

Gideon understood that Eric's voice had gone cold and hard. So he nodded. Then took his time approaching the desk. "It would help if I was given more background on her."

"Aspen will tell you everything she wants you to know."

That was nice and vague. "Not usually the way it works." He motioned toward the closed laptop. "Don't you have a dossier prepared on her? One that tells me everything I could ever want to know and *more* about the client?"

"Not in this case. In this case, you are being told that Aspen Gray is a criminal defense attorney from Pensacola, Florida. She is single, has no children, and currently has a stalker in her life."

His back teeth clenched. He hated stalkers. Stalker cases could go bad—very bad—fast. Obsession was always dangerous.

"As for any other material in Aspen's life, she'll tell you what she wants you to know."

And that was some bullshit. "I'm walking in blind?" *Because she's some magical VIP?* "I need to know more in order to figure out the stalker's identity!"

"I'm sure she will reveal more when you're down in Florida with her." It seemed to be a dismissal. "Don't forget your sunscreen."

It *was* a dismissal. "Damn, man. What…does she know where you buried bodies or something?" This was *not* standard operating procedure.

A muscle flexed in Eric's jaw. "When my brother was in his first year of law school, he was partying at a local club."

Sure, fine, he knew Ben enjoyed a good—

"A man tried to rob him when Ben left that night. Ben was with some friends, including Aspen. Most of those friends ran away at the sight of the drawn gun. Aspen lunged in front of my brother right at the same time the robber decided to fire his weapon because he didn't like that Ben wasn't turning over his wallet."

Gideon rocked back on his heels. "Damn."

"She took a bullet to protect my brother. So, yes, she's VIP. She will always be VIP. I don't care what secrets she wants to keep. She can tell me as little or as much as she likes. She'll have protection, and Wilde *will* eliminate any threats that come after her." His eyebrows rose. "Any other questions?"

"Yeah, why the fuck didn't Ben marry her right then and there?" A woman who would jump in front of a friend to protect him? *Put a ring on her finger.*

"Aspen has never been interested in Ben that way. He told me the first day they met, she shut him down on that score. For the best, of course, because we both know how insane Ben is for Courtney."

Yeah, they did.

And Eric was right. The *friend* relationship between Aspen and Ben was definitely for the best because...*I want her.*

*Ben's loss. My gain.* He'd felt the attraction the instant he'd seen her. The surge of awareness that had crackled through every nerve and cell in his body. He'd faked his relaxed pose when Gideon had really wanted to surge to his feet and rush to her and ask...

*Where the hell have you been? I've been waiting for you.*

Ridiculous. Madness.

But the whole world was a little mad.

When the door had opened, her lips had parted. Her eyes had flared. Gorgeous eyes, deep and dark. And she'd sucked in a quick breath. He'd been sure she felt the same attraction, too, but then she'd said, "I think there's a mistake." Her voice had been cool and poised and sensual as she'd tried to fire him...before he'd even really gotten the job.

*You won't get rid of me that easily, sweetheart.* "Don't worry," Gideon assured Eric. "I'll make sure she gets the deluxe treatment from us."

"Yeah, that is not reassuring." Eric's eyes had narrowed. "Your job is to *pretend* that you're involved with her. Not to actually *be* involved with her. There is a difference."

"Sure. Right." He was great at pretending. Did it all the damn time. Acted like he was normal and that a consuming darkness didn't eat at him as he thought of all the battles he'd faced. The friends he'd lost. The lives he'd taken. Yep, he pretended constantly. Smiled when he was supposed to. Headed out with work buddies so he wouldn't look like a hermit. Did all the things while being ice cold inside.

Except he hadn't felt cold when he was near *her*.

It was past time that he went and found his new client. Gideon turned on his heel and marched for the door. Then stopped. "One more question."

"Just one?"

For the moment. Gideon looked over his shoulder. "What happened to the guy who shot her?"

Eric's face tightened. "He got away. Ben was busy stopping the blood flow and working to keep her stable. He didn't see where the bastard went. By the time the cops got there, the shooter was long gone."

The back of Gideon's neck prickled. That happened sometimes. When something felt off. "A robbery," he said.

"Yeah."

"And you *never* tried to find the man who nearly shot your brother? And who *did* shoot your friend? You, with this giant, million-dollar business...?" He wasn't buying it.

Eric's fingers were still pressed to the closed laptop. "I looked."

Sure, he had. "And?"

"And I couldn't find him."

Red flag. Because Eric had a ton of resources.

"The client is waiting," Eric murmured.

"Can't have that." He saluted the boss. "Don't worry, she's in good hands." Once more, he made for the door.

"You're not supposed to put your hands *on* her."

Gideon whistled.

"Gideon! Stay on your best behavior!"

Didn't he always? Oh, no, wait, he didn't. His bad. Gideon opened the door and headed out to find Aspen.

# CHAPTER TWO

Someone was knocking on her hotel room door. Aspen frowned as she glanced over at the clock on the nightstand. Ten p.m. She hadn't ordered room service. There was no reason for anyone to be tapping on her door this late.

She slipped from the bed. Crept for the door.

*What if he followed you? What if he's here?*

She'd thought coming to Atlanta would buy her a few days of safety. A chance to sleep without jerking awake in the middle of the night because she was sure she'd heard someone slipping into her house. It was an old house, a true historic gem that she'd spent months renovating, and it was prone to creaking and shuddering. Cute quirks that she'd once adored. Only now, those quirks terrified her because maybe...maybe the house *wasn't* creaking. Maybe someone was inside with her.

More knocking at her hotel room door. Harder. Louder.

She pressed her palms to the wood of the door and peered through the peephole.

Gideon peered back at her.

She immediately jerked a few inches in surprise. Her fingers flew over the locks, and she hauled the door open. "What in the world are you doing here?"

"Strategizing."

"What?"

He walked forward, and she instinctively fell back a step. Then caught herself. Dammit, no. Her hands flew up and pressed to his chest. His super muscled chest. She could feel the muscles through the soft fabric of his cotton t-shirt. "You can't come in!"

"Well, we can hardly have our conversation in the hallway. That's just inconsiderate when there are other guests nearby." He kicked the door closed and dropped two duffel bags to the floor.

The duffel bags distracted her. "Are you planning to stay the night?"

"Well, I got word that you *did* sign the contract with Wilde this evening..."

Yes, she had. After pausing to think about things once more, she'd finally decided to do it.

"You signed the contract, I packed my stuff, and now I'm reporting for duty."

He wasn't serious. She squinted at him, decided there wasn't enough light to adequately read his expression so she leaned over and punched the light switch near the door. Illumination flooded down on him and...yes. Serious. "You don't need to be here *now*."

"You hired me. Where else would I be?"

"Your home? A bar?" Anywhere else? "Starting tonight is completely unnecessary. You can meet me at the airport in the morning, and we can go over plans as we fly back to Pensacola."

"That's a super short, direct flight."

Granted, but...

"And I think it would be better if we discuss things privately."

Grudgingly, she had to agree on that point. "Fine. We can strategize and then you can leave and I'll go back to bed." That sounded like an excellent plan to her.

He shook his head. "I'll be staying the night."

She threw her hand behind her as she exclaimed, "There is one bed. I don't plan to share it with you." Even though it was a massive, king-size bed.

"Fair enough. I'll just sleep on the floor."

"But—"

"That way, if anyone ever asks, the people at the front desk will be able to say they saw us check-out together. That we'd obviously spent the night together. That you came up to Atlanta to connect with your boyfriend."

"Wh-who would ask?"

"Whoever the hell sent you running to Atlanta." His gaze was steady. "Finding out his identity is part of the strategizing I discussed." Then he walked past her and lowered his big body onto the bed. "Nice jammies, by the way."

She looked down at the silk, black pajama shorts and matching shirt she wore. Hardly super sexy.

"Elegant. Feminine. Classy. Totally you."

He had no idea what she was like. Instead of sitting next to him on the bed, she wheeled over the chair from the desk and placed it a foot away from him. "What do you need for this strategy session?" They'd already talked—albeit briefly—

when he came to find her in the break room at Wilde. She'd gone over some bare-bones details.

She'd started getting late night phone calls. Calls she couldn't track. At first, the caller hadn't said anything but then...

*You're going to pay.*

Then she'd been followed home from work one night. Maybe two nights. Could be more. She hadn't been paying enough attention at the beginning...

"I need to go back to the first point of contact." Gideon's stare was steady. The covers were rumpled behind him, and she tried not to focus on the fact that he took up way too much of her bed. He still wore jeans—faded, casual—and the t-shirt he'd worn earlier, only now he'd also donned a long-sleeved button-up, except it was currently *unbuttoned* and loose. "When did the first phone call start?"

"A month ago."

"And he didn't say anything?"

"Not at first."

A nod. "When he did start talking, what did he say?"

She licked her lower lip. "General, threatening stuff. You know the 'I'll get you' kind of deal. That he was watching me." *That I'd pay.* "That sort of thing."

"Uh, huh." He leaned forward. Put his elbows on his knees. "So, it doesn't work like that."

"Excuse me?"

"If I'm going to do my job, you don't get to lie to me."

It took all of her self-control not to leap out of the chair. "I don't follow." She did. Perfectly.

"If I'm going to help you, I need to know everything. Holding back makes the investigation harder, and it just puts you in more danger. So don't do that."

"What makes you think I'm holding back?" Careful. Tight.

He smiled. "I get this little prickle in the back of my neck when something is off."

"You're not serious."

He shrugged.

"You cannot be serious."

"Call it a primitive response. Instinctive reaction. When things are off, I know."

She started to laugh.

"That primitive response has saved my life more times than I can count."

Her laughter died away.

"Of course, I could also tell you that I know you're lying because when you started speaking, your whole body tensed. You looked away before answering. Your breathing got a little heavier. All signs of deception."

Well, well. There was certainly more to Gideon than met the eye. "They teach you to read body language when you were in Delta Force?"

"No, but I might have picked up some tips on that when I got my undergraduate in psychology." He pursed his lips. "Or maybe it was when I got my Master's. Who knows? Either way, when it comes to deception, when it comes to omission, and when it comes to general shit that doesn't make sense, I *know*. One of the many reasons why

Eric loves me so much." His stare held hers. "So let's try again. What, exactly, did the caller say?"

"He told me that I'd pay." Goosebumps rose onto her arms. "Then he *did* say all the other stuff. That I wouldn't get away from him. That he was watching." This time, she made sure not to look away from his gaze.

"What are you paying for?"

"I have no idea." She jumped to her feet. Immediately regretted the action. Probably looked to him like she was being deceptive. *I am.* "My job is to defend accused criminals. I'm very good at my job, so many of my clients never see the inside of a prison cell." She began to pace. Too much nervous energy fueled her. "Perhaps we're looking at someone who is angry that I got a client off the hook. Or, conversely, could be that it's someone who is furious because a client *did* go to prison. It's not uncommon for defense attorneys to be threatened." More pacing. Her bare feet padded quickly over the carpeting.

"Nice toenail polish. The red is sexy as hell."

Her steps faltered.

"Sorry." He didn't sound sorry. "Just getting into the boyfriend persona. You should expect me to say things like that to you."

Her head whipped toward him. "Not while we're alone."

"Saying them when it's just us gets me in the habit of complimenting you. Makes it easier when others are around."

Suspicion filled her.

"Trust me," he murmured. "I'm the professional. I know how to build a believable cover. You need to get used to me complimenting you." A hesitation. "And touching you. That *will* be expected if you want people to believe I'm your boyfriend."

"Yes, I know you holding my hand or hugging me occasionally will be necessary—"

His bark of laughter cut her off. Her eyes immediately narrowed because the laughter...continued. She waited. Tapped the toes that he seemed to like so much, and, when his laughter finally died away, she gritted out, "So glad I can amuse you."

"Sweetheart..."

Her eyebrows shot up.

Gideon cleared his throat. "That's just me getting into the habit of using endearments."

Uh, huh.

"No man in his right mind—no guy who is *actually* involved with you—would ever be happy just holding your hand or getting the occasional hug. He'd be constantly trying to get you naked and in bed. He'd be kissing you. Caressing you. Trying to get you as hungry and eager as he was. Hell, he'd be worshipping that perfect body of yours."

Now she was the one to swallow. The hotel room was hot, just as Eric's office had been too heated. What was up with these Atlanta rooms? She should adjust the temperature. "Just remember this is all pretend. Nothing real at all about it."

"Pretend. Check." His head cocked to the right. "If acting like my lover is too much for you, I could always pretend to be a long-lost brother."

"No. Everyone knows I have no siblings. Lost or otherwise."

"A friend? A down-on-his-luck guy who is crashing at your place for a few days?"

That was an option, only it was not one she was willing to take. "I need you to pose as my boyfriend."

"Why?"

Aspen realized he'd pushed her directly to this admission. He was staring at her all intense-like, and she understood that Gideon was someone she could not underestimate. To do so would be dangerous for her. "Because my stalker has made some...sexual references to me." *Tread carefully.* "I think having a boyfriend as a shield would work better."

"Because you think this guy might be someone you were involved with in the past?"

She stopped pacing. "It's a possibility."

"You know I'll need a list of all former romantic partners. Those you slept with. Those you didn't."

"How very intrusive."

"Yep." Just that.

She glowered.

"Intrusive is the business. I have a partner on this case, and he'll be working in the shadows, digging up intel on all our suspects. He'll check out the exes and the current associates—business and friends—in your life. He and I will also check out all your past court cases to see if anything shakes loose."

She was the one nearly shaking at the moment. "I just need this to end."

Gideon rose and stalked toward her. "It will. I give you my word—"

A shrill alarm filled the air. So high-pitched and blaring that her ears seemed to tremble. Her heart immediately lurched into her chest then began a frantic, wild rhythm.

"Fire alarm." Gideon reached for her. His fingers curled around her wrist. "We need to go, now."

The blaring continued as he pulled her toward the door. *In her jammies.* "Wait! I need to get clothes—shoes—"

"We need to get *out.*" He yanked open her door. People were already filling the hallway. A wild, nervous din of voices tangled in the air. "Stairs only, and we've got lots of flights waiting."

"But—" Someone bumped into her from behind. Someone who was *running* for the stairs.

"Orderly exit, asshole!" Gideon snarled. His body shifted, and his arm moved to curl around her waist so that he was pulling her closer. Shielding her with his massive form. Then it was pretty much chaos. The alarm was blaring. Kids were crying. And Gideon was a huge wall between her and everyone else.

He got them to the stairwell.

He got them the hell out of there.

*∗∗∗*

Everyone had gotten out. The fire trucks had rushed to the scene, and the firefighters had raced inside. All the hotel guests stood in a designated "safe" zone. People in all stages of dress. People of all ages. Some people who were pissed at the inconvenience. Some people who were crying out of fear.

Aspen wasn't crying. She didn't look pissed, either. Her face was expressionless as she stared up at the hotel. The wind caught her hair and sent it blowing lightly over her delicate cheek.

His gaze swept the crowd. This whole scene bothered him. He didn't smell smoke, and, sure, maybe the alarm had just gone off in error. But...

*We're out of the hotel. We're in the open. Uncontrolled environment.* Because as far as the parking lot truly being "safe" for them? Ha. Safe, his ass.

A man with sandy-brown hair kept glancing over at Aspen. And that gaze of his kept dipping down her body.

*What the actual fuck?* "Keep your eyes somewhere else, buddy," Gideon snapped.

The guy's gaze jerked toward him. Fear flashed on his face, and he hurriedly stepped back into the crowd.

"You know him?" Gideon demanded as he surged forward.

"Know who?"

*The guy who was eye-fucking you.* "Jerk in the plaid shirt and blue jeans. He was staring at you for the last three minutes."

A shiver slid over her. "Probably because I'm in my damn jammies. I told you I needed different clothes."

And he'd needed to make sure she was safe.

He shrugged off his button-up. The thin fabric of the shirt wouldn't provide much protection, but it was better than nothing. Especially with her shivering. He put the shirt around her shoulders.

She frowned at it. Then him. "What are you doing?"

"You shivered." The shirt had long sleeves and it fell almost all the way to her knees. "Thought it would keep you warm." And he still had on a t-shirt, so he was fine.

She bit what was truly a plump and perfect lower lip and shoved her arms into the sleeves of the button-up he'd given her. "Thank you." She hurriedly buttoned it. Aspen gave a quick inhale. "It smells like you. And it's...warm."

Were those two things good or bad?

"And, no, I don't know that guy. But I see him talking to a woman and child, so I'm guessing that's his family?"

The bozo had a family and the jerk had been drooling over Aspen? *Mega asshole.*

"All clear!" Gideon heard one of the firefighters exclaim as he strode out of the building. The man was gripping a radio tightly in his hand. The hotel manager ran toward the firefighter, and they huddled together for a moment.

"Guess it was a false alarm?" Aspen's cute toes curled over the concrete. She wasn't the only one who was barefoot out there. Plenty of disgruntled guests were starting to twitch.

As if on cue, the manager rushed toward them all. She lifted her hands into the air. "Thank you all so much for your patience. We needed to wait for the green light from the fire department before we could allow guests to re-enter the building."

Gideon cast a critical eye over the crowd. The man who'd been watching Aspen before was now focused on the manager.

"It appears that one of our alarms malfunctioned on the fifth floor."

That was Aspen's floor.

"Everything is safe, and you can all return to your rooms. As an apology for the inconvenience, we will be offerings guests a twenty percent discount on tonight's stay."

That offer seemed to mollify folks, and everyone began to slowly make their way inside. When Aspen stepped forward, Gideon curled his fingers around her shoulders. "Let's give them some space."

She looked back at him, curious. God, she was gorgeous. The kind of crazy gorgeous that hit a man like a punch to the gut. Those eyes of hers seemed to stare right through him. Her lips were pure sin, and her thick, dark hair...

"Are you still planning to stay the night?" she asked softly.

"Yes." The word came out sounding more like a growl than anything else. Dammit, he was supposed to be *reassuring* the client, not scaring her. Eric had sent him over just so he could work his charm. "Yes, I'll be bunking on the floor."

"We could probably get a rollaway sent up for you."

He shook his head. No, because if they did that, then the manager would know he wasn't sharing her bed. Gideon wanted to start planting their cover story.

When he was sure they wouldn't be packed in like sardines with the other guests, he headed inside. The elevator waited, and it was just him and Aspen in the small space when the doors closed. He pulled in a breath and... "Why do I smell candy apples when I'm close to you?"

She fiddled with the too-long edge of his borrowed shirt's sleeve. "That's my body lotion. Sorry."

"Don't be. I fucking love candy apples."

Her gaze held his. Was it his imagination, or did the tension in that elevator notch up?

Her lips parted. She—

*Ding.* The elevator doors slid open. Aspen immediately surged out. The hallway was clear. Most folks had hauled ass to get back to their rooms. He'd snagged her room key before they'd left, a quick move when he'd seen it waiting near the door, and he had the door unlocked and them back inside seconds later.

She started unbuttoning his shirt. He jerked his gaze away because the sight of her doing that— yeah, he needed to look somewhere else. *You're supposed to be reassuring. Not drooling.* He could do this. He *had* done this. Worked plenty of undercover cases since joining Wilde, and Gideon had never, *ever* gotten involved with a client. He could play the game. Could keep his control. No problem.

"Don't you want it back?"

He realized Aspen was holding the shirt out to him, letting it dangle on the edge of her fingertips.

"Sure. Yeah." He snagged it. Put it on and—*candy apples*. His back teeth clenched. "Thanks."

"I'll go get some extra pillows for you. I think I saw a spare blanket in the closet." She turned away.

He didn't intend to go to sleep immediately. There was a hell of a lot more they needed to discuss. "Aspen..."

*"Gideon!"* Fear broke in her cry.

He immediately leapt toward her as she stood near the edge of the bed. He caught her shoulders and pulled her back even as his stare swept forward so that he could figure out what in the hell had frightened her.

Then he saw the knife. A knife that had been plunged into one of the pillows on the bed. "What the fuck?"

"He was in here! While we were outside, he was *here*."

Yes, it damn well looked that way.

She'd backed up several more steps, and her shoulder hit the doorframe near the bathroom door. Automatically, his gaze slid over her—and behind her. *Sonofabitch.* He reached for her.

Aspen stiffened. "What is it? What's happening?"

He gently moved her to the side. Flipped on the light in the bathroom. He'd been able to see the letters that had been written on the mirror, but he hadn't been able to clearly make them out, not until the lights had turned on.

A swift gasp escaped Aspen.

Her lipstick tube was open and on the edge of the sink. And on the mirror? The prick after her had left a message.

*You will pay.*

# CHAPTER THREE

"She's asleep," Gideon growled. "Where? In my bed. And I'm taking the couch."

Aspen inched open the bedroom door so that she could peek at Gideon as he talked on his phone. Obviously, she wasn't asleep. How was she supposed to just drift off to sleep after the night she'd had so far?

"I immediately got her the hell out of there and back to my place. No, I knew it wasn't safe at the hotel. Called in Elijah so that he could supervise a team to check out the room. He'll be getting any footage that the hotel has and doing a crime scene sweep."

They hadn't called the cops. He'd wanted to, but she'd refused. For reasons that she *could* not explain. Gideon had told her that the Wilde techs would do a thorough sweep of the hotel room. She knew he was checking the lipstick and the knife for prints. As for the rest of the room? Hundreds of people—thousands—had stayed there. The place was probably covered in prints. She hadn't needed to be told that the odds of turning up anything useful were slim to absolutely none.

"Yeah, yeah, I do think the alarm was triggered so that he could get in her room. Hurting her physically wasn't the objective tonight. He wanted to scare her. That means this jerk likes games." A pause. "You don't have to tell me. I know how dangerous that shit is. Predators who like to play with their prey are always the worst."

Goosebumps rose onto her arms. She didn't particularly like being called prey, even if that was exactly what she felt like she was. Prey being stalked. *He followed me all the way to Atlanta.*

"I won't leave her. We'll board the flight tomorrow just as we planned, then when we arrive in Pensacola, I'll make sure my cover is ready to go. But we need to keep eyes on everyone on the flight. For all we know, he flew up on the same flight with her and will return that way, too. Guys like this—guys who get so obsessed—they like to be as close as possible to—"

*Don't say prey. Don't say—*

"Their targets. It gives them a rush to be that near to the object of their desire. It's obvious he doesn't like for her to get far away from him. That will work to our advantage. It will help us to catch him." The floor creaked beneath his feet. "Sure, I've considered that possibility."

What possibility?

"And I want the bastard to come for me. I'll put up as big of a target as I can."

Her shoulders stiffened.

"I hear you. Good night, Eric. I'll check in again soon." He lowered the phone to his side. Stood there with his back to her.

Releasing a quick breath, Aspen began to push the door closed—

"Do you engage in a lot of spying?"

Crap. Her fingers tightened around the doorknob. "It wasn't spying. It was more like casual eavesdropping."

He looked back at her. "That's semantics."

She sniffed. "It was actually me being polite. I was having trouble sleeping, but when I opened the door, you were on the phone and I didn't want to interrupt your conversation. So I just waited patiently—and quietly—for you to finish up."

He smiled at her. "That's a really nice try."

He could tell she was lying? This was starting to be a problem.

"How about a shot?"

She hadn't expected that question. "Excuse me?"

"A shot of whiskey might help you sleep." He was already walking away from her.

Aspen found herself hurrying after him.

"Got this old buddy of mine who is obsessed with fancy whiskey. He likes the really old stuff. Fifteen year. Twenty-three year. Always Pappy's." He was in front of a vintage, wooden bar. "Gives me a bottle every time he sees me." Deftly, he pulled down two shot glasses and snagged a gleaming bottle of whiskey. "If you can't settle down, this might be just what the doctor ordered."

Aspen watched him fill the shot glasses. "I don't think we go to the same doctor."

His laughter came, all warm and rich. It seemed to ease some of the coldness inside of her. He handed her a glass. Her fingers brushed his as she took the drink. A surge of electric energy zipped through her. It wasn't the first time she'd felt that awareness when they touched.

But perhaps it was time for her to acknowledge it.

Then, again, maybe not. *Do not go down that path.*

Gideon took the other shot glass. Tapped it to hers. "To keeping you safe."

Yes, she could certainly drink to that. And she did. A quick downing of the amber liquid in the glass, and the whiskey burned in the best possible way.

Gideon was still flashing his half-smile right before he downed his drink, too. His glass clinked down on the bar. "Feel better?"

Her hold tightened on her glass. "No." The whiskey had certainly warmed her up, but the idea that someone was out there, that she was *prey*...very little could make her feel better with that hanging over her head.

"If you aren't feeling better, then are you at least drunk enough to tell me your secrets?"

It was her turn to release a laugh. One that she certainly had not intended. "It takes a whole lot more than one shot to get me drunk." She'd been hanging in bars long before she was legal. But that was another story. One she'd probably never tell him.

"Duly noted." He snaked the glass away from her. Once more, his fingers tangled with hers. Once more, that awareness danced over her nerve endings.

"It would be a terrible idea," Aspen told him as she turned away. His couch looked like the most comfortable thing in the world, so she settled in and tucked her legs under her body. She peered at him. "It's probably best just to go ahead and say it."

"It?" His eyebrow quirked as he lowered onto the couch next to her. He'd turned on the fireplace, and the flames danced in the most beautiful of ways.

"It." A nod. "Us. Getting involved. Crossing the lines that I am sure exist between a big, bad security agent and his client."

Gideon's finger tapped against his chin. "I tend to make my own rules."

She just bet he did. "Do you often have personal relationships with your clients?"

"Ah, *counselor,* I can see that I walked right into that interrogation, but, no, for the record, that is a line that I have never wanted to cross."

Oh. Well—

"Until now," he added, his voice all dark and rich and deliciously rumbly.

She wet her lips and realized she could still taste the whiskey. "It would be a bad idea. Yes, I find you vaguely attractive." *Understatement.* "In an...arrogant, I-work-out-too-much kind of way."

He chuckled. "No, please, flatter me more."

She liked the way humor would sneak out of him. Not that she'd inform him of that. "You know you're attractive."

"A man still likes to be told."

"And maddening."

He winked.

Her gaze jerked away. "This is a temporary situation. It will be complicated enough without us letting physical attraction get in the way—"

"And you believe I'm attracted to you?"

Her gaze whipped back to him.

"Someone thinks highly of herself," he murmured.

Her cheeks flushed. She could feel the burn igniting her skin. "I thought, I—" Aspen stopped. She did *not* get this flustered. Usually. "My mistake." The things he'd said to her before—had he really just been getting into the role? "I will certainly not say anything else when you obviously—"

"You're right."

Her eyes narrowed.

"I am attracted to you. You're striking. Not pretty in that flashy, magazine way. You have the kind of face that once a guy sees you, I don't think he can ever forget you."

"Thank...you?" Had that been a compliment?

His gaze was intense. Watchful. "You're probably used to getting everything you want. You smile, and men fall at your feet."

Hardly. He had *zero* clue about her life.

"And that's why you're giving me the talk."

"The what?" He'd lost her.

"The talk. The friend-zone talk. The it-will-go-nowhere talk. The same talk that I suspect you once gave to Ben Wilde and that you've probably given to dozens of guys who thought they might have a shot with you, but didn't."

She held his gaze. Didn't speak. *Did* assess.

"But what you need to realize is that there's a difference between me and your buddy Ben."

Yes, obviously. Ben was always an absolute gentleman, while Gideon...she wasn't so sure what he was yet.

"I don't care about rules. I don't care that we'll both probably go our separate ways as soon as the case is wrapped up. I get you're not looking for something long-term. That's fine. But you should know I do want you. I felt the attraction from the instant you walked into the Wilde office and told me that I was a mistake."

Oh, had she said that? Aspen winced. "Um…"

"You do seem to like using the 'mistake' word."

Actually, she didn't.

His gaze dropped to her mouth. Lingered. Then slowly rose until that green stare of his was locked with hers. Voice low, he told her, "I can be the best mistake you ever make, I assure you of that."

Aspen had to swallow the lump in her throat. She'd intended to deliver her lines and put this tension between them to bed. But, now, things seemed worse than ever.

His gaze seemed to see straight into her as he added, "You'll be the one who makes the call. You'll be the one who decides how far we go and what we do. You trying to figure out where I stand? That what you want to know?"

"Ah—" Yes? No? She was floundering. Her heart racing. Her body aching for something that she could not have.

"I'd love to have you." Said bluntly. Fiercely. "I'd love to give you so much pleasure that you scream again and again."

Her flush was getting worse. Her drumming heartbeat also filled her ears.

"But you have some heavy shit going on right now. You might not want any involvement, even if it is just physical."

*Just physical.*

"So there is no pressure. There never will be. I'll do my job. I'll play any role you want, and I will keep you safe. As far as anything else is concerned..."

He leaned forward. Put one arm on the cushion behind her head. He was so close that she could feel the warmth of his body wrapping around her.

"You tell me what you need, and I'll be more than happy to give it to you."

*Oh. Wow.*

"I'll be your bodyguard, I'll be your hunter, I'll be your pretend lover...or I can be your real one. Whatever you need, I can be."

This conversation had gone way off track. Hadn't it?

His eyes were on her mouth once again, and she was about ninety percent sure he was going to kiss her. She even found herself stretching toward him. An instinctive movement. Her lips began to part.

"Think you can get to sleep now?" Gideon pulled back.

Probably not. "Absolutely." Her voice was too sharp. "The whiskey did the trick." She practically jumped from the couch. "See you in the morning." Aspen fled toward the bedroom.

"Secrets have a way of wrecking a person's life."

She'd almost made it to the doorway. His low words stopped her.

"When I start hunting for him—and believe me, I am a very good hunter—I will uncover your secrets, too. That's just the way this thing works. To know him, I have to know you."

*No one really knows me.* They just knew the image she gave. Forcing a smile, she turned back toward him. "There is nothing in my past that will wreck me." *Lie, lie, lie.* "Good night, Gideon. Thanks for giving me a safe place to crash tonight." Once more, she turned away.

"Good night, Aspen." A soft rumble. "And I will be your safe place to crash anytime."

\*\*\*

Her scream woke him two hours later. He'd just managed to fall asleep, after an extremely cold shower and after getting a disappointing update from Elijah—the guy had turned up nothing at the hotel. And *someone* had turned off the security cams on the fifth floor right after the fire alarm started screeching.

Aspen's scream was loud and sharp, and it jarred him from his dream. A dream about her. Even as he shot up, Gideon thought he heard her try to say something else.

He kicked in the bedroom door. It flew back and thudded into the wall.

"Dead," Aspen gasped as she sat up in bed. "Dead. I—"

He caught her shoulders. "You are *not* dead. That shit will not happen on my watch," he swore.

She felt too fragile and delicate, and dammit, too *breakable* in his hold. "Aspen?"

Her eyes were open, but she didn't seem to actually see him.

"Aspen," he said her name again. Harder. Sharper.

She jerked. Her long lashes fluttered. "Gideon?"

"Yeah, yeah, it's me." His heart thundered in his chest. When he'd heard her scream, he'd nearly lost his damn mind. Part of him had been terrified that the stalker had gotten to her. Gotten *past* him and to Aspen.

But she was safe. Just a bad dream. "You're not dead," he said again, "and that will *not* be happening."

She drew in a shuddering breath. "Of course. Just a very dramatic night, that's all. Not every night that a woman finds a knife shoved into her pillow." Aspen sucked in a deep breath and looked down at his right hand. "You can stop holding me now."

He hauled his hands back. "I heard you scream, so I came running in here —"

"I appreciate your effort. Thank you very much."

Her voice was off. Too stilted and tight. "You want to talk about the dream?"

"No. Absolutely not."

He believed she was telling the truth...*then*.

"I think I'll stay away from the whiskey from now on." She eased back on the bed. Pulled the covers up to her chin. "Seems that it doesn't agree with me."

Gideon rose and stood by the bed. He was lingering, dammit. "You sounded afraid."

"Bad dreams make people afraid. But bad dreams can't hurt you. Just like ghosts can't."

What an odd thing to say. "You worried about ghosts?"

"No, of course not." She yawned. "But I am tired. Sorry I woke you."

"Part of the package deal." He didn't want to leave her. She was still afraid. He could feel it. "You scream in the middle of the night, and I'll always come running." He turned away. Took three steps for the door.

"Promise?"

So low, he barely heard her. But he still spun around. "Aspen?"

"Nothing. Good night."

He didn't move. "Yes, I promise." Gideon meant this, and she needed to understand it. "You call for me, and I will *always* come running."

She didn't say anything else. He was pretty sure she'd closed her eyes. It was only then, as he stared at her on the bed, that he realized...

She'd slept with the light on. She'd left the lamp turned on as it sat on the bedside table.

*Afraid of the dark?* With a creep on her trail, she probably was afraid. Slowly, he backed out of the room.

He didn't close the door fully. Instead, Gideon left it cracked open. If she called out again, he wanted to be able to hear even the faintest of cries.

\*\*\*

*Bad dreams can't hurt you. Just like ghosts can't.*

That had been a screw-up of epic proportions. Aspen blamed it on the whiskey. Or maybe her sleepiness. Or the fact that she'd been terrified.

*A knife stabbed into the pillow.* That message had been very deliberate. The threat undeniable.

*Tomorrow, you have to convince Gideon to do what you want.* She had created *her* confidentiality agreement before she'd left for the initial meeting at Wilde. Sure, she'd signed all their paperwork, but when she arrived in Pensacola, Gideon would be signing hers.

Then she would finally tell him why she had truly hired him.

It wasn't for protection. Aspen was quite good at protecting herself. She'd never been afraid to get her hands dirty. Her father had always taught her the value of hard work. He'd also taught her how to use a knife, how to shoot, how to fight. How to take care of herself in the most dangerous of situations. Because, unfortunately, too much of her life had been spent in those exact situations.

Her father had worked for one crime boss after another. He'd sold his skills out to the highest bidder. Violence and danger had been a part of his life. But he'd always wanted more for her.

*And I had more. I'd put all of this behind me...*Until the past had come back.

So she'd made a plan. Gone to Wilde. Hired an agent who could pretend to be her lover. Someone with enough skills that he wouldn't be taken out too easily.

No, Gideon wasn't there for her protection. She'd hired Gideon because she needed him to spring her trap.

To catch a monster, sometimes, you had to be willing to fight extra dirty. Luckily for her, Gideon seemed to be the dirty type.

*Maybe he isn't a mistake, after all. Maybe he's exactly what I need.*

# CHAPTER FOUR

A limo waited for them at the airport. Gideon raised his eyebrows when he saw the vehicle. "Someone likes to drive in style."

"I didn't want to leave my own vehicle here. For all I knew, the creep would key it or sabotage the engine. Seemed like a better plan to have the limo waiting. And the driver—he's someone I know." Technically, the owner of the limo was someone she knew, too. Someone she was very much hoping *not* to involve in this situation. As she approached the limo and waiting driver, Aspen smiled. "Hi, Jimmy. Thanks for picking me up. I owe you."

"You don't owe me a thing," he quickly assured her as he opened the back door. A broad smile lit his face. "You got me out of that bogus B&E charge and didn't let me pay you a dime."

"You had an alibi." An air-tight one. But the cops had been focused hard on him because of Jimmy's past. A past Jimmy was trying to bury. "I was glad I could help."

Jimmy's gaze slid to Gideon. Some of the warmth faded from his eyes, and his smile definitely tightened. "And who are you?"

Right. Cover time. Another reason she'd planned for Jimmy to be the one to pick her up. She adored the guy, but he was one of the biggest gossips in the area. "This is my boyfriend, Gideon."

"Boyfriend," Jimmy repeated. He whistled. "Does Ramsey know about this?"

She felt the slight stiffening of Gideon's body behind her. "I might have mentioned it to him," she replied airily. No, she hadn't. But she was sure Jimmy would. All part of her cover. If Ramsey just thought she was spending lots of time with a new guy, he wouldn't pry and poke in his way. His oddly protective, big-brother way. "Gideon and I had a long-distance relationship for a while but—"

"But I got tired of being away from her," Gideon finished as he stepped up to her side. He caught her right hand in his. Brought it up to his mouth. Pressed a kiss to her knuckles. "So I said screw it. I'm coming to stay with Aspen. I want to be with her."

Her head turned toward him.

"All the time," Gideon continued as he looked straight into her eyes. "I want something permanent, and I'll do whatever it takes to prove myself."

Well, well. He certainly was good at acting. Color her impressed.

"Ramsey will want to meet him," Jimmy noted. He didn't sound impressed at all. He sounded more like he was warning her.

"Well, Ramsey is out of town at the moment, off enjoying his time with Whitney, and I don't really think they care overly much about my social life." She laughed lightly. Gideon was still holding her hand. He wasn't laughing. "So I'll just tell Ram and Whitney my good news when they get back.

No big deal." She eased into the car. Since Gideon still had her hand, he had to follow her or let her go.

He chose to follow.

Jimmy shut the door behind him.

She saw that Gideon checked to make sure the privacy screen was in place. She had no doubt that the car had been vetted thoroughly by Jimmy to make sure it was secure before he'd picked her up. That was his standard operating procedure. Since it was so safe, she knew this would be the perfect time and place to have her little chat with Gideon.

"Who the hell is Ramsey? An ex?" He stretched his arms out across the back of the leather seats. "And just how long are you planning to wait before you give me a list of exes and suspects so that I can begin investigating them?"

"Right, about that." Jimmy had stopped to get coffee for her. She grabbed the mug that he'd thoughtfully placed in the back for her. *Still warm.* Jimmy was awesome. "I won't be providing that list to you." She sipped. *Heaven.*

"Excuse me?"

"I...may have misled you a little bit."

"No shit."

Her eyes narrowed. She took another sip. Then a longer gulp. She'd deliberately waited until they were in Florida before revealing this bit to him, thinking he'd be less likely to immediately jump on a plane and leave. *I have him here so...* "I don't want protection."

His brow furrowed. "Someone left a knife in your pillow last night. Wrote a threat on your bathroom mirror. Unless you're in some serious denial, you need to realize that your life is in danger."

"I know a threat is out there." *Believe me, I know.* "But it's not your protection I want."

His stare held hers. "What is it that you want?"

"About that..." She leaned forward and unzipped her bag. Her hold was steady as she drew out the manila file. "It would be better to go ahead and have this completed before we get into a full discussion."

A furrow appeared between his eyebrows. Gideon opened the file. Began to read. She saw the surprise flash across his face and braced herself for the questions that she knew would be coming. The limo rolled easily through the streets. Her head turned as she watched the familiar sights of the city come into view.

"What in the hell? A confidentiality agreement? About 'discoveries made during the course of my employment' with you? Is this shit even legal?"

Debatable. But she'd done her best and she was a very good attorney. Often, most people were so intimidated by legal jargon that they thought contracts were ironclad. In her experience, there was always a little wiggle room, though. She'd tried to eliminate as much wiggle room as possible.

"You already have an agreement with Wilde. It's standard practice." He shut the file. Stared at her with vague curiosity glittering in his eyes. "You know I'm not going to run to the media with your story. If that kind of thing happened at

Wilde, celebrities and VIPs would stop beating down our door."

"This isn't an agreement with Wilde. It's with you, specifically."

"The one you have with Wilde covers me, specifically." He put the file on the seat next to him. "Just what is it that you think I will discover? What are you so afraid of?"

*My life being destroyed.* "Will you sign the agreement?"

"I haven't even read it all."

Yes, and it was hard to read when the dang thing was in a closed file next to him. "Take all the time you need. When you are done, I will tell you exactly why I went to Wilde and what it is that I need from you." He was her solution. She hoped.

He didn't look down at the file again. He kept her pinned with his stare. "How about you tell me what you need first, and *then* I'll see about signing your papers."

She couldn't tell him everything. Probably never would.

"You are not the first client with secrets. I can handle anything you throw at me."

Yes, but it wasn't so much about *handling* things as him not running to the authorities because he felt duty bound to report her. *Tread lightly.* He wanted a little more info. Fine. She'd give him a little. "On the phone last night, I heard you telling Eric that you wanted my stalker to come after you. I believe you said that you would even, ah, 'put up as big of a target' as you could."

"Got that when you were spying?"

"Eavesdropping," she retorted, voice crisp. "Not that I even had to really do that. You have a very strong, clear voice."

Gideon grunted.

She tucked a lock of hair behind her ear. "I don't want you investigating my exes or my associates. That is unnecessary, and frankly, if my clients thought that they were being investigated, I'd lose them."

"Because your clients are criminals."

"*Accused* criminals," she delicately corrected.

"Uh, huh."

"There is no need to tear into the lives of people close to me. Instead, all we have to do is set a trap."

He leaned forward. His hands dangled between his legs. "Fascinating. Do tell me more."

Was he mocking her? Aspen couldn't be certain. "Look, you are the one who said he wanted to be a target."

"Yeah, I've got zero problem with that."

Wonderful. Finally, this conversation was headed in the right direction. "Then we just continue as we agreed—we pretend to be lovers. You don't investigate people close to me. Instead, we make sure that we are noticed. This man after me—he is very intent on making sure that I do not get involved with anyone else."

"You didn't mention that before."

No, she hadn't. She was mentioning it now. "By bringing you here, I'll basically be waving a red flag in his face."

"Because you want the bull to charge?"

"Because I want him out in the open. I want him to make a mistake. He can think he's the one in control, but I'll be pulling the strings and pushing him to the edge."

"Pushing him to make a mistake."

Her smile bloomed. "Exactly."

A slow nod. "Let me make sure I have this straight. You don't want me to investigate your clients, your friends, your lovers..."

She nodded in response, pleased to see that he was following along.

"And I'm guessing you don't want me looking at all into your own life."

"What's the point in that?"

"Sure. Right." He gave her a hard grin.

A chill skated down her spine. There was something about that smile of his. It held way too much of a tiger's edge. "I had wanted him to think you weren't a threat," she rushed to add. "That's why when I initially saw you, I said you were a—"

"Mistake," he finished, voice all silky. "I see. You wanted someone who was..."

"A little less of a physical threat. I'd hoped you would be less physically intimidating. Don't get me wrong, I needed you to have plenty of fighting skills and street smarts because I do *not* want you hurt during the course of this project."

"So it's a project now. Got you."

Her jaw hardened. "I had thought that if you were less physically intimidating, our perp would be more likely to engage, believing he could, ah..." No delicate way to put this. "Take you out."

"Uh, huh."

"But Eric kept insisting you were perfect, so I decided that we could make things work."

"Super."

Anger pushed through her careful control. "It's highly annoying when you mock me."

"Sorry." He did not sound even a little sorry. "Just coming to terms with your newest secret. Wondering how many more you'll drop on me before we're done."

*Done.* Her stomach twisted. "You can walk away if you don't want this case. I can find someone else."

He seemed to consider that option for a moment. A moment that had the twist tightening and then he said, "There are PIs and security agents in this town. Why'd you go all the way to Atlanta? I'm guessing it was not just because of that close relationship you have with Ben and Eric."

The relationship had been part of the reason. And she'd thought that if her past was discovered—well, maybe they'd help her to keep it hidden. "I didn't want anyone in this city to know what was happening. Going to an agent outside of the area made sense."

"When the stalker is turned over to the cops, don't you think everyone will realize what's been happening?"

She squared her shoulders. "I will cross that bridge when I come to it."

His expression hardened. "You *are* planning to turn him over to the police, right? Not like you're just going to make him disappear."

Her light laughter filled the air. "Well, of course, not. What do you think I am, a killer?"

Gideon's hand lifted and rubbed over the back of his neck.

*Uh, oh.* Unease slithered through Aspen, but she kept her smile in place. Was he getting that warning prickle he'd told her about? Was he realizing that her words might not hold the most honesty in them?

To distract him, she leaned forward and snagged the manila file. "There is no pressure here. If this situation doesn't work for you, then you are certainly welcome to leave. I'll just tell Eric that we didn't mesh, and we'll both go our separate ways."

His hand flew out in a lightning-fast move and curled around her wrist. "If I leave, you'll still go through with this plan."

Yes, she would. She wasn't the one with an out option. "I'll find another partner to help me."

His hold tightened. "I already accepted the job." His other hand pulled the file from her grip. "Don't think I need to sign this in order for us to have a deal."

"But it would make me feel so much better." They were leaning close together. So close that he could kiss her. Or she could kiss him.

Neither one of them moved, but she was sorely tempted.

And it took her a moment to realize the car had stopped.

That drive had been way too fast.

The door opened. "You're home, Aspen," Jimmy announced. "Safe and sound."

For the moment, yes, she was. She didn't look toward Jimmy, not yet. Her focus remained on Gideon. "Review it, then sign the contract," she whispered.

Jimmy poked his head inside the limo. "Everything okay in here?"

"Ah—"

Gideon kissed her. His hand freed her wrist and flew up to curve under her chin. She'd instinctively turned her head toward Jimmy, but Gideon used his careful hold to force her to look back at him. And then his mouth took hers. The kiss was sudden and fierce, and it caused a surge of sensual awareness to flood through her body.

"Oh, damn. My bad." Jimmy's rushed and awkward apology. "Didn't mean to interrupt. You just—you take all the time you need. I'll be out here when you're done."

Gideon didn't seem to be done. His mouth lingered on hers as he used his hold to tip her head back. Her lips had been parted because she'd been about to reply to Jimmy before Gideon had taken her mouth, and he used that openness to his advantage. Gideon's tongue dipped past her lips. Tasted her. Teased. Then took.

Her body quivered. Dammit, *quivered*. She kissed him fiercely. Held nothing of herself back. Just let the desire crest and take over and—

"I'm sure he'll take this back to the mysterious Ramsey and let him know that you are definitely involved with someone new." A rasp against her mouth.

Holy hell, had that kiss been an act? Just part of their cover? *Get yourself together. Now.* She pushed against Gideon's shoulders. Even managed a brisk nod. "Excellent job."

A muscle jerked along his jaw.

"If you hadn't kissed me, I was planning to kiss you. Jimmy is a notorious gossip. He's also the seeing-is-believing type, so this will cement the plan nicely." Provided that Gideon actually agreed to her amended partnership.

Time to get moving. She turned and reached for the door.

"When you said 'excellent job' a moment ago, were you complimenting me on my undercover skills or my kissing technique?"

*Play it cool.* Her nostrils flared as she exhaled. Her hold tightened around the door handle. "Both."

Before he could say anything else, she pulled on the handle and jumped from the car.

***

"Ramsey," Gideon said flatly as he gripped his phone.

"You got more than that? I mean, is that a first name, a last name, or a—"

"It's a starting point. Not like it will be hard to research Aspen and see when the guy's name pops up in her life."

There was silence on the other end of the line. Elijah didn't usually go much for silence so Gideon knew the guy must be up to something.

"Um, did you spend like even five seconds doing an internet search on this guy before you called me?"

"No, because about five seconds ago, Aspen walked away after telling me that she did *not* want any of her associates or exes investigated."

A hard beat of silence. "Come again?"

"Seems Aspen has another plan in mind."

"Yeah…" A long sigh. "Did you explain to her that stalkers are often people already in her life? And that someone she was previously involved with would be at the top of our suspect list?"

"She's refusing to tell me about her exes."

"Well, that makes shit hard," Elijah returned, disgruntled.

"Tell me about it." He looked to the left. He was inside Aspen's house. Not exactly the type of place he'd expected for her. She was all cool class and poise, so he'd figured she'd have a pristine condo. They were pretty damn close to the beach, so he'd thought she'd maybe even have a place on the water.

But, no, she'd surprised him. The house was historic. Hell, it *felt* old. In the very bones of the house. Two massive oak trees surrounded the home, with their long limbs towering and stretching in every direction. The house had been painted a dark blue, with a crisp, white trim around the windows, on the heavy, thick columns that lined the wraparound porch, and on the second-floor balcony. Once he'd entered the home, Gideon had seen a snaking staircase that waited beyond the foyer. Aspen had disappeared up those stairs just moments ago, and he'd yanked out his phone to make contact with Elijah.

Gideon raked a hand through his hair. "What do you have on this Ramsey guy?" Because he *knew* Elijah had already found something based on the way his partner had asked about the internet search. Obviously, Elijah had already gotten a hit.

"I thought you just said that you weren't supposed to dig—"

"I'm not digging. You are. See how I worked around that issue?"

"So, yeah, I don't think that's the way it is supposed to work."

Too bad. "It's the way it's working. Hurry up, buddy. She has a tendency to eavesdrop."

"Okay." Elijah cleared his throat. "When I typed in her name and the name Ramsey, I got lots of hits in my search. The most recent result was about some kind of fire that happened at his bar. She is quoted in the article as saying that her client was 'happy to act as a Good Samaritan yet again' and that she hoped—"

He heard the creak of the stairs. One thing about historic houses, they sure did love to creak. "Right," Gideon said loudly. "I'm glad to hear that you're settled in town, too. We will plan to meet up and go over the situation. Talk soon."

"But there's an implication that Ramsey is some sort of crime boss. Jeez, there's so much more—"

Gideon hung up. He'd be getting to that *more*, ASAP. First, he had to see if he was still employed by Aspen or if she was about to kick his ass to the curb. His bags waited near his booted feet. He looked up and saw her slowly descending those gleaming stairs. The light fell through a nearby window and hit her dark hair. The way the light surrounded her, she looked like some kind of damn fairytale princess.

If you were into that kind of thing. He wasn't. He liked flesh and blood women. Women who weren't afraid to get wild and passionate. Women who—

"What are you staring at?" She frowned at him.

*You.*

She may have stolen his breath. Hell.

He sucked in deep breath to replenish. "Your contract is bullshit."

She stopped on the bottom stair. Her fingers trailed over the mahogany banister. "Which one? The one I signed with Wilde or the one I presented to you?"

"The one you gave me," he gritted out.

"I see." The delicate column of her throat moved as she swallowed. "Then you have decided not to continue working with me." She squared her shoulders. "I understand. My demands were certainly unusual, I will grant you that."

"Yep, unusual." He tasted that word. "It is *unusual* when a client tries to tie my hands behind my back and stop me from doing my job."

"I am *not* trying to stop you!"

Wasn't she? "The stalker is quite possibly someone you know. Sure, he could be a stranger, could be some guy who saw you on the news or at the grocery store. Someone who developed an obsession and built himself into your life." Gideon watched her expression carefully. "But we both know you've been holding out on me. I think he's said something to you—something that made you think that, yes, you *do* know him. I'm guessing you might even know the stalker's identity. Or suspect that you do."

Her nostrils flared. Her lips parted the faintest bit.

*Pay dirt*. She did have a suspicion. "It would honestly save us all some time if you just cut through the bullshit and gave me a name. I won't blab your personal business to the world. I'm not exactly the kissing-and-telling type, contract or no contract. I want to keep you safe. I want to eliminate a threat."

Her hand smoothed over the banister. "I wish you'd sign my contract."

"And I wish you'd think about what I said." Now his gaze left her. Looked up at the second level of the home. "Just how big is this place?"

"About three thousand square feet."

That gave someone a lot of room to hide. He eased onto the step beside her.

She immediately inched back from him. "It was built in 1898."

He absorbed that info for a moment. "A house this old...it must come with plenty of ghosts."

Aspen flinched. "I don't believe in ghosts."

"No?"

"No."

Gideon looked up again. He could have sworn that he just heard another creak. "My first order of business is to thoroughly search the house. While I do that, why don't you reconsider giving me that name?"

"No one is in the house. I was just upstairs."

"I need to get the lay of the land." He needed to see every security flaw she had so he could fix them. Gideon headed up the stairs.

She caught his arm. "If you're not agreeing to sign my contract, why even bother?"

He liked the way her fingers felt against him. "Never said I wasn't signing, and I am definitely *not* leaving you on your own."

Hope lit her face. Brightened her eyes.

She'd actually thought he would walk away?

"I'm here until the job is done," he assured her flatly.

"No matter what you find out?"

"I've handled plenty of secrets that are far scarier than the ones you're hiding."

Her head tilted forward. Her hair slid to shield her face. "Don't be too sure of that." She stepped off the stairs. Moved to the center of the foyer. She stood beneath a big, glittering chandelier. The thing appeared to be draped with hundreds of glass droplets that caught the light and shimmered.

She stood there, with her arms wrapped around her stomach, and her head bent forward.

*You are keeping so many secrets.*

He could practically feel them. He could...

A red light flickered on the wall about five feet from her head. "What in the hell...?" Gideon bounded off the stairs.

Her head jerked up. "Gideon?"

Then he heard a strange, almost musical rush of sound. Kind of like a xylophone that he'd once heard. A cacophony rose and wind seemed to rush at him, and in a sudden, stark wave of panic he realized what was happening.

*The chandelier is falling down on us.*

All of that gleaming glass...coming straight for them.

He locked his arms around Aspen's waist, tucked her under his body, and hurtled across the marble tile.

The chandelier crashed and shattered.

# CHAPTER FIVE

"Oh, my God!"

"Are you hurt?" Gideon's head lifted, and he stared at her with wild, green eyes.

Blood dripped down his cheek.

She reached up to touch him.

"Are you hurt?" he repeated. "Did the glass get you?"

"No, it got you!" Because he'd covered her with his body. They'd managed to get out of the middle of the foyer—he'd accomplished that feat by hurtling them forward—and then he'd covered her with his much bigger form.

When the chandelier had crashed, the shattering of the glass droplets had filled the air— and she'd known they were breaking and flying everywhere.

"You're bleeding," Aspen whispered as she feathered her fingers over his cheek.

"Barely a scratch. Forget it."

Not likely. There was nothing about this event that she would ever be forgetting.

"Stay here, got me?"

Her eyes widened. "Why? Where are you going?"

Growling, he rose. Gideon shook his shoulders and shards of broken glass dropped off him. As he marched across the foyer and toward her bookcase, more glass crunched beneath his boots.

She carefully pushed herself up so that she was sitting. What was he looking for on the shelf? "Gideon?"

"Sonofabitch."

She kicked away chunks of glass.

"He was watching you." It looked like Gideon had some kind of device in his hand. She couldn't quite make it out, but if her stalker had been watching her...*Must be some kind of camera.*

Gideon glanced up at the ceiling—or rather, at the spot where the chandelier *should* have been. "He must have had it set to fall. All he had to do was wait until you were in the right spot."

Now she pushed to her feet. Glass crunched beneath her heels. "How did you know?"

"I saw a flash from the transmitter. Clever bastard." His head turned toward her. "And *this* is why I need to do a full sweep of your house. If he has more devices in here, I need to get rid of them."

*He'd been watching me?* Aspen wondered just how long the jerk had been spying in her home.

"I need Elijah. He's great at spotting these things." Gideon's hold tightened around his prize.

"If the stalker is watching and listening..." Then their ruse was over. He knew she'd hired an agent.

"I don't know that it was transmitting audio. I have to do more research."

"If he *was*," she continued grimly, "then he will know you're not really involved with me. He'll know everything here is a set up." Her voice was low, whispery, but she knew Gideon heard her. "He could be watching us right now from another camera."

A nod. "I hope he is."

Why?

Before she could ask, he was striding back to her. Didn't even seem to notice the glass on the floor. His free hand reached for her. Curled around her. "I hope he is," he rasped again.

Then he kissed her. His mouth crashed onto hers, and the intensity of this kiss? Even stronger than before.

Fear beat inside of her. Adrenaline pulsed in her blood. Her breasts thrust against Gideon's muscled chest and for a moment, all she could do was feel. Feel *him*.

He was kissing her like he was desperate for her. Like he'd been terrified and needed reassurance that she was safe. Alive. And she kissed him back the same way because her emotions were so raw and out of control and—

*Pretend.*

The one word rushed through her mind and had ice filling her veins. He was just putting on a show. If the stalker was watching, Gideon wanted him to see the embrace. Gideon wanted to throw the guy off.

A red flag, waving in front of the bull.

Gideon's head lifted. His lips were barely an inch from hers. She could still taste him.

"Read an article once," he said. His voice was so low. Low and rough and sexy. "Bulls can't actually see red."

What?

His mouth moved, going to rest beside her right ear. His breath blew lightly over it. "They respond to movement, to the jerk and wave of the bullfighter's cape, not the color. If you want this bastard after you to respond, then we need to show him how real this is." His mouth brushed against the shell of her ear. "How real we are." He pulled back. Stared down at her.

The blood gleamed on his cheek. He'd been hurt, protecting her. She'd told him that she didn't want protecting, but he'd literally just saved her life.

So how could she thank him?

Aspen shot onto her toes. Her hands wrapped around his broad shoulders. And she hauled him back to her for another hot, deep kiss. Something inside of her felt almost savage and so very out of control. Maybe it was because she'd almost died. Maybe it was because she was terrified to realize that whoever was after her—this time, he *had* meant to hurt her.

She'd thought he would come from the shadows when he learned she was with someone else. She'd thought she'd push him into taking action.

Well, she'd pushed him, all right. Apparently, he'd decided to just kill her.

And it was a very, very good thing that Gideon had been there. He'd saved her life.

The kiss was consuming and scorching. Arousal pulsed through her body, blending with the adrenaline and fear, creating a mix that was enough to make her feel drunk. Gideon was strong and hard against her. She wanted to hold as tightly to him as she could.

And she *was* doing just that.

Kissing him passionately, madly, with every bit of her being.

He was kissing her back just as hotly, and the man certainly knew how to use his lips and tongue. Skilled didn't even begin to cover it. And if they were at a different place, if they'd met under different circumstances...

*But we didn't.*

She forced herself to pull back. To look into his eyes. She could see his desire staring back at her. "Thank you," she whispered.

The faint lines near his eyes tightened.

Aspen knew she probably shouldn't say more. Not if they were being monitored. So she took another step back. Her body had felt hot when she was close to him, but chill bumps immediately rose onto her arms as she surveyed the wreckage in the foyer. Broken glass littered the floor, and the heavy remains of the chandelier's brass body slumped to the side.

Gideon had his phone out and was texting someone. She figured he'd be calling that partner of his, Elijah something. They should talk about a cover for Elijah to use. If he just waltzed in the door and promptly started searching...*that will compromise us even more.*

Gideon put the phone down. Pulled a small black device out of his pocket. The same device he'd found on her bookshelf. It *looked* like a small camera was on the end.

He scanned the device carefully. Snapped a pic of it and texted it off, presumably to Elijah.

She rocked back onto her heels.

His phone dinged. He read the text. Nodded. "Like I thought, video only. Didn't see anything for audio, but I wanted a second opinion. Doesn't mean there aren't listening devices hidden around your house, though, so we'll be doing a full sweep, ASAP. In the meantime..." He shoved the phone back into his pocket. Raised the black device so that he appeared to be staring into it.

"Let's see if you can read my lips..." He glared. "*Fuck. You.*"

Aspen sucked in a sharp breath.

Gideon's head whipped toward her. "Baby, be careful. You don't want to slip and cut yourself."

*Baby?*

He dropped the black device. Let it fall to the floor and mix with the shattered glass. His arms slid around her, and he swooped her up against his chest. "I've got you."

"You...don't need to have me." She could feel the flex of his muscles. "I can walk."

"Glass is everywhere. I'm getting you someplace safe." He turned for the stairs. Carried her up the steps in what was truly a hot show of strength. She certainly could have walked. Why not? But, hey, if he was in the mood to give her a ride, her jittery knees would gladly accept.

He stopped at the top of the stairs. "Where is your bedroom?"

"To the right." She'd looped one arm around his neck. His scent teased her.

Gideon promptly turned to the right. She'd left her bedroom door partially open, and he shouldered inside. But he barely seemed to glance at the bed or the furniture that she'd so carefully picked up from her antique store hunts. Instead, he made his way to the bathroom. Carried her over the threshold. Put her down so that her feet touched the tiles, then he shut the door. Locked it. And immediately turned on the shower.

A frown pulled at her mouth. "Are we...dirty?" She did need to clean that cut on his cheek for him, but...

"If there is a listening device up here, the water will drown us out," he told her.

Yes, of course. She should have thought of that. Aspen nodded. They were back to business.

Or maybe they'd always been back to business.

"He fucking tried to kill you," Gideon gritted out.

Steam drifted from the shower. He'd obviously turned on the hot water.

"This wasn't about scaring you. If I'm right, he was watching on the camera, he saw you go under the chandelier, and then he probably triggered the damn thing to fall."

"We don't know that..." Okay, yes, it looked helluva suspicious. "I mean, maybe it was just a freak accident." The words sounded weak to her own ears.

His doubting expression said the same thing. "He would have seen me find the camera, too."

*If* he'd been watching, yes...

Voice low, Gideon added, "I wanted to make sure he kept on believing we were lovers, so I kissed you."

She licked her lower lip. "That's why I kissed you, too." *Lie.*

"I found the camera so fast, he might suspect I'm security. So maybe we need to adjust our background story. Say I'm a bodyguard *and* your lover. Someone you met through your court cases. Someone you met and fell hard for, and as for me...I just can't keep my hands off you."

He was working on their cover story? Then? When her mind was in chaos and her body felt like it was shaking apart?

She could still hear the shattering of all the glass...

Could feel the hard floor as they'd slammed into it.

"We need to get ahead of this bastard. We need—" Gideon broke off when his phone pealed and vibrated. He yanked it out of his pocket and frowned down at the screen. "Elijah ran the model number. The thing only has a transmission range of two miles." His head lifted. "The sonofabitch is *close.*"

Close? Yes, within two miles was *very* close.

"Stay here," he barked at her.

First, he needed to settle that tone down, way down, and second—

*Stay here?* As in...he was going somewhere else?

"Lock the bathroom door behind me. Don't open it until I come back."

"But—"

But she was talking to air because he was already long gone. He'd apparently completely forgotten her plan. Her plan involved them luring out the bad guy together and not Gideon leaving her in the dust, dammit.

She peeked out of the bathroom.

*Long. Gone.*

\*\*\*

The fucker was close. Gideon burst out of the house. He looked to the left and to the right. It was the middle of the day, and it was bright as hell out there. The street was lined with houses and massive oaks. He didn't see anyone outside. The kids would be in school. Adults would be working or inside taking care of cleaning and the million other things people did.

He scanned the scene. Searched for anything that was out of place. The guy could be in one of the houses. He *could* be one of her neighbors. That was why the first part of the investigation should have involved taking a hard look at everyone close to Aspen.

The perp could also be some creep who was close by, some jerk who had driven his ride onto her street, then pulled out his monitoring equipment. The camera had been an interesting bit of tech. Not anything that would need a network to use. The wireless transmission had relied on—

A car hurtled down the street. A black Dodge Charger with darkly tinted windows. Gideon strained to see past those windows even as he stepped into the road.

The car kept coming straight for him.

"What in the hell are you doing?" Aspen screamed.

His head jerked toward her.

Why wasn't she in the bathroom?

She was surging toward him. Running fast. The Charger was revving and—dammit—

He grabbed Aspen and hauled her off the road. The Dodge didn't brake. Didn't slow at all as it surged past them.

*Fuck.* "Great," Gideon snarled as he held her closer. "You let him get away."

"*What?*" She squirmed in his hold. "Are you mad?"

Yeah, he was feeling pretty pissed at the moment. *No tag on the car.*

"You were standing in the middle of the road!"

More like on the edge of the road.

"He could have killed you!" she snapped. "I was trying to save your life!"

"You were supposed to stay in the bathroom," he groused.

"And you're supposed to be my partner!" She shoved harder against him. "Dammit, he's getting away! We need to follow him!"

She wanted to give chase? Nice but... "Don't worry. Elijah is on it."

Aspen stopped struggling. She glanced up at him. "Excuse me?"

"Me stomping outside, making a target of myself? That was to get the perp's attention.

Remember, that *was* the plan you had. For me to get his attention."

Her gaze was suspicious and dark.

"Elijah is close by. Elijah is watching. He has him."

"Let me go."

He did.

"How long has Elijah been close?"

"Since the first time I texted him?" Elijah had been there every step of the way. "He was on the same flight with us. He's just been hanging back."

She looked down the road. No sign of the Dodge. "You're sure he has the driver?"

He was reasonably sure. Elijah knew his shit. But Gideon still pulled out his phone. Dialed his partner. He expected Elijah to answer with an annoyed snap of something along the lines of, "Busy now," but instead...

The phone just rang. And rang. And went to voicemail.

"Gideon?"

He swiped his finger over the screen. As per Wilde protocol, every agent could always track the phone of a partner. He used the tracking app and... "Shit."

"What's happening?" Her arm brushed against him.

He looked to the left, the way the Dodge had just gone. Then to the right. Where his app was telling him that Elijah's phone was stashed. *Shit.* "Come on." He caught her hand and took off running.

"You keep asking so nicely," Aspen huffed as she ran with him. "And running in heels is so easy, it's—"

He shot through the bushes at her neighbor's house.

"Don't trample those azaleas! They aren't blooming, but Mrs. Mayton is super protective of—"

He hauled ass around an oak, then swore at the sight that greeted him. Elijah was slumped near the side of a black SUV. "Elijah!"

"Oh, God," Aspen gasped, then *she* was the one running helluva fast—in her heels—to get to Elijah.

She fell to her knees beside him, and Gideon was right with her. He saw the blood on the back of Elijah's blond hair, matting it, and swore, low and viciously. Using as much care as possible, Gideon turned the other man over.

Elijah let out a ragged groan. "What...?" His eyes fluttered open as he groaned again.

"Easy, buddy," Gideon cautioned him. "You've got one hell of a knot on the back of your head."

Elijah lifted his hand as if he'd touch his head.

"No, just take it easy a minute," Gideon ordered him. Okay, this was bad. Bad as in...someone had managed to get the drop on Elijah. Bad as in...

*There had to be an audio device in the house. Someone knew I had backup outside.* Or...or whoever the hell they were after was so skilled that he'd managed to make Elijah and take the agent out from behind.

"He...got the jump on me?" Elijah shook his head. Immediately groaned again. "That shit...doesn't happen."

No, it didn't. Not usually. Elijah was a former Fed. He'd worked high profile cases with some of the most dangerous criminals out there. In order to catch him off guard...

Gideon slanted an assessing glance toward Aspen. This wasn't some amateur they were facing. This was a guy who knew his tech, who knew how to slip up on a trained agent, who knew how to stalk his prey out of state...the list just kept going on and on. In a *bad* way.

"Who in the hell are we dealing with?" Gideon wanted to know. The fierce twist in his gut told him...*a professional.* Someone with deadly experience and skills.

Aspen's gaze darted toward him, but she didn't answer.

He knew she had a suspicion. Wasn't that the whole point of her master plan? To draw out the creep she suspected they were after—a man she obviously knew since she didn't want Gideon investigating any-damn-one else?

"You're telling me," he warned her. "You will tell me *everything.*" One way or another.

# CHAPTER SIX

"We have to figure that he tailed you to Atlanta and saw you go to the Wilde office. He'd been threatening you, so he could assume one of two things with your visit..." Gideon tapped his fingers against the bar top in front of him but made no move to actually touch the drink that he'd been given moments ago. "Assumption one would be that you went there to hire an agent. If he's thinking that, then our cover story is moot at this point."

She swiveled to the left and right on her stool. He'd insisted they come out that night even though she would have been much happier staying at her place. But, he'd wanted her out—in a very public setting. "What's assumption two?"

"Assumption two is that he doesn't quite know what to make of me yet. He'll get that I'm a Wilde agent, but he may believe that you and I have a personal relationship. Based on your job, it stands to reason our paths might have crossed in the past. A savvy lawyer like you could have hired Wilde to dig for info on some of your cases. That happens all the time at our business."

Okay, going with that line of reasoning... "He'll think we met before. Maybe hooked up. And when I started getting the threats from him..."

"You turned to someone you could trust for help. Someone with a personal investment in you. Someone..." Now he leaned toward her. "Someone who would be willing to do just about anything to keep you safe."

Voices rose and fell around them. The band was playing from the raised stage, and drinks kept flowing.

"The more physical we get with each other, the more he'll continue to believe that second assumption," he told her. "What you have to do is decide if that's what you want. You want us to keep pretending? Or do you want me to show him who I really am?"

Her heart drummed hard against her chest. "He doesn't want me involved with anyone else." On this, she was certain. "If he thinks we're together, from a psychological stand-point, that will prey on him." *I want him to be prey. Not me.*

"You're playing a dangerous game."

As if she had to be told that. Her lips pressed together as her fingers slid over the stem of her wine glass. Like Gideon, she hadn't taken a sip of alcohol yet. "Elijah's okay?"

"Hardly. He's pissed as hell and determined to bring down the bastard who got him. But as far as injuries are concerned, he'll be fine."

Her breath shuddered out.

"Elijah is former FBI. Did a stint in the Army before that. He's trained in Krav Maga, Ju Jitsu, and a dozen other damn things that he usually likes to brag about." A shake of Gideon's head. "Someone getting the drop on him? That will *not* sit well with Elijah."

She didn't imagine it would. Getting a concussion probably didn't sit so well with him, either.

"And it royally pisses me off." One of Gideon's arms draped over the back of her stool. The way they were sitting, they had to look like lovers. Maybe that was what he wanted others to see— and maybe it was also so that he could speak softly to her in the din around them. "This guy after you has training, doesn't he?"

Her lashes flickered. "You haven't signed—"

"Fuck the contract."

Well, okay then.

"You either trust me to keep you safe and to do my job, or you don't."

He didn't get it. The situation wasn't just about safety. *It's about my whole life. Losing everything I worked so hard to get.*

"Aspen?"

Tension burned between them. Hot enough for Aspen to feel it sliding over the edge of her skin. This would not do. This—"Dance with me," Aspen blurted.

His head pulled back. Gideon frowned.

She was already jumping off the stool. Reaching for his hand. "Dance with me." For show. For anyone watching. For her. Aspen turned her back and tugged him onto the dance floor. His hand was strong and steady in her grasp, big and powerful, and soon they were on the dance floor. The other couples eased back, maybe because Gideon appeared so large and menacing.

Dressed all in black, wearing his thick jacket, with his hair tousled and his green eyes blazing...

She exhaled slowly and moved into his embrace.

"You do like a show," he murmured.

No, in truth, she didn't. When she'd been a teen, attention had been the last thing that Aspen had ever sought out. She'd wanted to blend. To be just like everyone else.

That hadn't been possible, not in the world she'd lived in.

"I think he is someone very dangerous," she said softly. She pressed close to Gideon. "Someone who doesn't hesitate to hurt others. Someone who can kill easily. Someone who has done so in the past."

"Yeah, I'm liking him less and less, and, Aspen, dammit, why haven't you gone to the cops?"

"Because they can't help me."

"What? I'm not sure I heard you..."

They were even closer to the band and to the blaring music. Keeping her voice just as soft, she said, "Because they can't stop a dead man."

He stiffened. He'd caught her words. Somehow, even over the barrage of music and voices, he'd heard her low confession.

She wanted to stay right there, with her body swaying lightly in tune to his. His arms were around her, one hand splayed over her lower back, and in his embrace, she felt safe.

*Protection is not the worst thing ever.*

Elijah could have been killed when he was outside her place. Collateral damage had never been on the agenda for her. She knew the attack on Elijah had been yet another message for her...

*This is what happens when you bring others into this game.*

Only it wasn't really a game, was it? It was more just a straightforward matter of revenge.

She'd killed him.

He wanted to kill her.

*No, no, dammit, you know it doesn't work like that. Once a bastard is dead and buried, he can't hurt you any longer.*

Or at least, he shouldn't be able to. Just how many times was she going to have to kill this particular asshole?

"We're being watched," Gideon said, his fingers pressing a bit harder to her back. "Eight o'clock. Guy with the white shirt and glare that says he'd gladly put a knife in my back."

She didn't want to glance that way—too obvious. Aspen waited, knowing Gideon would slowly work her around until she could casually see their watcher, and sure enough, a moment later, her breath expelled as she caught sight of him. "That's a friendly," she murmured.

"He hardly looks friendly."

That was because Darius Addams only had one expression. Not a resting bitch face, more of a resting *I-Will-Kick-Your-Ass* face. "He's one of the good guys."

"Something makes me highly doubt that." Gideon maneuvered her again, and this time, she saw him toss a cold smile toward Darius. "In fact, I think he may be someone who should be on my suspect list. You know, that nonexistent list I have since you won't tell me jackshit while my partner gets ambushed."

Anger vibrated in his voice. Justified anger considering what had happened. "Gideon..."

"I'm thinking that asshole over there needs to be on the list. And so does your *client* Ramsey. Didn't take much work at all to learn that guy is trouble from the word go. If someone is out for you, if someone wants to hurt you, I'd put money on it being him—"

She stopped in the middle of the dance floor. "No."

His arms were still around her.

"What have you done?" Aspen shook her head even as a heavy dread filled her. "I told you not to dig into the lives of the people close to me." She cast a quick glance toward Darius. His *I-Will-Kick-Your-Ass* face was even fiercer as he shoved away from the wall he'd been leaning against and began a hard march toward them.

*Time to leave.* "We're getting out of here." Once more, she grabbed Gideon's hand. Only this time, it wasn't to lead him onto the dance floor. It was to get his ass out of there. "Just how much research did you do?" she snapped.

"After Elijah was hit, I called in to Wilde and got their tech teams to dig. Ramsey was my starting point."

*No, no, no.* "I asked you not to do that. I *told* you Ramsey was no threat to me."

He pulled back on his hand, which pulled *her*, and Aspen staggered to a quick stop. In the next moment, he'd whirled her around so that she faced him. "You're terrified of him."

Frantic, Aspen shook her head. Over his shoulder...*Darius is moving in like a missile.*

"With good reason." Gideon nodded grimly. "If half the shit that Wilde has already unearthed about Ramsey is true, he should be rotting in a cell some place."

"You should lower your voice. It's not a good idea to say bad things about Ramsey." Everyone in the area knew that.

"Fuck him."

Her head jerked. "You should—"

"I'm not scared of Ramsey. I get that you are, but I'm not. I will stop him."

"You are so off target here. I'm not afraid of Ramsey. Why on earth would I be?"

Darius was almost on them.

She grabbed Gideon's shirt front. "Come *on*."

And, wonder of wonders, he came. She basically dragged him outside into the night. They'd hit a bar in downtown Pensacola, an area that was always packed on Friday nights. Aspen kept her tight hold on him as she maneuvered through the crowd. They headed right past another bar, Armageddon, that had a line snaking out the door. She didn't even slow down. Her goal wasn't to hit another bar. She needed to get to their vehicle and get out of there.

But he stopped. Again. Stopped far too close to Armageddon and the crowd that was so eager to get inside. Sighing, she spun back around. "Will you just get in the vehicle and then I will explain everything?"

"Is he behind me?"

She darted a peek around him. Yes, Darius was there. Hardly a surprise that Gideon had realized he was being followed. Her efforts to get away had not exactly been casual. "He's not a threat. Do not hurt him."

"Will he follow the same rules? Or is he going to try and hurt me?"

Excellent point. Darius was nearly on them so she let go of Gideon and hurtled around him. Her goal was to put herself between the two men.

"Oh, that shit is not happening." Gideon grabbed her by the shoulders. Lifted her up. Put her behind him. "You stay out of the line of fire."

"Gideon—"

"Is this man giving you trouble, Asp?"

Her eyes narrowed at the nickname. Both Ramsey and Darius used it occasionally. They'd said she wasn't cold like snow, so they preferred the shorter version of her name and believed that she fit it better. They said she could strike like a snake and destroy the enemies in all their paths.

*If only.*

"No trouble," she rushed to say as she tried to rise onto her toes and look around Gideon's big form. "Just tired. We're heading home for the night."

"Are you." Not a question. She saw Darius cross his arms over his chest. "This guy must be Gideon."

Of course, Jimmy would have passed that along.

"Gideon Ranier," Darius continued in the deep, rumbling voice that had always reminded her of Vin Diesel. "An agent with—"

She shot around Gideon once more. Actually managed to whip past him because he probably thought she was going to stand back there and listen to orders. Nope. She threw her body against Darius's. Held tight. She was on her toes, trying to get as close to his ear as possible as she whispered, "Not another word. Not on the street. *Please*."

"Yeah, you'll want to get your hands off her. Now. Before I take them off," Gideon growled. There was a lethal intensity in his growl.

Darius's hands were on her shoulders. At Gideon's low threat, his hands released her. His face hadn't changed expression, but curiosity lit his eyes.

Gideon's hand closed around Aspen's shoulder. *"Asp,"* she knew he deliberately used that nickname because there was an edge of steel in his voice. "Why don't you introduce me to your friend? An introduction seems fair, since he seems to know all about me."

"This is Darius." She didn't give a last name. Darius wouldn't want her to do that. "We've been friends forever."

"Have you now?"

Oh, Gideon was *pissed*. Check. She stared into Darius's eyes. "We're in the parking garage around the corner."

"Then let's walk," he responded flatly.

And they did. Their quiet group strode through the crowd and around the corner. As they entered the garage, she noticed that both Gideon and Darius swept the scene. No one else was there. It appeared safe enough to talk so...

Darius went first. "You're digging into Ramsey's life. He doesn't appreciate that." His stare was on Gideon. "This is your only warning to stop."

"Are you shitting me right now?" Gideon gaped at him.

"I shit you not." His focus dipped to Aspen. "You should know better than to trust a boyfriend. You know he's probably using you in order to get to Ramsey. He's barely in town one day, and Ram gets tipped off about the inquiries coming from that bullshit Wilde agency."

Gideon cleared his throat. "Excuse me, but Ramsey is aware that Wilde was researching him? How?"

"The usual way."

Gideon didn't appear to understand what the usual way was. That was because he didn't understand Ramsey. Then again, few people did.

"Dump him," Darius directed her.

A laugh sputtered from her.

"Seriously," Darius said. He frowned. "He's using you. Didn't you hear what I said before? He's an agent from—"

"I know where he works. But he's not using me."

"No? Then why is he digging up dirt on Ramsey?"

*Handle with care.*

"Because—" Gideon heatedly began.

She reached for his hand. Curled her fingers with his. "Because he's jealous." She smiled. "He doesn't...ah, understand my relationship with Ramsey. I told Gideon it was nothing to be concerned about, but I guess he didn't believe me." Her head turned. She met Gideon's stare as a flickering overhead light shone down on them. "For the last time, Ramsey and I are not, nor have we ever been, romantically involved."

"Bro, that would be gross," Darius said with a shudder.

She shot him an annoyed glare.

"I mean, she's the closest thing to a sister that Ram and I both have. So don't go there, got it?"

They were her family, too. Another reason she wanted them kept *out* of this mess.

Darius stepped forward. So did Gideon. Some kind of ridiculous male standoff that she didn't have time to handle.

"You treat her like a princess, understand?" Darius threw out. "Like a fucking fairytale princess that you are lucky to have in your life. You so much as hurt her feelings, and I will wreck you."

Aspen cleared her throat. "Darius, as your lawyer, I would caution you to..." Her voice trailed away. *Not make threats that I know you will carry out.*

Darius slapped a hand on Gideon's shoulder. "Just getting chummy with my new friend."

Gideon looked at the hand on his shoulder. Then at Darius. "Out of curiosity, where were you today around noon?"

"Noon? What is this? Alibi time?" Darius laughed.

Gideon didn't.

"I was out looking at a bar I think I'll buy. Since Ram's out, I'm in the market for my own place. Had a real estate agent showing me around." He let go of Gideon's shoulder. "That lady that Asp recommended to me, Fran Ray. Saw some nice spots." His eyebrows lifted. "Anything else you want to know?"

"Actually, a lot," Gideon assured him. "I want to know—"

"When you can come over for dinner!" Aspen pressed her hand to Gideon's powerful chest. "He'd like for you to come over. He's been wanting to meet the important people in my life, so I said that once things are settled down, we'd have everyone over for dinner." Her smile was so wide her face hurt. "How about I call you in a week or two and we'll sort things out?"

"All right." Darius rolled back his shoulders. "A meeting is waiting on me now."

She did *not* want to know what kind of meeting. Probably better not to ask.

Darius pointed at Gideon. "Remember what I said."

"Yeah, and how about you remember a thing or two that I say?"

Her eyes closed. Gideon was not letting things end easily.

"Like what?" Darius wanted to know.

"Like you don't glare at me across the room. You don't stalk after me and Aspen in the night. You don't act like you have some control over her life. Aspen chose me, and that means she believes I can take care of her."

"Is that so?"

"Yeah, it's so. She's also not a fucking fairytale princess. She's a flesh and blood woman—strong, smart, beautiful—and the last thing I ever intend to do is hurt her."

Darius smiled. A real smile, one that he gifted to very few. "Then you might be worth keeping alive."

He was joking. Did Gideon get—

Gideon lunged forward. She grabbed him. Held him back. Darius vanished into the shadows that always seemed to surround him. "The last thing we want is to antagonize Darius," she warned Gideon.

"Don't want to make your *brother* mad?"

Darius was like her brother. As was Ramsey. "You shouldn't have dug into Ramsey's life. Call your people at Wilde. Make them stop, now."

"Why? Why the hell should I do that when he's the most likely—"

"You read some internet stories and you think you know him. So you took that and you got your people to dig deeper. It's a mistake. And Ramsey doesn't like it when people dig too deep." The breath she sucked in chilled her lungs. "I wanted him kept out of this mess. Ramsey *and* Darius. Because if they find out what's happening, I'm worried the town will be red with blood." Did that sound dramatic? Too bad. She felt dramatic. "Either get out your phone and tell your associates to stop or we end this partnership right now."

His nostrils flared. "That's not how it works."

"Actually, I'm afraid it is the only way it will work." She clenched her hands into fists because her fingers were shaking too badly. "Ramsey cannot know about what's really happening here. That is my number one rule. You want more information about me? About who I truly think might be behind this mess? Fine, I'll give it to you, but Ramsey is off-limits."

"You *are* afraid of him." Gideon shook his head. "I will protect you. I don't care if he is the big, bad crime boss. I don't care—"

In a flash, she shot toward him. Her right hand had unclenched, and she pressed her index finger to his lips. "Do not talk about Ramsey." A bare breath of sound. "You never know who is listening."

His lips parted. His stare blazed down at her. And his tongue slid over the top of her finger.

She was the one to suck in a sharp breath. Her whole body tightened. Automatically, she went to jerk back her hand, but *his* hand flew up and his fingers closed around her wrist. They were staring at each other, she felt as if she was breathing him in, and all she wanted was to put her mouth against his. To taste him and let the rest of the world burn around them.

*No. Stop it.* "We should...get in the car."

"We should go home."

*Home.* The place she'd always longed for. Aspen managed a jerky nod. He didn't let go of her wrist, but he turned and led them through the garage to the waiting truck he'd rented. At least this wasn't an SUV that screamed undercover operative like Elijah's ride.

He opened the passenger door. She slipped past him. Climbed inside. But he kept standing there. "Gideon?"

"I heard what you said in the bar."

Her heart surged faster.

"When I asked why the police couldn't help, I *heard* you."

"It was extremely loud in there, so easy to misunderstand—"

He slammed the door. Stalked around to the driver's side. She never took her eyes off him.

He slid inside. Had the vehicle cranked and growling moments later. But he didn't reverse. His fingers curled loosely around the steering wheel. "I didn't misunderstand anything."

No, she hadn't thought that he'd go with that ruse. But it had been worth a shot.

His head turned toward her. "You said they couldn't stop a dead man."

Her face felt frozen.

"Who is the dead man, Aspen?"

*Oh, no one, really. Just a man who swore he loved me. He was still swearing that, even as I drove a knife into his chest.*

And it wasn't as simple as one might think to stab someone in the chest. Not like you were just cutting into warm butter. She'd had to shove that knife hard to get it hilt deep. Aspen hadn't been prepared for the amount of blood that had followed the attack.

Or for the fact that even after she'd stabbed him, he hadn't stopped coming for her...

"Aspen?"

"I want to show you an area that used to be my favorite spot near the water. I'll give directions, and you can drive us there."

"I need answers." Growled.

Yes, he did. "I'll give them to you." Some of them. "But first, make the call about Ramsey."

He slowly pulled out his phone. The engine kept growling. He looked at the phone, looked at her, and Aspen realized she was holding her breath.

But he made the call. Spoke tersely with someone. Ordered all current lines of inquiry on her case halted.

And she could breathe again. When he hung up the phone... "Thank you."

"Don't thank me yet. I can just as easily get the investigation going again. Or, I can go straight to the source."

Gideon and Ramsey in a face-off? No, thank you. Bad idea. Terrible.

"And I will," he swore, "if I don't get real, straight answers from you." He reversed the vehicle. "No lies, no half-truths. I want *everything.*"

That was a pity. Because she wasn't even sure she knew how to tell the full truth any longer. All her life was these days...lies, half-truths. Desperate deceptions as she just tried to hide the horror of what she'd done.

And to think, she'd started with the best of intentions. But then again, didn't everyone always say that the road to hell *was* paved with good intentions? That was the saying.

At this rate, Aspen figured she had to be banging her fists at hell's gate.

# CHAPTER SEVEN

The beach was beautiful and deserted. The full moon shone down on what appeared to be miles and miles of pristine, white sand. His boots sank into the sand as they walked, and Gideon knew he probably should have ditched the damn shoes. Aspen had kicked her heels off as soon as they cleared the long boardwalk that led out to the beach. She'd just left them there, carefree, as the wind tossed her hair, and she'd pulled the salty air deep into her lungs.

Her skirt blew lightly in the breeze. She was down at the shoreline, letting the waves rush up to caress her bare feet. The waves in the distance rolled and dipped, not too rough, but a soft, easy rhythm in the night.

"I would come to this place all the time when I was a kid. It's so beautiful at night. No tourists, not even any locals...except me. A perfect spot to slip away."

She wasn't looking at him as she spoke, her gaze was focused on a point in the distance.

"I didn't have a lot of money growing up. My dad...he didn't exactly get what you'd call vacation time with some of his employers. The hours were odd, and the benefits package was shit."

He wanted to touch her. Hardly surprising. Gideon was discovering that the longer he was with her, the more he wanted her. But he needed answers.

*The cops can't stop a dead man.*

"My dad—Saul—he was a big guy. He had a massive bear tattoo on his right shoulder because some of his old buddies gave him the nickname of bear. A lot of people thought he was scary and dangerous, but he was never like that to me." The waves crashed into the shore. "No one can overhear us at this spot, and we can see clearly for miles. If anyone approaches, we'll know."

True enough.

"The first time my dad went to prison, I knew he was innocent. I was ten years old, and he'd been accused of a robbery down at a convenience store that was just a few blocks away from the place we were renting. The guy who committed the robbery was big, too. Real big like my dad. And he wore a ski mask, so no one saw his face. My dad became the chief suspect, and no matter how many times I told them that he was home with me that night, no one would listen." Her head cocked as she stared out at the water. "That was the first time he went to prison, and the first time I had a stint in the foster care system."

"Aspen..."

Her head whipped toward him. "It wasn't bad. Quite the opposite. The people who took me in were great. I had a room of my own. Plenty of food and clothes. They were always kind to me. They were the ones who eventually helped me to get my dad out. My foster dad was a lawyer, and he was the one who finally *listened*. But by that time, Saul had been in prison for seven months."

Her voice had gone cold and stiff. He'd heard it do that a few times and knew that it was a technique she used when she was trying to shut down her emotions.

"He got out. I went back to him. Because he'd been in prison, even if he was innocent, a lot of people wouldn't hire him. So he had to go back to doing protection work. Guarding men and women who were quite dangerous." She caught her hair as the wind whipped it and shoved it over her shoulder. "One day, he started working for a guy named Ramsey. Ramsey was so young back then, but my dad told me he'd be going places."

Saul certainly hadn't been wrong about that.

"Saul eventually worked the bar for Ramsey. He also worked protection for him, whenever Ramsey would need an extra hand. Ramsey liked my dad, and he liked me."

*What the hell is this twisting my gut?* But Gideon was pretty sure he knew. It was the same acid bite that had hit him when she'd hugged Darius.

Jealousy.

*I'm sure Ramsey liked you.* He forced his back teeth to unclench.

"Just a few weeks before my eighteenth birthday, my father was killed in a hit and run. It was just a few miles away from Ramsey's bar. The police assumed it was a drunk driver."

His eyes narrowed.

"Ramsey insisted on paying for my college. First college, then law school. He told me that my dad always had big dreams for me, and Ramsey wanted to make sure I succeeded."

Now that surprised him. From what he'd gathered, Ramsey wasn't exactly the giving type.

"I asked Ramsey once if he thought my dad's death was an accident." She turned away from the water. "He didn't answer. I knew then that he believed my father had been murdered."

Fuck. "Did Ramsey go after the killer?"

"Ramsey sent me out of town immediately after my father's funeral. Sent me off to college. Made sure I wasn't anywhere near here. I heard there was...a spate of violence after my departure."

He could read between the lines. Ramsey had sought retribution. Gideon yanked a hand through his hair.

"I wanted to know the truth for myself. I needed to know *why*. Had my dad been caught in the crossfire? Was killing him some sort of message that was sent to Ramsey? It was the not knowing that ate at me the most."

Yes, he was sure it had. Gideon could practically feel her pain, almost like the waves hitting the shore.

"When I graduated college, I...I reached out to some people that my father used to know. I didn't tell Ramsey because he would have stopped me."

*Or did you not tell him because you fear him?*

"I followed the intel I'd gathered and made sure that I fell into the path of a man named Braden Savage. Braden's father was known in certain circles as being a man with a great deal of power."

"You're doing such a good job at revealing but not actually *saying*," he pointed out gruffly. "The guy's dad was a crime boss, just like Ramsey?"

That seemed to give her pause. "Why would you think Ramsey was a crime boss?"

He moved ever closer to her. His fingers curled around her shoulders. "It's just you and me. No one else. You picked the location so that we wouldn't be overheard. If you don't trust me, then why the hell—"

"I didn't pick the location because we wouldn't be overheard here. I picked the location because if you look about a mile off-shore, that's the spot where Braden attacked me."

His hold tightened. "What?"

"We were on his boat. Like I said, I put myself into his path."

"Holy hell."

"According to all the intel I'd gathered, Braden wasn't supposed to be involved in his father's business. He owned an art gallery. *He* was an artist. A sensitive, passionate soul who wanted to make the world a better place." Her laugh was mocking. "Funny because once upon a time, I wanted to be an artist, too. That was how I first got into his life. Shared interest, you see."

Gideon choked back the rage that wanted to drown him. The SOB had attacked her?

"Braden was also the man who stared straight into my eyes and told me that *he'd* ordered the hit on Saul. But that we certainly couldn't let that get in our way. He loved me. He knew I loved him. And if anything, I should thank him for helping to free me of the burden of being tied to someone like my father."

He wanted to haul her closer. Her voice had gone colder. She *hurt*.

"He thought Saul was a failure. A weak man who'd never risen up the ranks. My dad didn't rise because he *wasn't* a criminal. He protected people. He protected *me*. And Braden wanted him taken out because when some of his guys had come at Ramsey, Saul had stopped them. Saul had *embarrassed* him. An older guy like that, wiping the floor with his team." Her breath shuddered. "Braden confessed right to my face, and then he offered me more wine."

Screw it. Gideon yanked her into his arms. Wrapped her up tight. Held her.

She immediately stiffened. "What are you doing?" Aspen's voice was muffled as she turned her head.

"Hugging you."

"*Why?*"

"Because you're hurting, and I'm realizing I don't like it when you hurt." Not one damn bit. The feelings he had for Aspen were growing more complicated by the moment. And what the hell was he supposed to do about *that*?

*No damn clue. But I want her safe. I want her in my arms. I want to stand between her and any threat out there.*

Oh, yes, huge trouble was coming his way.

She pushed against him. He eased his hold so she could put a little space between them, but he didn't let her go.

She stared up at him as if trying to figure him out.

He stared down at her and was fucking grateful she was alive before him. "The prick attacked you."

"I didn't want his wine."

It took a moment for her words to sink in, and despite everything, she *almost* made him smile.

"I threw it back at him. Tossed it right into his face and told him I'd go to the cops."

"Hell, yes, you did." He could see the scene in his head.

"And he told me that no one would believe me." She pulled against his hold.

Reluctantly, Gideon let her go.

"The daughter of a petty criminal, a woman who had her way to college paid for by someone like Ramsey—he was sure the press would love to hear that tale. Said it made it look like I'd been screwing Ramsey for years."

Okay, he *would* be finding this Braden bastard, ASAP. "Where is he?"

Her head tilted. "Ramsey? But—"

"Braden. Where is the bastard?"

She looked over her shoulder at the soft waves.

*Oh, fuck.* "You killed him?"

The moonlight showed him her slow, sad smile as she faced him once more. "Now why would I ever answer a question like that one? Do you think I want to find myself tossed into a cell?"

"You think I'd do that to you?"

Her smile slipped. "I think I don't know what you would do."

"You brought me out here, told me this story..."

"I brought you out here and told you that a man named Braden Savage confessed to killing my father. When I became angry over that confession, Braden got rough with me."

"What did the sonofabitch do?" Red-hot fury tore through him.

"He hit me with the wine bottle. Slammed it into my left arm. Broke the arm when he snapped the radius and ulna."

He reached for her left arm. His fingers slid tenderly over her.

"He's a dead man." Tenderly, he stroked her once more.

"That's what the stories say." Flippant.

"Aspen..." He knew flippant was the last thing she really felt.

"I didn't exactly stick around that night. I got the bottle away from him. I jumped overboard. Even with a bad arm, I'd always been a good swimmer. You grow up at the beach, and water is your friend. It has to be. It was only a mile, so I swam back to shore even as he screamed at me."

*Only a mile.* But with a broken arm?

His jaw locked.

"The boat was found washed ashore the next day. Braden wasn't there. The Coast Guard looked, but they didn't find him. His dad offered thousands and thousands of dollars in reward money, but no sign of Braden was ever discovered. After a while, folks just thought he was dead." A pause. "His father passed away fairly recently. He was found dead in his own study."

A soundless whisper escaped him. "What is it that you believe happened? You think Braden has come back and is stalking you?"

"I think he is someone who feels I deserve to pay. I think..." She swallowed. "I think the second time my stalker called me, he said that we would finish our wine together..."

*What. The. Fuck.* She was mentioning this now?

"And I think that either Braden is back or someone else is out there, someone who knows what happened that night..."

"Someone who wants you to pay," he finished, voice hard.

Her head inclined. "I would have said all of this was completely impossible a while ago..."

He would have said it was impossible *now*...

"But someone else I know cheated death out in the Gulf—the love of Ramsey's life."

Wait, back up, since when did Ramsey have a love of his life?

"Dr. Whitney Augustine was left for dead in the Gulf. Despite the serious injuries she suffered before going into the water, she survived. She made it out. She made it *back*."

Okay, yes, Whitney's story was ringing some bells for him, but he'd had no idea that woman was tied to Ramsey. *The plot twists and twists.*

"And another thing that asshole on the phone told me...another reason why..." But she stopped.

*Another reason why you think it's Braden?*

"He told me...he actually said, 'Whitney isn't the only one who escaped a watery grave.'"

Double fuck. "This guy wants vengeance on you."

"So it would seem." A roll of her shoulders. "If it is Braden, I don't know where the hell he has been for all these years. If it's not him, then I don't know who it is or why I'm suddenly being targeted."

He flipped back through everything she'd told him. His nape was prickling. Something just wasn't fitting. "When did the dad die?" She'd said recently, but he wanted specifics.

She rocked forward. "About a month before my stalking began."

Yeah, like it took a genius to connect those dots. "Another reason why you think it's Braden?"

"I think it's possible his father had him hidden. Or at least contained. Without that containment, maybe he's free now. But I can't say for certain. Not until we catch him." A low sigh that was almost immediately swallowed by the wind. "I got close to Braden. I made it my mission for him to fall for me. I found out what Braden liked, and I acted as if I was everything he'd ever wanted."

"Shit."

"Exactly." She turned away and stared out at the water. "When I told you before that this stalker would respond to someone else—to another man—getting close, I was working under the assumption that it could be him. Braden thought I was perfect for him because I made him believe that lie. I made him believe me because I wanted the truth about what had happened to my father. Everything that this stalker is doing—it reminds me of Braden. Every. Single. Thing." A bitter laugh. "Even the chandelier falling right after you got home with me. Braden was possessive and jealous, and when we were t-together, if he thought I was stepping out, if I was interested in anyone else..." She wrapped her arms around her body. "He let me know how very unhappy he was."

*Braden was possessive.* She'd just slipped up. A few times she'd slipped and talked about him in the past tense. As if she'd been certain he was gone, too.

*What really happened on that boat?* Gideon would bet his soul far more had gone on than she'd revealed so far. "You played a very dangerous game." And it infuriated him. She'd put herself into the hands of a sadistic bastard who'd *hurt* her.

She glanced over at him. "It was no game. Then or now. My father was murdered. I found his body the next day when he didn't come home from work. I walked along the road near the bar until I found him. Back then, our house wasn't too far from the bar, and my dad would always walk home." Her voice thickened as she said, "He was still alive. Barely breathing and clinging to life, and if I had found him sooner, he would have made it. Or at least..." She looked away. Her head tipped back and her body shuddered. "At least he would've had a fighting chance. Since I didn't give him that, he deserved for me to make sure justice was served."

"He wouldn't want you in danger." The words snapped from him because she was in very real and fucking grave danger.

"No, he wanted me safe. He wanted me away from criminals and dangerous bars and safely in some cute neighborhood that featured well maintained lawns and potluck parties. Instead, I spend my days defending criminals and my nights...well, I guess I spend those baiting ghosts and getting Wilde agents ambushed." A shudder worked over her. "I'm very, very sorry about your friend."

"Elijah is fine." And would *not* be caught off guard again. "But there is one thing that doesn't make sense..."

"One thing?" She went back to the water's edge. Let the waves hit her toes.

"You told me this Braden was an artist. The man who came after Elijah was trained." He'd *had* to be.

"That was a lie."

His gaze sharpened on her. She was staring down at her feet.

"Braden *was* a talented artist. He used to sketch me, and the images were quite good." She moved her right foot lightly in the water. "But he was more than merely an artist. Despite appearances, he was involved in his father's work. He had been for a very long time. He'd been trained since he was a kid, and he could be deadly when he wanted to be."

Good to fucking know. So he was facing a ghost with some skills. "Not a problem."

The waves crashed. They were getting a little rougher. The surf sucked some of the sand beneath her feet, and she swayed. "Excuse me?"

"You got a dead ex who thinks he's gonna mess with your life? He has some passable skills?" Gideon nodded. "Fine. Noted. But it's not a problem."

The waves hit again. This time when she swayed, he was there. His hands closed around her waist to steady her.

"You say that so easily," Aspen murmured.

Yeah, well, he'd read between the lines. Nothing was *easy* about this case. But if she'd thought that her confession was going to make him turn and abandon her, she needed to think again. "I'm in this until the end."

She turned toward him. Curled into his embrace. "No matter what?"

*No matter what lies or half-truths you tell.* Because he knew there was more to the story. Just as he knew that he would not be abandoning her. His nape prickled again, and he ignored it. Aspen was scared. She was in danger. She needed him.

Gideon wasn't sure anything in the world could have made him walk away from her. "No matter what."

She stretched up toward him. His head lowered toward hers. He wanted her mouth.

He wanted *her*. So badly that he could already taste her. So badly that if he took her mouth right then and there, Gideon feared he wouldn't want to stop. He feared that he wouldn't be satisfied until he had her. Naked and moaning and coming beneath him.

One man had been obsessed with her to the point that he cheated death...

And for Aspen, it had all been pretend.

*It won't be the same for me.*

Gideon straightened his shoulders. "It's getting cold out here. We need to get home." And he needed to brief Elijah.

Her lips had parted. Her head had tipped back. She stared at him a moment, then slowly nodded. "Yes, you're right. It does feel cold now." Aspen pulled from his hold. With straight shoulders and a stiff spine, she began walking back toward the boardwalk.

She didn't look back.

\*\*\*

"Well, of course, he doesn't want to sleep with you," Aspen muttered as she glared at her reflection in the bathroom mirror. "Gideon thinks you attempted to kill your ex, after lying to him and manipulating the guy." Fine. She *had* lied and manipulated Braden, but he'd been a psychotic asshole. "Only now Gideon probably thinks I'm doing the same damn thing to him." *Lying and manipulating.* Aspen shoved her hands into the pockets of her fluffy, white robe. And glared at her reflection some more.

It was well after midnight. She should have been sleeping, and while not necessarily having *peaceful* dreams, she should have at least been resting. But, no, instead, she kept reliving those moments on the beach over and over again.

She'd bared her soul to Gideon. He might not get that. But she had. For her, it had been huge. And then, when she'd thought they were having a moment...

He'd pulled back.

"He thinks I'm a killer." Not that he was necessarily wrong, but...

A knock sounded on her bathroom door and had her jumping.

"Hey," Gideon called out—*from the other side of the door.* "You okay in there? I thought I heard you talking."

Yes, dammit, guilty. She talked to herself. Side effect of living alone. Sometimes she muttered and there was usually no one around to call her on her particular brand of crazy. *Not* that it was crazy, but, oh...*screw it.* Aspen yanked open the door. Glared at him. "Why are you in my bedroom?"

And he was. Because in order to get to the bathroom door, he'd needed to walk *through* her bedroom.

"Shouldn't you be downstairs," she added, "sleeping in the guest room?"

His gaze swept over her. Slowly moved from the top of her head down over her enveloping robe and all the way to her toes. "That looks...comfortable."

Her jaw nearly dropped. Was he serious? That was just insulting. "Thanks. It's super comfortable." Her own gaze trailed over him. The bare chest. The rippling muscles. The soft fabric of his gray sweatpants that rode low over his hips...and as she dipped her gaze down a bit more...

Something was very much shoving against the front of said gray sweatpants.

She swallowed. "You look..." *Aroused. Hard. Lickable.* "Tired," Aspen finally decided. But he didn't. He was practically screaming alert and aware.

And aroused. That, too.

"It is after midnight," he allowed. He had one arm pressed to the doorframe.

"It is," she agreed, "and you're blocking my way."

"Am I? Sorry." Gideon immediately stepped back. "Like I said, I thought I heard voices. I came to check on you."

Had he really heard her? Her voice had been *low*. And he'd been downstairs.

Hadn't he?

She hurried around him and climbed into the waiting bed. "I'm perfectly fine. You can go to sleep. I'll just be here. All comfortable-like."

He laughed. "What's wrong with being comfortable?"

Nothing. Why had she even said those words? *Because you want a gorgeous guy like Gideon to tell you that you look sexy. Hot. Not...comfortable.*

But he was heading for the door, pausing only long enough to send her a wink. "Night, Aspen. If you need me, you know where I am."

The door closed behind him.

Her body was as stiff as a board in the bed. The lights were still on in her bedroom. She'd hauled the covers up to her chin. And...

*Damn it all to hell.*

She jumped out of the bed—comfortable robe and all—and stormed for the door. She yanked it open and double-timed it down the stairs. Her gaze *did* cut briefly to where the chandelier had been, and a quick chill darted over her. But then she was on the ground floor. Hurrying toward the guest room and—

*Oof.*

And slamming into the rippling, muscled chest she'd seen moments before. Before she could stagger back, Gideon's hands flew up and closed around her shoulders. The heat from his touch scorched through her robe and straight to her skin, and Aspen hissed out a breath.

Almost instantly, he let her go.

*And there it is again.*

"Something you need?" Gideon's deep, darkly sensual voice asked.

"Yes." A brisk nod. "There is absolutely something I need."

He waited.

Right. She should tell him. "It's not the same thing."

"Excuse me?"

"Me and you. This partnership. Us pretending to be lovers. It's not the same thing that happened before."

One eyebrow rose.

"What I was doing with Braden. It's...it's *not* the same thing. And despite what you may be thinking, I didn't sleep with him."

Another eyebrow lifted. "That's fucking good to know." Even rougher.

"He was my target. Every bit of intel I could find pointed me toward him." She didn't go into how she'd gotten that information. She'd been a part of that world for so long, she'd known how to get people to talk to her. How to pick up whispers. Known who would spill for the right cash and for the wrong reasons. "I was doing what I had to do for my father. I needed Braden close. I needed him to trust me so that I could search his life."

"And you did a very good job of getting close. Of—"

"Do *not* say 'pretending' to me right now," she snapped. Her hand flew up and her index finger poked him right in the middle of his powerful chest. "I hated every moment with him. When he touched me, my skin chilled. I had to smile all the time, and it felt like my face was breaking. I didn't want to be anywhere near him. What I was doing then was *nothing* like what is happening between us, and I don't want you thinking it's the same thing." *I don't want you pulling away from me.*

He looked down at her hand. Then back at her face. "How's it different?"

"What?" Her head shook. "You *know* that we're pretending. He didn't. He thought I was into him, that I was falling in love, and every time he revealed something new and twisted that he'd done, he thought I was fine with it." No, she never had been. "I wanted evidence to lock him away.

That was my goal. To get evidence I could use." Her plan had seemed so perfect, a lifetime ago.

Then everything had gone to hell. It had spiraled far too fast...

"And what is it like with me?" Gideon asked, voice gruff. "What does it feel like when I touch you?" His hand lifted, and his knuckles skimmed over the edge of her cheek.

A shiver rippled over her body.

His jaw locked, and his hand began to fall.

She grabbed his hand. Held tight. "It feels like..." A deep gulp of air. "I want more."

# CHAPTER EIGHT

He'd worked at Wilde for eighteen months. Eighteen months since he'd grudgingly accepted the job from Eric even as he told his old buddy that he might not be sticking around. He'd been drifting, looking for something—for somewhere that he belonged.

Eric had assured him he belonged at Wilde.

During that time, Gideon had never crossed the line with clients. Never been tempted. In fact, the greatest temptation of his life had only come...*when I met her.*

He knew his attraction to Aspen was dangerous. It made him reckless. Made him want to bend and break every rule out there so he could have her. And the problem? As if everything else happening wasn't already enough...

Gideon knew with a bone-deep certainty that having Aspen once wasn't going to be enough for him. He'd never been the love-them-and-leave-them type. He thought those guys were assholes. He didn't screw partners and move on without a backward glance.

*There will be no moving on from her.*

He took a woman to his bed when he knew her, when he liked her. When things were ready to go to the next level. There was usually a whole getting-to-know-you phase that involved wining and dining.

With Aspen, it was different. He'd pretty much wanted her naked from day one. Pretty much? No, he *had* wanted her that way. He wanted to strip her. He wanted to take her until she screamed his name.

And he wanted to protect her. From every threat out there. He wanted to erase every single bad thing that had happened to her before they'd met and make sure that nothing bad ever happened again.

Except he wasn't sure he could trust her. Mostly because he knew Aspen was still keeping secrets.

"My whole body heats up when you touch me." She stared into his eyes. Her dark gaze seemed to see right into his soul. "My skin doesn't chill. It warms. I don't feel cold on the inside, the way I do so many days. I feel alive."

Her delicious scent surrounded him. Her body was so close to his. She was still holding his hand. Leaning toward him.

"The cover is pretend," Aspen said. "What I feel for you isn't. You need to understand that."

She needed to go back upstairs. Fast. Before he pounced. He had never, ever been the fucking pouncing type until now. He wanted to grab her, lift her up, and drive into her right then and there. He could have her against the wall. Could shove that robe out of the way and let her wrap her gorgeous legs around his hips as he drove them both straight into oblivion.

"No one else has to know what we do," Aspen told him. Her voice was breathy. Such a husky temptation that teased and tormented him. "It's you. It's me. We're alone here, and you made sure no one was watching."

Damn straight, he had. There would be no more cameras in the house. No more peeks into her world.

"So why don't you kiss me?" Her head tilted, and her thick, dark hair slid over her shoulder. "Kiss me like you mean it and not like you're just doing it for show."

Every muscle in his body locked down. Well, not *every* one. His dick surged eagerly up and forward. If the thing got much harder, it would be out of the sweats he wore.

She pressed up onto her toes.

It would be so easy to close the distance between them. But... "No."

Her lashes fluttered. He heard her suck in a sharp breath of air. "I see." A brisk nod.

No, she didn't see. "You kiss *me* like you mean it."

Her lashes lifted. She met his stare once more.

"And you tell me to stop when you've had enough."

Her tongue slid over her lower lip. "I won't have enough."

*Neither the hell will I.*

She grabbed for his shoulders. Pulled him to her. He leaned over her, and her mouth crashed into his.

\*\*\*

*Aspen had a new friend.* Ever so casually, he drove down the road in front of her house. Why she'd bought such a big monstrosity, he had no clue. She was far too refined for that old, sprawling house. She needed elegance. Sophistication.

Power.

Once upon a time, he could have given her all of that. But she'd been lying to him. Aspen was very, very good at lying. Wasn't that why she was such a good attorney? Everyone knew they were liars.

Aspen wasn't alone in her ugly house. The security agent was there. A man who was too familiar with her. Not someone she'd hired for protection. No, when he'd watched them together, the man's expression had given too much away.

*You're under her spell, too.*

That would be why she'd brought him in. Because the new player was a man she could manipulate and control. She probably thought the fool would do anything to keep her safe. That he'd cover up all her dirty, little secrets.

*Wrong, Aspen.* No one would protect her. Not this time. She'd have no one to hide behind. No one who could make her sins disappear.

In the end, she'd pay for what she'd done.

He reached the end of her street.

*I won't forgive you, Aspen.* No matter how much she begged and pleaded.

\*\*\*

She tasted so damn sweet. Her tongue was sexy as hell as she kissed him and the little moan she gave as her mouth met his with such wild need...freaking hot. His hands were on her, clamped tightly around her hips, and he hauled her even closer. She kissed him with no hesitation, just raw desire, and Gideon knew she wasn't holding anything back.

Neither was he.

He'd let go of his control. Grabbed hard to the lust that surged through him. Maybe it was time to stop toeing the line all the time. No more good soldier. Maybe it was time for more.

For her.

His hand dipped toward her waist. Caught the belt of her robe and tugged. The loose knot gave way, and the robe slipped open. His head lifted, and he glanced down at her.

The drumming of his heartbeat filled his ears. She wore a black bra, one that displayed her breasts in a manner of sheer perfection. Matching black, bikini panties curled over her hips, and he wanted to skim his fingers over that silk. Correction, he *would* be skimming his fingers over the silk.

Her breath rushed out. "It doesn't have to mean anything," she told him.

Maybe not. Or maybe it would mean everything. He took her mouth again. Kissed her deeper and harder even as he lifted her into his arms. The robe gaped open, and she wrapped her legs around his waist. She pressed her sex against him, riding him through the silk of her panties and over the cotton of his sweats. He didn't push her to the wall as he'd imagined.

*I want her in my bed. I want to touch and kiss every inch of her.*

He carried her to the guest room. Kicked the door shut behind him. Kept returning to her mouth over and over again. She was just as eager as he was. Kissing him with a fierce hunger that fanned his desire all the more.

He sat on the edge of the bed and pulled her down with him. Aspen straddled him, her knees sliding onto the mattress on either side of his hips. Gideon began to kiss his way down her neck, and she tipped her head to the side in order to give him better access. When he pressed his mouth to the hollow of her throat, Aspen dug her nails into his shoulders and gasped.

He licked her. Kissed her. Pulled the robe off her shoulders and caught the straps of her bra as he shoved them out of his way. When the bra fell away from her breasts...

*Perfect.*

He caught her nipple in his mouth. Sucked. Licked. Had her arching and digging her nails into him even deeper. Her hips twisted and her sex pressed to him as he savored her. His fingers eased between their bodies. Eased under the top of her panties and went down, down...

She was wet. Hot. Aspen felt like heaven against his hand.

"Gideon...I don't want to wait."

He didn't either. His hand pulled back, and he twisted and pulled her so that she was on the bed. A quick move that had a surprised cry breaking from her even as he had her flat on the mattress in the next instant.

"Gideon?"

He stripped her completely. Yanked her panties down her legs and then spread her thighs.

"We need...protection." Her eyes gleamed. "Dammit, it's upstairs! Give me just a moment to—"

"Got it covered." He did. But first, he put his mouth on her because he couldn't stare at her as she was spread before him and *not* taste all of her.

With the first stroke of his tongue against her sex, she nearly surged right off the bed. Her body shuddered and her hips arched and her hands flew down to clamp around his shoulders. "Wait! I mean, you don't have to—"

He lifted his head. "I *want* to."

She stared at him.

"Do you want this?" Gideon asked. Her sensual taste made him feel drunk.

A nod. "I want everything with you."

He put his mouth back on her. Stroked her again. Licked and kissed and teased her with his fingers and just wanted so much more. He felt her come against his mouth, heard the sharp cry of his name, but he was enjoying her far too much to stop. He kept tasting her. Working her clit. Dipping his tongue into her...

*"Gideon!"*

A second orgasm. Hell, yes.

He couldn't hold back any longer. He surged off the bed. Yanked open the nightstand and hauled out the box he'd put inside earlier. He ripped open the packet and had the condom on moments later. She reached for him. The head of his cock lodged at the entrance to her body.

He wondered if he should take a breath. Try to slow down.

"Now," Aspen told him.

*Now.*

He drove into her. There was no slowing down. She squeezed him so tightly he was sure he'd lost his mind. and Gideon didn't care. She was hot and clamped so fiercely around him. He withdrew, thrust, and was lost. Over and over again, he pounded into her. He caught her legs and lifted them over his shoulders so he could go in even deeper. She met him, her hungry cries urging him on, and he felt her come again around him. *Holy fuck.* The way she squeezed him...

He exploded right after her. A long, body-shuddering orgasm that he swore was going to obliterate him. The pleasure wrung through his whole body as he growled her name.

\*\*\*

Aspen stared up at the ceiling and tried to calm her racing heartbeat. She'd just had the best sex of her life. Hands down, the best. Not that she'd had a ton of experience, so it was really easy to say with one hundred percent certainty...

*Way better than anything else.* No comparison. She'd come three times. Insane. Addictive.

And what was supposed to happen now? She was just supposed to go back to awkward fumbling in the dark with her carefully selected lovers in the future? Um, no.

"What are you thinking?"

His voice had her jerking because she'd thought Gideon had *maybe* drifted off to sleep. After that body-shaking climax, he'd gone to the bathroom and ditched the condom. He'd come back and pressed a warm cloth to her core and asked if he'd hurt her.

*Hurt* had been the last thing she'd felt.

"You seemed to be a million miles away."

Her head turned on the pillow, and she found Gideon staring at her. "I'm right here." Here was where she wanted to be. Here she could pretend as if the danger outside wasn't pressing down on her.

She was very good at pretending.

But it wasn't as if she could stay there with him forever. Aspen doubted he wanted her getting cozy in his bed all night long. "Will this happen again?"

A little furrow appeared between his eyebrows. "This?"

"You. Me. Sex. Was it just a one-time event or will there be repeat performances?" She wanted to know exactly what she should expect.

"You're very direct."

"I find it avoids miscommunications later."

His lips hitched. "I'm down for repeat performances." Spoken ever-so-casually.

She could be casual, too. "Me, too. Not like I'm involved with anyone else at the moment. And we already said it wasn't going to mean anything So..." So they would be having awesome sex again.

Excellent to know.

But that little furrow had grown deeper. "*You* said that."

"What?"

"You said it wasn't going to mean anything. Does sex always mean nothing to you?"

This conversation had seriously derailed. Or maybe it had never been on the right track to begin with. Keeping her voice light, she responded, "I hardly think you're looking for some lasting tie while you're down here on this case."

"Can't say I've had any lasting ties in a very long time. Not even certain my apartment in Atlanta is unpacked. Pretty sure the closets are full of moving boxes that I shoved in there after I returned to civilian life."

"And...when was that?"

"A little over eighteen months ago."

She tugged the sheet closer to her chest. "Why did you leave the service?"

"Got tired of seeing people I care about die in front of me."

Aspen flinched. Automatically, her hand reached out and curled around his arm. "I'm sorry."

"Not like I joined thinking the work was safe. But the longer I was in, the more dangerous the missions became. I realized there had to be more out there for me. But hell if I knew what that more was."

She was still squeezing his arm. Still hurting for him and wishing he'd tell her exactly what painful memories had just chased shadows into his eyes.

"Turned out, though, that I came out of service with a mind and body trained for war. It's hard to adjust when everyone else has been living life one way and your world is a million times removed from that."

So he hadn't unpacked. He'd kept his boxes while he looked for...what?

"A place where I belong."

She'd whispered her question to him, half-mumbling because she hadn't even realized what she was doing. Now she cleared her throat and spoke louder. "Do you belong at Wilde?"

"Eric says I do."

"That's not really an answer."

"No, counselor, it's not." He stared back at her. "But then, you didn't answer my question earlier, either."

"I didn't?"

"Um, no, you didn't."

"And what question was that?"

"Does sex always mean nothing to you?"

Oh. Right. That question. She could have tossed out a flippant answer. Could have refused to answer at all. But as she gazed into his eyes, Aspen realized that she wanted to give him the truth. "I can count the number of lovers I've had on one hand. I carefully chose them. Picked men that I thought would give me what I need."

"And what is it that you need?"

*Control.* Boundaries. No messy emotions. No ties that would bind too quickly or too deeply. But she couldn't say all of that, could she? The silence stretched between them.

"I don't think you've ever gotten what you really needed," he finally said.

"Oh, really? And let me guess, you're the guy who can give me what I need?"

"I don't know."

Well, that was...

"Do *you* know what you need? Do you know what you want? Really, deep down, do you know?"

Yes.

She rolled away from him. Slid from the bed, and, thankfully, managed to find her robe pretty quickly. Once she'd donned the robe, Aspen took two quick steps for the door.

"Are you running away?"

"I was letting you go to sleep." After schooling her expression, she glanced back at him. "Big day tomorrow. We get to hunt a dead man, remember?"

He'd sat up in bed. He looked all sexy and tousled and instead of storming away because his questions were hitting way, way too close to home, Aspen realized that she should have stayed in that bed. Probably pulled some sort of super sexy move and convinced him to go for round two.

Now she was mid-storm away and living with regret. Fabulous. "Good night." She spun for the door.

"What do you really want?"

His voice wrapped around her. "A home." How sad did that sound? Her hand flew up and she motioned vaguely around the room. "Why do you think I bought this place? I bought it when it had a sagging roof, a rotted front porch, and paint peeling in every room." She stared straight ahead, and in her mind, she saw the house as it had been. "Some people wanted it torn down. They said it was an eyesore, but when I looked at it, that's not what I thought."

The floor creaked behind her. She knew he'd gotten out of the bed and was closing in on her. "What did you see?"

"I saw a house that had been a home to people for years and years. Families had played here. Kids had grown up. There had been more dinners and parties than I could ever count. People had belonged here. It had been great once, and it could be great again, and it could be a...*home*." A spot where she could belong. "My father wanted me to have the picket-fence life. I wanted a place that made me feel like I fit." Slowly, she faced him once more. "This house fits me. And as for what I need? I need roots. I need closure on my past, and I need to be able to hope for my future." Hard to do when you felt so hunted. "I need safety, and I need someone who can give me that safety."

So when she'd asked if he was the man who'd give her what she needed...

No, she hadn't been joking. Hadn't been sarcastic. Not really. And when she talked about safety, she didn't mean *physical* safety, though, hell, yes, that was important, too.

But she wanted someone she could confide in. She wanted a man who would keep every secret that she had. A man who would let her confess all—and when he knew her secrets, she'd never fear that he'd turn on her.

Like that would happen. Some wishes were impossible. "I should get to bed." In addition to their hunting, she had actual legal work to do for her job. "I need to be at the office at eight tomorrow. I've got briefs to review. Clients scheduled." She should go to bed. So why hadn't she moved?

"I traveled all over the whole world looking for a place to belong."

She swallowed. "Sometimes, those places just don't exist."

"Maybe. Maybe not."

Her gaze dropped to the floor. "It's late." Way past late. "I should get to bed."

"You said that already."

Yes, she had.

His hand curled under her chin. "You don't need to run from me."

She wasn't running. Aspen was certain she'd been conducting a very slow walk.

"You want to set rules for us? Go ahead."

"Rules?"

"Yeah. Seems like you're telling me that fucking is fine, but there will be no sleeping together."

Heat burned her cheeks.

He laughed. "How can you do that?"

"Do what?"

"Blush like that...when you were just clawing your nails down my back moments ago."

Her throat cleared. "I just—" She stopped. "I thought you were breaking rules. Isn't that what the whole...ah, fucking bit was about?"

His hand still held her chin. Ever so carefully. "No, the whole fucking bit was about me needing you so much that I wanted to devour you."

She would not tell him that he'd been the first man to go down on her. Letting a man do that—in her mind, it took trust. She was at her most vulnerable then. She'd worried she'd never be able to fully let go and just be in the moment. Until...Gideon.

*Wait. Am I saying that I trust him?* But...didn't she? Wasn't that why she'd told him about Braden? Wasn't that why she'd had sex with Gideon in the first place?

"The rules are for you," he explained quietly. "Because you are a woman who values control."

Her spine stiffened.

"You believed I didn't know that?" His thumb brushed over her lower lip. Her mouth parted and she thought about licking his thumb. About nipping him. But his next words had a bit of fear snaking through her heart.

"I know far more than you realize."

Was this his psychology background coming into play? Or had he been digging into *her* life with his Wilde friends?

"You want control. Rules give you that feeling of control. Personally, I say screw the rules. But if they make you happy..." His hand dropped to his side, and he shrugged. "Tell me your terms. I'll tell you mine. I'm sure we'll be able to work out a deal.

You're a lawyer, after all, so that means you're all about the details."

Yes, she was. "Fucking is fine." Crisp. Like she talked about this sort of thing all the time. Uh, no. "But I thought you'd prefer your privacy for sleeping."

He stared back at her.

Determinedly, she continued, "Sleeping implies a degree of intimacy..."

"And fucking doesn't?"

Her lips thinned. "We're vulnerable when we sleep."

"And when we fuck. In fact, I'd argue that a man is at his weakest then because all of his attention is focused..." His gaze swept her. "Elsewhere."

Her whole body had heated beneath his sweeping gaze. "Well, I can certainly promise not to go after you when you're at your weakest, if that's a rule you want to add."

One eyebrow quirked. "Good to know."

She crossed her arms over her chest. Her knees felt a wee bit shaky. "Did you have any other items to add?"

"Sure." An easy reply. "No lies."

She would not stiffen.

"And I'm not talking about you telling me things like I'm the best you've ever had or that I've totally ruined you for any other man. You can tell me sweet shit like that all night long."

She wouldn't, but...

*God, it's true.*

"See, I don't want lies from you. I don't want half-truths. I don't want partial stories. I don't want the back of my neck prickling because something is off. I want to be able to believe you completely, and in order for that to happen...no lies."

Her chin lifted. "You are the best I've ever had."

His eyes immediately narrowed.

"Is your neck prickling?" Why had she thrown out that taunt?

"No." His gaze glittered. "And I can sure as hell tell you that I've never wanted a woman more than I wanted you, and nothing has ever felt as good as the way *you* feel when I'm balls deep inside and your nails are digging into my back."

It was hot in there.

Or, maybe that was just him.

"What are your other rules?" he asked. His voice had gone a little hoarse. She darted a glance down.

His sweatpants were tenting. Or had they been doing that all along?

He wanted to go again?

*Yes, yes, please.* But... "You never signed my contract."

"Yeah. Screw the contract. You trust me to do the job or you don't."

That wasn't exactly how things worked.

"Is the contract part of the rules?" Hard. Rough. "If I don't sign it, then I don't get you?"

Her stomach clenched. "If I said yes..."

He stepped closer. Brought his mouth right over hers, just an inch or so away. She wanted to taste him. Wanted to let go of everything again and get lost in that wild passion that burned between them.

But Aspen shook her head. "No."

His mouth was still above hers.

"It's not part of the rules," she whispered. He wanted no lies? She could give him some truths. "I want you. The agreement I have with Wilde has nothing to do with how I feel. My contract has nothing to do with it. I want you, you want me. We keep going this way and no one gets hurt. That's my rule. *No one gets hurt.*"

"I would never hurt you." His words almost sounded like a vow.

She wanted to believe him.

But another man had once told her the same thing. Braden had sworn that he loved her. That he could make her happy. That he'd never hurt her.

He'd been lying.

Should she tell Gideon that she hated lies just as much as he did?

But she didn't get the chance. His mouth took hers, and she stopped wanting to do anything but feel.

*** 

Gideon stared up at the ceiling. Aspen was in the bed beside him. Her breath came lightly, and he knew she'd gone to sleep.

He'd been too rough. Too hungry. Next time, he'd try to do better.

*Next time.* Because they had a deal now. A bargain struck on mutual desire. Maybe she thought the lust would burn out.

He didn't think so.

She didn't realize that he was just pulling her into his web. She wouldn't see the truth, not until it was too late. By then, he was hoping she'd be well and truly caught.

"No!" The cry burst from her. Strangled and rough, but distinct enough to understand.

Another of her bad dreams?

He stroked her arm. "You're okay."

Her eyes opened. Her head turned toward him. The lamp was on nearby—Aspen had insisted on it being left on—and as she looked at him, she said, this time, quite clearly, "You're dead."

Then her eyes closed, and she went back to sleep.

# CHAPTER NINE

"I'm perfectly safe here," Aspen assured Gideon for what had to be the tenth time. "Go to the hospital. Get Elijah." Because the doctors had insisted on keeping him for observation, and she knew he had been way less than pleased. She knew it because he'd shouted his disapproval so loudly she'd heard him while he talked on the phone to Gideon. "There are two security guards on the ground floor, and they check everyone before allowing admission to the office building. And in *my* office, my assistant will be waiting, and my investigator will also be on hand. I will have plenty of company, and again, I will be—"

"Perfectly safe," he growled back. "Yeah, you'd better be." Stubble darkened his cheeks. His hair had been finger combed back from his forehead, and he looked utterly delectable.

Not that she'd tell him that.

But she'd sure think it.

"I'll be back at lunch," he promised her. "Noon."

"Then you can be my lunch date." That would work well with their cover.

"Sounds like a plan."

She should go inside. Not like she could just linger on the sidewalk all day. But... "What all are you doing this morning?"

"Taking care of Elijah's grumpy ass. Then running down some leads."

She'd thought he would say that. *Hunting.* That had most definitely been on the agenda, but she'd rather hoped he'd wait until she finished up and could join him. "What kind of leads?"

"The kind of leads that tell me if your ex Braden is a dead man walking."

"Gideon..." She glanced around, but no one was close.

He pressed a quick kiss to her lips. "Better go inside. The security officers are starting to side eye me."

She grabbed tightly to his arm before he could back away. "Be careful."

"Hey, no worries. It will just be me doing a little red flag waving. Our original plan, remember?"

But that planned had changed. "Do not get hurt."

"Aw, now you sound as if you care."

She did. More than she'd expected. "If you get a concussion, if you get shot, if you get hurt in any manner, I will not be amused."

He flashed her that slow, sexy grin of his. "Duly noted."

And she had to let him go. Aspen turned on her heel and strode into the office building. The security guards greeted her with warm familiarity, but Aspen couldn't help glancing back over her shoulder.

She caught Gideon watching her through the window.

***

"I am going to rip him apart." Elijah slammed the truck's door shut and glowered at Gideon. "He got the drop on me. *On me.* Do you have any idea how embarrassing this shit is? When the other agents at Wilde hear about this, they will not let me live it down. I mean, dammit, I had a streak going. I was untouchable. I was—"

"I have a lead. Do you want to hear about it or do you want to continue to bitch at me?"

Elijah sniffed. "I would prefer to do both, thank you for asking."

Gideon slapped him on the shoulder. "There he is. I was hoping that hit on the head hadn't taken away that lovely spark of yours."

"Fuck off."

"We could be after a dead man."

Elijah squinted at him. "Maybe the blow to the head rattled me more than I thought."

"Braden Savage. According to Aspen, she had quite the run-in with him years ago. So many years ago, in fact, that she thought he was dead."

Elijah was still squinting. "Why would she think he was dead just because time had passed?"

"Oh, she thought he was dead..." *Because she may have killed him.* "Because his boat washed ashore without him on it," he replied carefully. "The Coast Guard searched and turned up nothing. People assumed he'd drowned."

"But we don't assume that any longer?"

"No, we don't."

Elijah straightened. "So where do we start?"

"We start by talking to some locals who will know more about Braden and his family. Turns out that his father Frank was quite the interesting individual."

"You say that in a bad way."

Gideon just smiled.

\*\*\*

"Want to tell me why we're stopping at a bar first thing in the morning?" Elijah asked wryly as he climbed out of the truck and stared at Armageddon. "Sure, I get that you're trying to cheer me up after my bad experience, and you definitely get buddy points, but I thought you wanted to track down leads."

Gideon slammed his door. "We are tracking down leads." He pointed up. "We're not going to the bar. We're going to the PI office located on top of the bar."

Elijah tilted his head back and peered up at the building's second floor. "How about that."

Gideon walked across the street. "The owner is an old buddy of mine. The man knows his whiskey and his intel." In fact, Warren "War" Channing had actually tried to lure Gideon away from Wilde and down to his PI office in Pensacola.

The offer had been tempting.

Especially since War was one of his oldest friends.

They strode up the exterior stairs that took them to the second floor, and before they could open the door there, it was already swinging open.

War stood on the threshold with a wide smile on his face.

"Gideon, you sonofabitch..." He hauled Gideon in for a bear hug. "You drop in my town and give me a text heads-up that you're five minutes away? Dude, why aren't you just staying with me and Rose? You know we have extra room."

He slapped War on the back before releasing him. Life post-SEAL service had been good to War. His friend had settled down. Gotten married of all things. And War's PI business was booming. So much so that even Eric was taking notice.

Eric would like to incorporate Trouble for Hire with Wilde. He'd made a ridiculously high offer to War in order to do just that.

War's response?

*Fuck off.*

War's gaze swept over him, then darted to a silent Elijah.

"This is my partner, Elijah Cross," Gideon said. "Elijah, this is War, one the best bastards you'd ever want to have at your side in a fight."

Elijah extended his hand. "Good to meet you."

"Likewise." War gave him a firm shake. His expression turned thoughtful. "This is *not* a social call."

No, it wasn't. "How about we go inside?" Where he knew War would have assured they had complete privacy.

Without another word, War turned and headed back inside. They followed him through a small lobby and into his office. He shut the door behind them. Let them take their seats, then War propped a hip on his desk as he lounged there in a seemingly relaxed pose. "Exactly what is this about?"

"You know everything that's happening in this town," Gideon began carefully.

"I try." A modest reply.

"I need to know about Frank Savage."

A ripple of surprise crossed War's face. His dark eyes glinted. "He's dead."

"Right, so I hear." *There's a lot of that going around...* "What was he like before his death?"

"A dangerous bastard. He had his hands in all sorts of illegal pies. The guy had enemies left and right."

Enemies. Check. "Enemies like...Ramsey Hyde?"

War's head cocked to the right. "Ramsey?"

"You know all about him, too, don't you?"

War gave him a careful smile. Then his stare drifted to Elijah. "Where are my manners? I should have offered you some coffee. There's a pot down the hall. Why don't you go help yourself, Elijah?"

"Uh..." Elijah shook his head. "Thanks, man. I'm good."

War's careful smile tightened around the edges. "Why don't you go help yourself? AKA, I don't really know you, so I want to have this talk with Gideon alone. Nothing personal, you understand. One just has to be careful with business these days."

Elijah raised his eyebrows as he turned his head toward Gideon. After a brief hesitation,

Gideon nodded. If War wanted to talk with him alone for a moment, fine.

"You know what?" Elijah said to no one in particular. "Suddenly, I feel the need for coffee. I'll go find some. Be back soon." He sauntered for the door.

It closed softly behind him.

Gideon waited a beat of time. "Do you even have coffee?"

"No, what the hell do I look like? A coffee shop? He wants coffee, there is a bakery down the street." War crossed his arms over his chest. "Why are you pushing into Ramsey Hyde's business?"

Hello, new red flag. Now he had to look at War with suspicion. "Don't tell me you're working for him, too."

"Too?"

Gideon unclenched his back teeth. "Are you on the guy's payroll?"

A dangerous anger lit War's eyes. "You know me better than that."

He did. He just... Gideon raked a hand over his face.

"What is this about?" War asked softly. "Be straight with me, and I'll give you as much help as I can. But you just waltzed into my office with a five-minute heads-up, and you immediately started grilling me about two of the most dangerous men I know. Granted, one of those guys is in the ground, but the other one—believe me when I say you don't want to suddenly be on his radar."

*Too late.*

"What you say won't leave this office." War waited.

Gideon exhaled. "You ever hear of a woman named Aspen Gray?"

A nod. "Sure, I know Aspen." Said easily. Casually.

Gideon stiffened. "You do?"

"Yeah, she's the best defense attorney in town, and our paths have crossed. Fairly recently, as a matter of fact." Now War straightened. "Is something wrong with Aspen?"

Gideon stared back at him.

"Aspen is Ramsey's attorney," War continued, voice slower, more thoughtful. "But you already know this because...?"

"Let's say I have a personal interest in Aspen."

War seemed to absorb that bit of info. "And the guy who just went looking coffee? Does he have a personal interest in her, too?"

"Elijah has an interest in helping me."

War rubbed his chin. "Has someone hired Wilde to take down Ramsey Hyde? Because if so, and you think you're going to use his lawyer to do the deed, I'd advise you to think again. Aspen has very deep ties to Ramsey, and from what I know about her, she's not the kind of woman who ever turns on those close to her."

Good to know. "My interest in Ramsey is only in how he relates to Aspen."

War studied him in silence.

"It's a *very* personal interest," Gideon added.

"Since when?"

*Since I had her in my bed. Since she went molten beneath me.* No, since...

*Since she stood on the beach, and I could hear the tremble in her voice. I knew she was only telling me half the truth, but I still wanted to pull her into my arms and keep her safe because I knew she was terrified.*

No, since...

*Since she chased after me at her house and grabbed me because she was afraid I was about to get hit. Since she'd stared up at me and yelled with worry in her voice.*

No, even before that...

*Since...fuck, since she walked through the Wilde office door?*

"Yeah, okay, you think on that," War advised him. "Obviously, it's giving you some trouble."

Gideon scratched his cheek with his middle finger.

War laughed, but the quick bark of laughter faded almost instantly when Gideon confessed—

"She's in danger."

War surged away from the desk. "Aspen is? Why the hell didn't she come to me? Everyone knows I'm the best freaking PI in town!"

Gideon rose from the chair. *Because she doesn't want people who know her getting close to the truth.* "Because she came to me. I'm handling things for her."

"Handling. Right. As in...?"

"As in I'm living in her house. I'm sticking close. I'm eliminating the threat that has started to plague her."

War's eyes narrowed. "What kind of threat?"

"How about we go back to what you know about Frank Savage...and his son, Braden."

"Braden? I thought the guy was dead."

And again...*there's a hell of a lot of that going around.*

"Frank Savage was an old-school bastard," War told him. "One of the big crime guys who had his fingers in every pie and didn't tolerate someone trying to take what belonged to him. It should go without saying that he and Ramsey did not get along."

*And is that why Saul was killed? A message to Ramsey?*

"Ramsey isn't in that world any longer. Aspen should have told you that."

"Aspen doesn't talk about her clients. She told me to stay the hell away from Ramsey and not ask any questions about him."

War blinked. "And you came straight to me...and started asking questions."

A shrug. "Figured that you wouldn't run to Ramsey and tell him about our talk. Also figured you'd give me the real intel on him." A pause. "Did I figure wrong?"

"No, you didn't. Look, there are plenty of people out there who will tell you Ramsey is as violent and twisted as they come..."

That wasn't Aspen's story.

"But you can't believe everything you hear," War said gruffly. "I swear, I will kick your ass if you repeat this outside of this room but, hell, I kinda like the guy. Might have even played poker with him a few times."

Unexpected.

"I can tell you that he and Aspen are tight. And if someone is messing with her..."

This was something he wanted to know. Because Aspen seemingly had Ramsey's powerful connections at her beck and call. *But she wasn't turning to him for help.* "Would he start a battle for her?"

"Even though he's supposed to be out of the game? Yes. If some of Savage's old team were to target her, he would but..." War began to pace. "Savage only had one son, Braden. There has been no word about him in ages."

"So, yes, let me stop you right there because I've got a problem with what I'm hearing." He rubbed the back of his neck. "Frank Savage is a badass, and his only son vanishes? You're really telling me that Frank didn't rip the world apart trying to find him? Because I'm having trouble with that part of the story."

War stopped pacing. He stared out of his window at the street below. "You don't look if you want people to vanish."

Surprise rocked through Gideon. "You're telling me that Frank *wanted* his own son to vanish?"

"A few other cases I've had put me in the Savage world. From what I picked up, Braden wasn't what he wanted the world to believe he was. His father kicked him out of the business. Braden didn't choose to leave because he was some upstanding citizen." War turned toward a watchful Gideon. "Braden was viewed by many in the inner circle—including his own father—as being dangerously unstable. Now you just take a minute and realize how bad that must have been, for *him* to get that label from a crime boss father."

"Wouldn't have thought that label was even possible," Gideon replied carefully.

"It's possible if you think your kid won't be able to handle business. If he blows up and can't manage control. If he crosses the line too much, gets violent too much, and thinks that no laws will ever apply to him. If his actions jeopardized everything Frank Savage had built..."

Okay, Gideon was getting the picture.

But War wasn't done. "Then, of course, there were the rumors that Braden wasn't even Frank's kid."

Well, well. "You do have good intel." *Call me impressed.*

"It was probably easier for Frank to kick Braden to the curb when he realized the guy wasn't his kid."

And easier to just let the mystery of his disappearance fade away?

War scraped a hand over his chin. "But Frank is dead, and Braden has been gone for a while now, so what do they have to do with Aspen Gray?"

Gideon squared his shoulders. "Does anyone have proof that Braden is dead?"

"Actually..." A frown. "No."

"Right. In that case, I think the sonofabitch may be stalking my lady."

# CHAPTER TEN

"Aspen?" Her assistant poked his head in the doorway and grimaced. "I'm sorry, but there is someone in the lobby insisting to see you."

She automatically glanced at her watch. Five minutes until her scheduled lunch break. "That's my boyfriend." Like that term didn't feel odd. "You can escort Gideon right inside, and, Zan, he doesn't ever have to wait, unless I'm meeting with someone else. You can send him directly in—"

The door shoved open.

"Hello, Aspen," a deep, male voice said, one with a slightly raspy edge. "I don't think I'm the man you were expecting."

No, he absolutely was not. Beneath the desk, her hands immediately fisted.

"Thanks for showing me in," the visitor said to Zan, "But I'm good now." He made a shooing motion with his hand toward the assistant.

Zan glared. "You do *not* have an appointment."

"Yes, but I have a history with Aspen, and I think she'll want to see me so..." He let his words trail away.

Aspen swallowed. "It's okay, Zan. I've got this. I am acquainted with Mr. Eros."

"Aw, come on, you know you can call me Jake."

She rose. "Thank you, Zan."

"Yes, well, I'll just go to lunch..." Zan hauled the door shut on his way out.

Silence.

Jake didn't approach her. She didn't take a step toward him. When a snake was close, it was always a good idea not to make any sudden movements. You never knew when it might strike.

"You look good, Aspen. Then again, you always do."

"Let's skip the fake pleasantries, shall we? I do have an appointment waiting."

"Oh, right." He snapped his fingers. "The boyfriend. We do not want to keep him waiting." He finally took a few steps toward her desk.

She flattened her hands on the hard surface. "I hear you've recently come into some power..."

"Oh, are you talking about the fact that when Frank Savage died, he left everything to me?" His smile was that of a satisfied cat. "Imagine my surprise."

Aspen doubted there would have been any surprise.

"With my change of fortune, I find myself in need of good legal counsel...which is why I am here today."

He'd caught her off guard. "You want me to be your lawyer?"

"Um."

That had not been a yes or no. "Are you currently being charged with any crimes?"

"Not currently. But I think it's probably a good idea to get you on retainer. I hear you're the best." His blue eyes gleamed. Very distinct eyes. "I want the best."

"I'm afraid my client roster is full at the moment," Aspen told him smoothly. "But I can refer you to some associates who are more than capable of handling any issues that might arise for you."

He stopped right on the other side of her desk. His hands flattened on the top, too, as he leaned toward her. "If you're my lawyer, then you have to keep everything confidential."

She didn't even try to touch that statement.

"Don't you think it's in our best interests if you and I make sure we have an ironclad agreement about the things we keep confidential?" he murmured.

Goosebumps rose onto her arms. "What happened?"

"Why?" A careful question. "Has something happened to *you* lately?"

"I am not in the mood for your games." She hadn't seen Jake in years, for a very specific reason. The man was terrifying.

"I'm not in the mood for games, either." His voice roughened even more. "So either you're doing some late-date screwing around that is not funny and will get you *nowhere* or..."

A sharp knock sounded at her door. It was followed immediately by a disgruntled, "Why the hell is no one at the desk out here?" before the door swung open.

Her gaze flew to the door. To the large, fierce man who filled the doorway. A man who didn't scare her at all, but instead, made the fear she'd felt moments before seep away from her. Her shoulders straightened, and a quick gasp of relief slipped past her lips.

*Gideon.*

But then Gideon took in the scene before him. The guy leaning forward with his hands on Aspen's desk. An aggressive stance. "What's going on?" Gideon stalked forward and circled the desk to stand at Aspen's side. "Who are you, and why does it look like you were threatening her?" A hard, deadly edge of steel underscored his words.

Jake pushed from the desk. Took a step back. "The boyfriend, I presume."

Aspen cleared her throat. "This is Gideon."

"Pleasure to meet you, Gideon."

Gideon grunted. "Who. Are. You?"

Jake offered his hand. "Jake Eros."

She felt tension sweep through Gideon's body.

"Oh, you've heard of me?" Jake asked.

Gideon took the offered hand. She had the feeling there was a whole lot of fierce grip strength being used in that shake even before Jake winced.

Jake also hurriedly tugged his hand back. "I'll take that as a yes," Jake concluded. "And you...haven't heard good things?" His gaze cut to Aspen. "I am wounded."

"Aspen hasn't told me a damn thing about you," Gideon responded.

Jake's eyes narrowed. "Then you have other sources?"

"Why are you here?" Gideon snapped.

"I needed a lawyer." Casual. "Aspen is the best in town."

"He's not wrong on that," Aspen agreed.

"Yeah, you're spectacular, sweetheart," Gideon flatly told her. "But that's not why he's here."

No, Jake was there because he seemed to be having the same problem that she had. *Some late-date screwing around...* "I believe someone might be stalking Jake."

"Why would you believe that?" Jake immediately returned. "Is someone stalking *you*? Is that why you have such a very large and determined boyfriend standing ever so protectively at your side?"

She reached for Gideon and curled her fingers around his wrist, silently signaling for him not to give too much away to Jake. "If you're in trouble, Jake—"

"What? Will you help me? In that case, you should certainly reconsider the offer I made to you."

The offer to be his lawyer. Because whatever he had occurring, Jake thought he needed legal protection? "What have you done?"

Jake smiled at her. "As always, I am the picture of innocence. Just, of course, as you are." He motioned toward Gideon. "Since you have that lunch date waiting, I'll see myself out." But first, he put a business card on her desk. A plain, white card that had a series of numbers printed in black. "My personal number. In case you change your mind and want to increase your clientele." After giving an inclination of his head, he headed for the door.

She reached for the card. Tucked it in her top drawer. She didn't need his number. She already had it. She'd called him once before, a desperate call in the middle of the night, and that time, he'd helped her.

Or, maybe he'd helped himself.

The door closed.

"Yeah, so..." Gideon began as he turned toward her. "That whole bit about you being perfectly safe here at the office? Sure feels like bullshit right now considering that Frank Savage's right-hand man and his top enforcer just happened to be in here, threatening you." A low, rough curse. "*Fucking threatening you.*"

"I...don't think he actually was threatening me."

"Sure as hell looked like he was to me. When I came in, he was looming over your desk and the two of you were going toe-to-toe."

"That's because I think we may have the same enemy." Something she should have considered before now. To a certain extent, her secrets were his.

And Jake's were hers.

She let go of Gideon's wrist, somewhat surprised to see that she'd still been holding him. "We should go eat. I'm starving." She reached into her desk for her bag.

"Yeah, baby, nice try, but I want to know what the hell is happening first."

Her fingers clenched around the strap of her bag. "You already obviously know so much. You leave for a few hours and then you come back telling me that Jake is connected to Frank

Savage." She swallowed. "I bet you had lots of enlightening conversations today." From the sound of things, his "hunting" expedition without her had certainly yielded results. So much for them doing things together—

He wrapped his hands around her waist and lifted her up onto her desk.

"Wait—what are you doing?" Her hands flew down onto the wooden surface.

He kicked her chair back—she figured it must have been in his way—and slipped between her legs. His hands kept their grip on his waist. "Making sure you don't run away before we clear up some things."

"I wasn't running." He seemed to accuse her of that a lot. "I was going to lunch with you."

"Why did Jake Eros come to see you?"

"I told you already. I think we have the same enemy. I think—based on the way he was acting— that Jake has been contacted, too. I believe it's likely he's being threatened as well."

"Doesn't strike me as a bright idea to threaten a man with his connections." A pause. "Or with yours. Because it seems that if you wanted a problem to vanish, all you have to do is turn to your buddy Ramsey, and he'll light the world on fire to protect you."

Gideon had definitely been busy. "I don't think I would go that far."

"No?"

"No, but…" *Give him the truth.* "I didn't want to see what he would do. And my problems aren't his."

"Even if those problems tie back to your dead father, who was probably killed as a message to Ramsey?"

Her lips pressed together.

"Uh, huh. Sure. They don't relate to him at all, got you."

She swallowed as her gaze cut away from him. His touch burned through her clothes. "Who did you go see today?"

One hand lifted from her waist. Caught her chin. Carefully turned her head back so that she was looking at him.

"You need to stop digging on Ramsey." She licked her lips. "I warned you..."

"Ramsey won't know what the hell I did. My friend is a vault. He's also someone with some serious knowledge of the people in this town. And a guy with one fine whiskey collection."

Her stomach clenched. No. No, no, no. A thousand times...*no*. He could not possibly be talking about—

"War clued me in and filled in some of the blank spaces for me."

*War.* The drumming of her heartbeat thundered in her ears. "You know War Channing?"

"Yes, and, apparently, so do you."

Oh, God. This was bad. She'd deliberately avoided War and the Trouble for Hire PI team because she didn't want anyone close to her knowing the truth. War was the freaking true-blue type. Ramsey always called him Captain Asshole, Captain America's cousin. "You told War about me?"

"Told War that I was worried about my lady. That someone was scaring her, and I wanted to know what the hell was happening. He had intel on Frank Savage and on Braden. He also filled me in on some details regarding Ramsey." His thumb slid gently over her chin. "And he gave me a file on Jake Eros. Because he told me that with Frank Savage gone and Braden out of the picture, everything in the Savage empire now belonged to Jake."

"It does."

"Because Frank's son wasn't around to collect his inheritance."

*Tell him.* "Frank's son did get what he deserved."

"I get that he was a bastard who—"

She wasn't talking about Braden. "You ever see a photo of Frank Savage?" Had War shown him a pic?

He frowned and then—

"He has quite distinct eyes," she added softly. "Shockingly bright. Incredibly blue. Sure, there are plenty of people who have blue eyes in the world, but not quite that shade. Just as there *aren't* plenty of people who have the same dimple in their chins, and the same thick, slightly curly hair..."

"Jake is Frank's son."

"I couldn't say that without seeing DNA evidence, of course," she told him. *But all signs sure point to yes.*

"But you think it."

She did.

"And Jake?" Gideon asked. "What does he think?"

"Jake has always known who his father is."

"Well, well..." He absorbed that info. "According to War, the rumor around town is that Braden wasn't related to Frank at all." He let go of her chin. Whistled. "Damn. I bet Jake was thrilled when Braden went missing. If Jake was the real son all along, if everything was supposed to be his, then when Braden vanished, and Jake finally got what he figured he'd been owed, hell, yes, freaking *thrilled*."

Thrilled didn't quite cover it.

*You tell no one about this night, got it?* Jake's voice pushed through her head. *I won't have your death on me, Aspen.*

Her hands rose and pressed to Gideon's chest. "Let me down."

"Aspen?"

She pushed harder.

He backed up. "What is it?"

She jumped off the desk. Turned her back on him. "There is so much involved in this mess. I want to tell you everything, but I'm afraid."

"Afraid of what? That I'll turn you over to the cops because you—"

Aspen whirled back toward him. Her hand lifted and her fingers pressed to his lips. "Don't say it." Tears stung her eyes. *If you don't say it, then I can almost pretend...*

It didn't happen.

She could pretend she hadn't killed Braden Savage.

Except...

She looked at her fingers as they pressed to his mouth. For an instant, she saw blood. *From when the knife went in. From the blood that poured out of Braden.* Gasping, she wrenched her hand back and stumbled away from Gideon.

"You have to trust me," he gritted from behind her.

It wasn't about trust. She didn't want him lying for her. Covering for her. When the heck had things switched and she started worrying about that? Aspen rushed toward the window and swiped at her cheek. For some unknown reason, her cheek was wet.

She stared blindly down below and tried to get her foggy eyes to focus.

Except when they focused...

Aspen saw Jake heading into an alley. And a man in a black ski mask ran toward that same alley. Right before the guy in the ski mask turned and disappeared from sight, she could have sworn that she saw the glint of a knife in his hand. Her own hand slammed into the glass of the window and instinctively she screamed, "Jake!"

But he couldn't hear her. She knew that. Just as she knew that Jake was about to be attacked in that alley.

"What is it?" Gideon demanded.

She spun. "Someone's after Jake in the alley below. A man in a black ski mask." She darted for the door. Gideon beat her to it. Blocked her path with his massive form. "We have to help him!" she cried.

"Tell me what you saw."

"I saw a man with a knife! Now, we have to go! Come on!"

But he grabbed her when she tried to dart around him. "No, you stay here."

"What?"

"Stay here. This could be a trap. Dammit, at least promise to stay downstairs in the lobby with the guard!"

Fine, yes, whatever. Just... "Go!"

\*\*\*

Gideon drew his weapon as soon as he entered the alley. A security guard was several steps behind him. One of the guards had stayed inside the office building with Aspen, but the other had insisted on following him.

A groan reached his ears.

Gideon tensed.

"H-help..." Weak.

Gideon kept his gun at the ready and hurried forward. When he slipped around the edge of the building, he saw a figure slumped near a dumpster. Jake Eros had his hand pressed to his stomach, and blood seeped from between his fingers.

"Shit!" A startled exclamation from the guard.

Jake's head lifted. "Get...ambulance..."

"Yeah, yeah, right, on it," the guard said.

Gideon scanned the area. He didn't see the attacker.

"G-gone..." Jake gasped out. "Bastard ran...after he...st-stabbed..."

Gideon advanced on Jake so he could better see the wound. "Search the area," he barked to the guard. But the guard mostly seemed to be just standing there and gaping. So much for the guy keeping the building safe.

The blood was pumping fast from Jake. His skin had gone ashen. "W-was...on my phone. Heard rustle behind me...t-turned..."

"It's okay. Save your strength." Gideon crouched near him.

Jake's bloody hand flew out and grabbed his shirt. "*Find him.*"

He would, as soon as he made sure the jackass before him wasn't bleeding out. Gideon studied the wound, the depth, the amount of blood pumping... "How about we keep pressure on this wound?"

"It's...because of her." Jake's voice was low.

After calling for help on his phone, the guard had rushed off to search toward the left, where the alley twisted and snaked behind another building.

"Her?" Gideon repeated just as softly.

"When he stabbed me...said...she...she did same..."

Gideon's jaw locked.

"She stabbed him." Jake's lashes fluttered and his eyes seemed to roll back. "He...he stabbed me. P-payback..."

"Aspen hasn't stabbed anyone. You are mistaken."

Jake tried to shake his head.

"*You are mistaken,*" Gideon snarled.

"I see something!" the guard yelled.

Gideon flew to his feet. He whirled to follow the sound of the guard's voice, only to see the fellow double-timing it back toward him. The guard clutched something dark in his right hand.

"Found his mask!" he proclaimed proudly as he held it up.

"What about the attacker?" Gideon thundered. "Did you find him?"

A quick, negative shake of the man's head.

Dammit. Gideon yanked out his phone. Had Elijah on the line moments later. "Got an attack in the alley near Aspen's office. Perp is on foot and armed with a knife."

Elijah had been waiting down the road at a restaurant.

"What the hell?" Elijah's shocked reply. "Aspen was attacked?"

Gideon looked back down at Jake. Shit. He'd passed out. "Not her."

"Thank Christ. Look, I'm on the way. I'll help you search!"

They'd search, but he had a feeling the attacker was long gone. All he'd needed to do was ditch his ski mask and then he could have blended with everyone else walking on the main roads. But maybe when they pulled the street cams from the area, they'd get lucky. Aspen had seen the man— so had Jake—and they could describe what he was wearing. If Gideon could find a man with the same outfit on the cameras, minus the mask...

*We'll ID you and track you down.*

He hung up the phone. Looked back at Jake. Dropped near him and put pressure on the wound. The deep cut wasn't going to kill the other man. It was bleeding like a sonofabitch, but didn't appear to be near anything vital. "You'll live."

"You sure?" Jake's low voice. His eyes were closed, but the guy was still aware.

How about that? Jake had seemed to be drifting out of consciousness moments before, but his current awareness was undeniable. *Just how hurt are you?* "No," Gideon snapped. "I'm no doctor. I have no idea if you'll live or die. Maybe you should say your prayers just in case."

Jake's eyes opened. "I pray...you can keep her safe."

"Don't worry about that, I will." Gideon pushed down harder on the wound.

Jake grunted.

"I will do anything I have to do in order to protect Aspen." And *his* words were a warning.

# CHAPTER ELEVEN

The ambulance rushed away with a scream of its sirens. The beat cops who were on scene turned to Aspen one more time.

"And you never saw his face?" Officer Kathleen O'Reilly asked her.

"No, I was upstairs." She pointed to her window and kept her voice steady as she added, "I looked down, and I saw Mr. Eros heading into the alley. He was followed by a man in a black ski mask."

"A man with a knife." The red-haired male in uniform rocked forward onto the balls of his feet. Officer Tommy Coggs. "You said you saw a knife."

"I said I *thought* I saw the glint of what could have been a knife." She'd been over this several times already. Her story hadn't changed. It wouldn't. "The man appeared well-built, muscled. Looked fairly tall, maybe a few inches over six feet. He was wearing black pants, a black sweatshirt, and gloves. I didn't see his face. Didn't glimpse his hair." She could only shake her head. "There is very little else that I can offer here."

Tommy nodded. "Probably a robbery," he figured as he looked back at his partner.

"Uh, the vic was Jake Eros," Kathleen pointed out.

Tommy nodded. "Yep, that's his name."

"You don't rob Jake Eros." Obviously, Kathleen was far more informed than the male cop. But Aspen had already pegged him as being new to the area, anyway. Kathleen continued with a grim air, "This won't end well. Someone will want payback."

Someone already did want payback. "If that's all, I need to go." The cops had already talked to Gideon, and he was waiting for Aspen near his truck. He and Elijah were speaking quietly to each other, and she wanted to find out what the hell they were saying.

She also wanted to see if Gideon had learned anything about the perp that he *hadn't* shared with the uniformed cops.

"Sure, go ahead," Tommy directed her.

She gave the cops a tight smile, then hurried toward Gideon. Was it her imagination or did he stiffen as she approached? And what was up with the shadows that she could see in his eyes?

He and Elijah also immediately stopped talking when she joined them.

So she blurted, "You saved Jake's life."

"Nah," Gideon's immediate denial. All casual. Like they were just talking about the weather. "You're the one who saw what was happening. If it weren't for you, Eros could be dead in that alley."

Because the attacker had run away. Had he been scared off when he heard Gideon's approach?

"Figure Jake Eros owes you both," Elijah added with a small inclination of his head. "Think he'll be feeling generous once the docs finish sewing him up?"

"Jake isn't the generous type," she replied in a low voice. "He's more the type to take everything that he can as he lets the world burn around him."

"Is that right?" Gideon's voice still seemed way too casual. "You and Jake go back far?"

"Far enough." She'd almost told Gideon everything about Jake in her office, and she wanted to tell him more, but on the street, with cops nearby? Not the best place for those confessions. "The police think this was a robbery gone wrong."

Gideon shook his head.

She sidled even closer to him. "I was afraid of that." The timing had been way too coincidental. "Did Jake tell you anything useful about his attacker?"

If possible, the shadows in Gideon's eyes grew even deeper. "A few things."

Okay, like what?

But he didn't speak. Her foot tapped on the pavement. "Why are you keeping me in suspense?"

Instead of answering, he shoved away from the side of the truck. He marched to the passenger side and hauled open the door. "We have a lunch date waiting." His voice seemed overly loud, and she knew he was putting on a show for the nearby cops.

Aspen's gaze cut to Elijah. "You coming with us?"

A negative shake of his head. "Got a few things to handle. I'll be catching up later." He gave her a little salute before he sauntered away.

She cast one more glance around the scene. Saw that the female cop was staring a little too hard at her. Right. Definitely time to go. Aspen hurried to the passenger side and started to hop in—

Gideon's head lowered toward her. Probably looked as if he was pressing a kiss to her cheek but really...

He whispered, "No more lies. You're in real fucking danger, and you are telling me everything."

She climbed into the passenger seat. He slammed the door.

\*\*\*

"Tell me. Now."

They were back at Aspen's. Gideon knew Aspen had to go to the police station later for a client—because she'd tensely told him that on the drive over as she sat ever-so-stiffly beside him in the truck—but they had a little time, and he *was* getting to the truth. He'd showered, gotten the damn blood off him, and changed into fresh clothes. Now it was time to clear the air. *No more secrets.*

He could still smell that stinking alley. Could still hear Jake's voice..."It's...because of her."

Fury burned through Gideon. Aspen sat on the couch and stared up at him, her expression almost fearful. What the fuck did she think he was going to do?

"Each time I feel like I'm getting close to the truth with you, I learn that you've been bullshitting me." Gideon's hands clenched and released. "I can't protect you if I don't know what threat is coming."

Her shoulders hunched. "I told you—"

"You told me that you didn't need to be protected. That's bullshit. Jake Eros even needed protecting today. If he hadn't gotten that help, he could be dead. You and Jake—I *know* you are both hiding something."

"Gideon—"

"Did you stab someone?"

She flinched.

*Shit.* He stalked to her. Glowered down at her.

Aspen's head tipped back as she stared up at him. "You can't intimidate a witness."

"What?"

She shook her head. "I-I didn't mean—"

His fingers curled around her shoulders, and he pulled her to her feet. "You're not a witness. You're my—" Gideon broke off because he wasn't sure what to say. Client? Lover? Partner? *Screw it.* "You're mine. I protect what's mine and—" *Dammit.* He let her go. Took a lurching step back as a sinking realization dawned. "Was that what it was fucking about?"

"Wh-what are you talking about?"

His gut clenched. "You coming down the stairs to me last night. The whole seduction routine."

Her eyes flared. Was it his imagination or had she just gone pale? "What are you implying?" Soft. Rasping.

He wasn't implying. He was saying..."You thought that if you fucked me, I wouldn't care that you'd killed—"

"*Stop it.*" Her face wasn't pale. It flushed crimson with fury. "Don't you *dare* say that to me! I did not fuck you for protection or to buy your silence or—or anything like that!"

"No?"

"No!" Aspen practically shouted.

"Then why did you fuck me? Why did you come to me? Why did you push for us to go to bed together when you were damn well not doing it before?"

Her delicate jaw tightened. "I get that it's been a big day."

A big day? A *big* day? An assault in an alley, yeah, that counted as big. His mouth opened—

"But you don't get to be a bastard about things," she snapped at him. "And you don't get to accuse me of sleeping with you just so I can what—control you? Is that it? Is that what you think? Because that's not what I'm doing. I told you, I haven't had a lot of lovers. I'm very particular about who I have sex with, and I sure as hell don't just jump into bed with a guy because I think I can convince him with my amazingly magical vagina that I am not some cold-blooded killer!"

He blinked at her. It had been pretty magical but...

"I had sex with you because I wanted you. Period. Full stop." Her dark eyes glinted. "Everything we did together was because I wanted you and because you wanted me. Don't mess up what was a great night by being an asshole and jumping to conclusions now."

Wait, were her eyes tearing up?

Gideon peered at her in horror.

"Stop looking at me like that!" She blinked rapidly. "I was going to tell you everything about Jake when we were in my office, but then I looked out of the window and saw his attacker. This is hard for me, all right? Hard for me to pull up one of the most terrifying nights of my life, and yes, revealing what went down makes me vulnerable. You *could* turn on me. You could go to the cops. You could decide I'm a terrible human being and walk out on me and that would *hurt* because I actually care what you think and I—" Aspen sucked in a breath.

He waited for more.

She clamped her lips together. The seconds ticked past in tense silence.

"Who did you stab?" he asked her softly.

"I was being attacked. Braden had already broken my arm, and his hands were around my neck." Her hand rose. Pressed to her throat. "I couldn't even beg him to stop because I couldn't speak. Black dots were dancing around my eyes, and my right hand just flew out and grabbed whatever was close." She wet her lower lip. "It was a knife he'd used earlier to cut some fishing line. I grabbed it and the next thing I knew, it was in his chest."

Gideon didn't let his expression change even as fury churned and burned within him. *The bastard had choked her?*

"His hold loosened, and I remember he looked so surprised. Braden glanced down at his chest and so did I, and there was so much blood." A shake of her head. "The blood kept pumping out, and I-I told him to leave the knife in because I knew if Braden took it out, the wound would bleed even more. I raced toward the boat's radio because I was going to call for help, but he screamed behind me. When I looked back, he'd taken the knife out. Braden was coming for me with that knife, even as his blood splashed onto the deck." She shuddered.

Gideon's hands were fisted again. Part of him wanted to pull her close and hold her tight.

Part of him wanted to destroy Braden Savage.

"I got to the back of the boat. I was just running, trying to get away from him, but he charged at me. He swung out with the knife. I ducked, then slipped because waves had crashed back there and the deck was wet. When I slipped, he was swinging too hard and he went..." A swallow. A loud click of sound. "He went over the back. He sank into the water, and I waited, I *looked*, but he didn't come up."

A very different story than the one she'd told him before. "You didn't go to the cops."

"I was on Braden's boat. His blood was all around me. It looked like a slaughter scene."

"But you would've had bruising on your neck. You had a broken arm. You could prove you were attacked."

Her lashes lowered. "Proving to the cops that I was a victim wouldn't be the same thing as proving it to Frank Savage. He and Braden had their differences, but just as a matter of reputation alone, he wouldn't let his son's killer go free. Not when I was standing there at the crime scene, covered in Braden's blood. And with my ties to Ramsey, I knew that if word got out about what I'd done, there would be no end to the violence that came."

She'd been alone on the boat. Surrounded by blood. Hurt. And... "You turned to Jake." Something dark twisted inside of Gideon.

A nod. "I called Jake. I knew him. I'd met him off and on over the years because he'd always been in the same bars where I was. Two kids who didn't belong, but who managed to sneak in, anyway. I thought that if I explained everything to him, he could help to calm down Frank. But..."

"But what?"

"But Jake said there was no explaining. He took me home, and he made the evidence disappear."

The back of Gideon's neck pricked. "You're a criminal defense attorney. You know you can't just walk away from the scene of a crime. You know you can't—"

"I wasn't a criminal defense attorney back then! I was a twenty-one-year-old woman staring into the water, looking for Braden—both hoping that he'd surface and praying he wouldn't—as I called Jake. I was crying, I was shaking, and I was in shock. Jake had recently gotten tighter with Frank. I knew who he was to Frank, who he *really* was, and I thought Jake might be able to make Frank understand...and as I stared into the water, I started realizing just how bad everything looked..." She wrapped her arms around herself and rocked forward.

"Aspen..."

A ragged sigh. "I stood on the back of that bobbing boat and realized that I could look innocent—I could look like a woman who'd been hurt, but I could also look as guilty as hell. After all, *I* was the one who'd inserted myself into Braden's life. I was the one who went after him. I was the one who asked to go out on his boat because I wanted him alone with me. I wanted to push him into confessing. And maybe...maybe I even wanted to kill him." Her lashes lowered. One tear slid down her cheek.

He hated that tear. He hated her pain.

"Before making contact with Braden, I had read the file on my father that the ME prepared. My dad had so many injuries. Bones that were shattered, not just broken. His body was twisted and mangled, and he was left that way for *hours*." Pain and grief burned in her words. "Looking back, a good prosecutor would say I wanted vengeance. The DA would say I wanted my prey to suffer." Her lashes lifted. "And maybe that's exactly what I did want. Even back then, before I'd gone to law school, I knew it wasn't going to be a case where the cops believed me. I was in a bad spot, and I was desperate."

"And Jake made it all go away."

Her lower lip trembled. "Jake wanted Braden to vanish. He'd always wanted it. He took me home, and the next morning, Braden's boat was discovered washed ashore, exactly as I described before. A search was conducted by the Coast Guard, but Braden wasn't found. He was never found."

# CHAPTER TWELVE

"So you and Jake just kept this secret for years?"

She knew Gideon was furious. The edge of rage cut beneath his words. Her chin angled up, and her hair brushed over her shoulders. "I would have kept this secret for the rest of my life." When it had all happened, no, she hadn't been familiar enough with the law...

*Isn't this just another reason why I worked so hard in law school? Why I wanted to be as good as I could be?*

Because she'd known she had to protect herself. Even if the cops bought her story about self-defense, she'd still covered up everything else. She'd still go to prison.

"No wonder you wanted me to sign that damn contract of yours when we were in the limo. You were covering your ass."

"Yes." She didn't look away from him. "Because you now have the power to destroy me."

He pulled her even closer. "Is that honestly what you think I would do?"

"We met days ago." And, yes, she felt closer to him than she had to anyone else, but that was just insanity. He didn't feel the same connection, and even if he did, she'd just confessed to covering up a killing. "I don't know what you'll do."

"Let me show you," he growled.

And he....

Kissed her?

His lips took hers with a ferocious hunger. A hot lust. An angry passion. The kiss was rough and consuming, and it was not what she'd expected. He should be raging at her. He should be calling the cops. He should be asking her question after question or storming away or—

"I will not give you up," he rasped against her mouth.

Give her up as in...turn her over to the cops?

Or...could he possibly mean...*he wouldn't let go?* That he wanted to stay with her, to—

Gideon lifted her up. Her mad thoughts stopped spinning because she couldn't focus on anything but him. His kiss had sparked a wild intensity within her. Her legs locked around his hips and her arms twined around his neck as her tongue met his, and the kiss sent pleasure and need surging through every cell in her body.

His arousal shoved at her core. Her skirt was in the way. A narrow pencil skirt that she'd picked for the office. Her heels had fallen away. She was twisting and arching against him, and all that seemed to matter in that moment was being as close to him as possible.

Her back hit the wall. He'd pushed her against the wall and his mouth tore from hers to kiss a hot path down her neck. One of his powerful hands gripped her waist while the other grabbed the edge of her skirt and shoved it up higher.

Maybe she should stop this. Stop him. Herself. But...

He yanked, and her panties tore. Then his fingers were pushing between her legs, pushing *into* her, and a gasp broke from Aspen as her body jolted and shuddered. Her shoulders pushed back harder against the wall even as her hips pushed down against his fingers. Two broad, long fingers were in her. Working her, stretching. And his thumb rubbed and teased against her clit.

Her heart thundered. She couldn't catch her breath, and her body just kept shuddering as the climax built closer and closer.

"Did you fuck him?"

Her eyes flew open. Green fury stared back at her from his gaze. "I-I told you..."

His fingers withdrew. Thrust back in.

Her inner muscles clamped greedily around him. "No! No, I never slept with Braden, I *told* you—"

"Not Braden." Another withdrawal of those wicked fingers. Then they drove back in and wrung a moan from her. "Jake. The man you called when you were desperate. The man you *trusted* in your darkest moment. Him. Did you fuck him?"

Her breath sawed out. She was on the edge of release and her emotions were frayed to hell and back. "*No!*" A shout.

"Good." His fingers pulled out.

Fury raked through Aspen, and her hands grabbed hard to his shoulders. "You don't get to play with—" *My emotions. With me. With—*

"Not fucking playing. Never with you." His mouth crashed back onto hers. Through his jeans, his hard dick thrust toward her.

The jeans had to go.

Her hand snaked between them. She yanked open his jeans, hauled down the zipper and was exceedingly glad he didn't have on underwear. Because while he might be able to rip hers away, she didn't think she could have done the same to his boxers.

Her fingers curled around his cock. Pumped. Squeezed.

His breath hissed out.

"The bedroom," she managed. "The condoms—"

He kissed her. Dipped his tongue into her mouth and had her heart racing even more. "Got one," he said.

What? Her brain was all foggy and lust soaked, but he pulled back and yanked something from his back pocket.

His wallet.

A condom *in* his wallet. Great. Wonderful. He did some maneuvering, she remained pinned to the wall, and he had that condom on in seconds.

Then there was no more talking or restraint. He sank into her with one long, hard thrust.

They both moaned. Their bodies heaved together as they raced toward release. It wasn't soft and gentle. Not tender and romantic. They were savage and hungry. Almost fighting for the pleasure. When it hit, when the climax tore through Aspen's body, she heard the echo of her own scream.

Then his roar of satisfaction.

***

*So much for being more controlled.*

Gideon's heartbeat drummed in his ears. His grip was too tight on Aspen's hips, and his too-eager dick was already getting hard again. Hard *inside* of her.

He had to ditch the condom. Had to get his control back.

Why the hell was he so savage when it came to her?

Gideon slid back, eased out of her body, and immediately wished he was driving back inside of her.

Aspen gave a soft gasp.

*Shit.* "Did I hurt you?"

Her lashes were down, covering her eyes. "No." But her voice was off. Not the prim tone she took when she was locking down her emotions. But...too weak. Almost with a sad note in it.

"Baby..."

Her lashes lifted. "You didn't hurt me." Her legs unlocked from his hips. Slid down. "You should go ditch the condom. I-I need to straighten up."

Straighten up. Because he'd just fucked her against the wall.

His jaw locked. "I will be right back." Back to apologize and try to regain the ground he'd lost with her.

"Of course."

*Hollow.* That was how her voice sounded. No emotion at all.

He hurried away from her. Nearly ran back to the guest bedroom and ditched the condom. He righted his jeans and hurried back but—

No Aspen.

Alarm blasted through him. *"Aspen!"* He whirled around. Where the hell—

She was on the stairs. Half-way up with her back to him.

"I need to get cleaned up." Again, her hollow voice raised alarm bells in his head. "I have a client that I'm meeting at the police station soon, and I can't go in...like this. I need a quick shower. I need fresh clothes."

He hurried to the base of the stairs. Gideon's hand reached out and curled around the banister. "What can I do?" He felt like the biggest ass in the world. Why the hell couldn't he be more controlled when it came to Aspen?

He saw her shoulders stiffen before she slowly turned so that she was half-way toward him. She looked down at him. "Why did it matter if I'd fucked them?"

*Give her the truth.* "Because I'm a jealous bastard."

"I don't ask who you've fucked."

"My exes aren't trying to kill me."

Her eyes narrowed. Yeah, shit, that had obviously been the wrong thing to say. He bounded up the stairs and reached out for her.

But she flinched away and that movement cut him to the quick. "Aspen..."

"I didn't have sex with Braden. I didn't have sex with Jake."

He believed her. But what still nagged at him..."Why did you turn to Jake?"

"I told you already, I thought he could talk to Frank. That he could *help* me."

Gideon shook his head. "It was the worst moment of your life. When you were at your darkest, you didn't turn to Ramsey or to Darius even though they are supposed to be like brothers to you. Instead, you turned to Jake, and he helped you. He kept your secret for you. I want to know *why*." Because that worried him more than anything else.

Worried him because...

When you turned to someone that way, emotions had to be involved.

"No more secrets," he added. "Tell me everything."

"I have." She stared into his eyes and didn't flinch. Didn't make any nervous movements. Didn't so much as flicker an eyelash. "It's up to you whether you believe me or not." Her mouth firmed. "For the official record, I didn't just have sex with you because I was trying to control you and stop you from running to the cops with this story."

Hell. Those words were pure ice.

She turned away. "Excuse me, I have to hurry."

"Aspen—"

She'd gone up four more steps. She tensed at his call. "Just so you know, that wasn't the worst moment of my life."

His heart seemed to squeeze in his chest.

Aspen threw a look back at him. "The worst moment of my life was when I found my dad on the side of the road. So broken and bloody. I called the cops. Called for an ambulance. And I waited for them to arrive as he struggled to take his last few breaths. *That* was the worst thing I've experienced."

Then she climbed the rest of the stairs.

He didn't call out to her again.

\*\*\*

The truck pulled to a stop in front of the police station. "I could have driven myself here," Aspen murmured as she unhooked her seatbelt.

"Twenty-four-hour service. That was part of the package, remember?"

She peeked at him, not sure of his mood. Or of her own, frankly. The explosive sex and the big emotional reveal had left her shaking. It had been all she could do to get up those stairs without showing him her weakness.

As a rule, she didn't do big emotional scenes. Didn't share with people. But there had been no choice. The time for secrets was over. She'd told him everything and now...

Now the police station was just a few feet away. "What will you do?"

"Find the fucker. Stop him. Keep you safe."

She released a fast breath. "I meant what will you do with the information I gave you?"

"There's no proof, is there?" Gideon's voice was musing.

Her head angled toward him.

"I'm sure you and Jake saw to that. I'm betting he cleaned the boat from top to bottom before he let it wash ashore, and with no body, it's going to be pretty hard to have a murder case, right?"

Not having an actual body *did* always make murder cases much harder, but...

"It would be my word against yours. And Jake's, of course. Because I'm sure he'd back up your story. Not like he will incriminate himself."

No, she didn't think that Jake would incriminate himself. It would take one hell of a lot to get him to ever do something like that.

"So, you aren't going to say anything?" Careful. Stilted. She pretty much held her breath as she waited for his response.

"You asked me the wrong question."

Her brows rose. "What question should I have asked?"

"You should have asked...what would I have done if you'd called *me* that night?"

She could only stare at him. "You didn't know me back then."

He reached over. Tucked a lock of hair behind her ear. "I know you now."

Yes, he did. Gideon knew all of her darkest secrets and that was why she was terrified to be with him in front of the police station.

"From here on out, if you have a dark moment, if you get scared, then you call *me*."

Her heart lurched hard in her chest. "And what will you do?"

"Whatever it takes."

She shook her head. "I don't—"

"Trust me."

"If I didn't trust you, I wouldn't have told you anything!" Didn't he get that? "But I know you, too." She'd learned a lot about him in the last few days. "You're not the kind of man who would—"

But she broke off because she didn't want to say...*You're not the kind of man who would kill.*

"You think I don't have dark parts, too, sweetheart? I do. If someone is trying to hurt you, if someone has his freaking hands around your throat and is trying to kill you, there would be no holding back for me." His lips curled down. "Holding back is an issue I seem to have with you. You might have noticed it."

"No." She cleared her throat. "Didn't see it."

"Not when I was taking you against the wall? Or when I was so frantic for you that I couldn't stop kissing you?"

Her lips pressed together.

"You hired me to find this bastard. That is exactly what I will do. And I am not going to hurt you. I am not going to turn on you. Believe me when I say that."

Sometimes, it was easy to say the words. But he'd just learned her secrets. Once he had a chance to think about them, to fully understand what had happened...*what will he do then?* "I need to go inside. I have to be there when they question my client."

"I'll park the truck and be waiting for you in the lobby."

Because he'd insisted on dropping her off at the door. "Thanks." She jumped out of the truck. Started to close the door. Hesitated. Aspen peered back at him. "I don't have any other secrets from you." She needed him to know that.

"If you did, I'd just uncover them."

Goosebumps rose on her arms.

"It's what I do," he added quietly. "It's why I'm very good at my job."

Before she could respond to those words, a cop she knew called her name. Aspen stepped back. Slammed the door.

\*\*\*

He whipped the truck into the nearby parking garage. Got out and pressed the button on the key fob to lock the vehicle. The truck's lights flashed and the honk of the horn seemed to echo around him.

Gideon rubbed the back of his neck as he advanced through the cavernous garage. Had Aspen understood that he'd meant exactly what he'd said? If she needed him, he would be there for her. Wilde agreement or not, he wasn't going to turn this back on her. He...

He heard the rustle of a footstep.

Gideon didn't stop walking forward, but he was suddenly, acutely aware that he was being watched. *Hunted.* He let his hand drop from his neck and hang at his side. He didn't see anyone in the garage, not on this level, but he knew eyes were on him.

He strode toward the elevator. Gideon expected an attack to come at any moment, and he was ready for it. But when he pushed the button on the elevator, no one lunged out from the shadows of the garage and came at him.

He kept his pose relaxed, as if he didn't have a care in the world.

*Are you there, you sonofabitch?*

Gideon didn't think he'd been followed which meant the watcher had known where he was going. The person hiding had realized that Gideon would be in that parking garage at that time. The watcher had been waiting. *He must have known about Aspen's appointment at the police station.* This garage was the closest one to the station, so it stood to reason that Aspen would have parked at the garage before going inside to be with her client.

And maybe *that* was the point...maybe the watcher wasn't approaching because he wasn't interested in Gideon. Maybe the SOB had thought that Aspen would be there, alone, and that he'd be able to get a jump on her.

*Screw this.*

Gideon whirled back toward the parking garage. "I know you're there!" he thundered. "Just show yourself!" At the very least, he thought his words would make the watcher nervous. Get the asshole to flee forward—

The elevator dinged behind him. He heard the doors slide open, and battle-ready tension thundered through Gideon's body. In a flash, he whipped back around. He lunged into the elevator.

The dark-haired man who'd been waiting inside raised his hands. "Easy. I'm not here to kick your ass...yet."

"Don't think that will be nearly as easy as you imagine." Gideon's hand flew out, and he hit the button to keep the elevator doors open. "And how about you tell your flunky to stop hiding in the shadows?"

The man in the elevator smiled. It wasn't a particularly warm and friendly sight. "I don't have a flunky out there."

Footsteps padded toward them.

"I have a *friend,*" the man continued smoothly. "And he's hardly a threat. He's here because he wanted to make sure Aspen got safely into the police station."

Gideon risked a quick glance over his shoulder and saw Darius casually strolling toward him. Great. *Darius.* If Darius was there, then he strongly suspected the dark-haired prick in the elevator had to be... "Ramsey."

"The one and only."

Gideon removed his fingers from the elevator's control panel. "I was hoping to chat with you."

"Then consider this your lucky day."

***

Aspen's heels clicked as she headed through the bullpen. Cops she knew tossed out greetings to her, and she flashed them quick smiles. Her destination was the second interrogation room, and she intended to be absolutely certain that no one pressured her client.

"Heard there was some excitement in your area earlier today," a female voice said as Aspen skirted around a large desk.

She paused—briefly—and glanced at the detective. Melissa Wright. Homicide. "I'm surprised you're interested," Aspen returned with a little shrug. "No one died."

"Yes, I know...because your new boyfriend raced to the scene and saved the day." Melissa swiveled her chair toward Aspen. "Just finished reading the preliminary report. How very interesting."

Aspen made a show of glancing at her watch. "I'd love to stay and chat with you." *I would not.* "But I have a client waiting."

"Is Jake Eros one of your clients?"

She let her brow furrow. "Why do you ask? He was the victim today. Not the attacker."

Melissa studied her with a too-intent gaze.

The detective was often like a very determined dog with a bone.

"Is there something I'm missing?" Aspen asked her. "Because I must confess that I—"

"I received an anonymous call a short time ago. Do you remember Braden Savage?"

Aspen's heart slammed into her chest. *Do not change your expression. Do not...* "Of course, I do. I dated the man." *As I am sure you know.*

"Right." Melissa smiled at her. "An anonymous caller said he knew exactly where Braden Savage was."

She took a step closer to Melissa. "Well, do tell me. His disappearance has haunted me for years."

"Really? Haunted you? Interesting word choice."

*Oh, shit. This is going to be bad.*

"Because my anonymous caller said that Braden is dead. That *you'd* murdered him, and Braden is currently in a watery grave out in the Gulf."

# CHAPTER THIRTEEN

"Why don't you hit that stop button?" Ramsey directed, posture relaxed. "It will give us a few minutes to chat."

Gideon hit the button. The elevator stopped moving.

"The security camera doesn't work in here," Ramsey added as he waved toward the far-right corner of the elevator. "Such a shame. Someone should get that repaired."

Gideon strongly suspected that the security camera had worked just fine until Ramsey arrived at the location.

"Darius tells me that you're involved with Aspen..." Ramsey began.

Gideon wasn't in the mood to bullshit. "And my sources tell me that you're a crime boss."

Ramsey made a vague, clicking sound with his tongue. "Your sources are incorrect. I'm an upstanding member of the community. A true Good Samaritan. Just ask Aspen. She'll vouch for me." His stare was ice-cold.

"I also thought you were out of town."

"Um, you just keep being wrong. Must be unfortunate to go through life that way."

"I get by."

Ramsey propped one shoulder against the elevator's wall. "You saved Jake Eros today."

"I don't know if I'd go that far."

"And I don't know that all people are worth being saved. You'd do well to remember that. Jake is not someone you can trust."

"Aspen trusts him." *Enough to call him when she was terrified.*

"Aspen remembers who he was when she was a kid. The scared boy who didn't fit at the bar and who desperately wanted to prove himself to a father who didn't want him."

Gideon was surprised Ramsey was being so blunt. "Let me guess, once upon a time, you were a scared boy, too."

Ramsey laughed. "Hell, no. Once upon a time, I was the one who did the scaring."

Okay. That Gideon could believe. "Is that why you're here now, to scare me?"

"Are you someone who scares easily?"

He kept his pose just as relaxed as Ramsey's. "No, I'm not."

A faint tilt of Ramsey's lips. "I didn't think so. If Aspen was getting serious with someone, she wouldn't waste her time with a dumbass who jumped when things got a little...intense."

*He thinks Aspen is getting serious with me?* Then their cover story with Darius must have worked. "Why exactly are you here?"

"Well, Wilde agent..."

Yeah, he got it. Ramsey was saying he knew about Gideon's past—

"I wanted to meet you myself, after Darius and Jimmy both passed along some details about you."

"Details like me working at Wilde."

A nod of Ramsey's head. "The same agency that has recently been prying into my personal affairs." He raised his eyebrows. "I'm a private man, you must understand. I don't like it when people start poking around in places they don't belong—and those places would be all of my life."

"Yet I suspect you've been poking around plenty in *my* life."

"Yes, I have, Delta Force."

Had Ramsey just called Gideon Delta Force? Like it was some kind of freaking nickname?

"I know about Egypt. I know about Sudan. I know about Russia."

Was he supposed to be impressed or intimidated? Gideon found he was neither. "You know the names of some countries. Good for you." Again, his pose stayed relaxed.

But Ramsey narrowed his eyes. "I'll give you points for bravery on those missions, though your methods certainly seemed risky. Tell me, do you think you're a hero?"

*He read my classified files.* "No. I don't."

"An adrenaline junkie then. Is that what you are?"

Gideon sucked in a breath. "Why don't we just cut through the BS and get to the real point of this little visit? I've got places to be."

"That place would be with Aspen, wouldn't it?" Lazy. Casual.

A lie. Gideon knew there was nothing at all casual about this conversation.

Ramsey's stare raked him. "Why is a guy like you, a former Delta Force man who must have a closet full of shiny medals at home, a fellow who is used to guarding the rich and famous...why are you so desperate to get back to the side of a small-town criminal defense attorney?"

Simple. "Obviously, because she's mine."

Ramsey's jaw tightened, a minute movement that was only noticeable if you've been watching. Gideon had been watching.

"Would have thought you got the memo," Gideon continued silkily. "Figured it was delivered by Darius and Jimmy. Aspen and I are an item. I came down here because I wanted to be close to her."

"Close?"

"I intend to marry her." The words just—shit, they flew out.

Ramsey jerked back and elbowed the elevator's wall. "What?"

"You heard me."

"Indeed, I did." Ramsey shoved away from the wall. Moved to stand toe-to-toe with Gideon. "Just not sure I believe you."

"No?"

"No. Because I tend to know quite a bit about what is happening in Aspen's life. I promised her father I would always watch over her, so I've taken a special interest in Aspen—and in the people who get close to her."

Gideon held his stare.

"Is Aspen in danger?" Ramsey asked softly.

That question *did* catch Gideon off guard. "I would never be a threat to her."

"Not talking about you, Delta Force." His voice was still low. "I can read the writing on the wall. I get what you are."

Not *who*. What.

"I also get that Jake was attacked while leaving her office. Jake has always had an unhealthy focus on her."

"What the fuck does that mean?"

Ramsey smiled. "What the fuck do you think it means?"

Gideon's back teeth clenched. "They haven't been involved."

"No, much to his never-ending disappointment." Ramsey shrugged one shoulder. "When they were younger and he was mooning so hard over her, Saul told him to stay the hell away."

*Saul.* "Her dad knew Jake?"

"Saul wanted more for his daughter than what Jake was going to give her. Saul wanted her out of our world. I wanted the same thing."

Gideon studied Ramsey. Ramsey was barely older than Aspen, or at least, that was how it looked so... "How the hell old were you when you started this business?"

Ramsey just smiled.

Gideon didn't smile back. "I'm not going to be intimidated by you."

"No, I can see that. Rather cute."

"You're a dick."

Ramsey merely laughed. But after a moment, his laughter faded. "Is Aspen in trouble?"

Gideon felt a muscle jerk along his jaw. "If you and Aspen are so close, if you're like her *brother*, then wouldn't she tell you?"

"No, not if she is afraid of what I might do, and not if she is trying to protect me." He rolled his shoulders. "She knows I'm trying to start new. That I want things to be better for Whitney and the baby."

*The baby?*

"So Aspen would do everything in her power to make sure that she didn't let me find out what is going on. She'd want to keep me as far out of trouble as possible."

If Ramsey was having a baby with his Whitney...hell, yes, more bits of the puzzle that was Aspen slid into place. *No wonder she was adamant that Ramsey not find out.*

"But Aspen is family," Ramsey continued as his expression hardened. "I always protect family. So I ask you again...is Aspen in trouble?"

\*\*\*

"Well, well, well...you must be the boyfriend."

Gideon turned at the feminine voice and found a woman in brown pants and a crisp, white button-up strolling toward him. Her gaze swiftly assessed him from his head to his toes. He did a quick survey of her, as well, and noted the badge clipped to her hip. He also saw the holster under her left arm.

"Figured you'd be showing up at some point." She offered her hand to him. "I'm Detective Melissa Wright."

He shook her hand. "Gideon Ranier." Her grip was firm. Solid.

She let him go. "Heard that you're quite the hero."

He felt tension gather between his shoulder blades. "I don't really like that term."

"I've found that real heroes rarely do." Behind her, the bullpen was a swarm of activity. "But you *did* save Jake Eros earlier today, didn't you?"

"Aspen is the one who saw his attacker going into the alley after him. She's the one who alerted me and the security guards at the office building. If anyone is a hero, it's her."

"Isn't that sweet." Her words said it was anything *but* sweet. "Just how long have the two of you been involved?"

He gave her a slow grin. "Why do I feel like I'm being interrogated?" *Because I am.* "Wait," he said, injecting some fake humor in his voice, "are you and Aspen friends? Are you trying to find out how serious we are? Because I can tell you...we're dead serious."

"We aren't friends." Flat. "Aspen is friends with the people who make life dangerous in this city. I, on the other hand, want to protect the community."

He let his grin vanish. "I see."

"I'm not so sure that you do." She edged closer to him. "It's been my experience that men can often be fooled by a pretty face. They don't see danger until it's too late."

His eyebrows shot up. "Are you trying to tell me that my girlfriend is dangerous?"

"What do you know about Braden Savage?"

The question came straight out of the blue, a surprise shot. And, damn, but he had to admire the detective in that moment. Because this whole scene between them *was* an interrogation, and she'd been deliberately setting him up with a line of questions so that he'd chat with her and then...bam, she'd delivered her main hit to catch him off guard.

*What do you know about Braden Savage?*

Now just why would the detective be asking him about Braden?

"What am I supposed to know about him?" Gideon returned as he let his brow furrow.

Her lips tightened. "Aspen was once closely involved with him."

"Huh." A shrug. "Well, she's closely involved with me now, so I'll assume the guy is history."

"That's what most people assume about him due to the fact that Braden hasn't been seen since he and Aspen were dating—and that was years ago. He vanished one night. Was never seen again."

He took a step back. "That's odd."

"We have a lot of boating accidents in the area. You can't live on the Gulf and not have them. People get drunk on the water, and tragic situations happen. One of those tragic situations was assumed to have occurred with Braden. His boat was found. He wasn't."

Gideon gave a low whistle. "Well, damn. Bet Aspen was torn up about that."

"You think so? I wonder if Aspen is ever torn up about anything."

Now the detective was pissing him off. "You definitely aren't her friend."

Her eyes widened.

"Because you don't know jack about her or how she feels." Before he could say more, Gideon heard Aspen's voice. She was talking soothingly to someone, and when his head turned, he saw her walking out with a teenage boy. She had her hand on his shoulder, and he was nodding quickly, *his* hands shaking at his sides. A woman trailed behind them, and the woman swiped at her wet cheeks.

"It's going to be fine," Aspen was saying. She turned back to the woman, a lady with faint gray near her temples. "I am taking care of everything." She glanced around the station, saw Gideon, and inclined her head.

A uniformed officer appeared and escorted the woman and boy down another hallway. Aspen squared her shoulders, lifted her chin, and marched toward Gideon and the detective.

"I thought you only dealt with the high rollers in town these days," Melissa said as Aspen approached.

"I deal with people who need me. Vincent needed me today."

"Vinnie? The car thief?" Melissa asked.

"The alleged car thief," Aspen returned. "And as I just explained to the investigating officer, I have ironclad evidence that Vincent could not have been involved in that theft. He has an alibi. The officers picked up the wrong kid."

"Vinnie has a history of this, he was picked up for joy riding before." Melissa shook her head. "He lives two blocks away from the theft, the car was found abandoned near his school, and he—"

"Vincent was at confession. His priest will back him up," Aspen returned crisply. "You see, Vincent wants to turn his life around. He is doing everything possible to achieve that goal, and hot-wiring a car isn't on his to-do list. He went to confession, and then after, he worked in the church gardens for two hours. He's trying to earn extra money to help out his mother."

Melissa frowned at her. "And his alibi wasn't checked out *before* he was arrested?"

"Things slip through the cracks sometimes. That's where I come in." Aspen gripped her bag. "Vincent's so-called friends pointed at him as being guilty because they were the ones who'd gone for the ride. They didn't like that he was trying to be different, and when the cops started questioning them, it was easy to throw him out as a target. Perps do that occasionally, you know, they say things to distract cops from the truth."

"Oh, right. I see what you're doing." Melissa waved one hand toward Aspen. "Clever."

"I'm not attempting to be particularly clever." Prim.

*Uh, oh.* He knew Aspen was locking down her emotions. He shot her a quick glance. Her hair was pulled into a tight knot at the base of her head. Pearl studs were on her ear lobes. She'd changed into black pants and a chic black sweater before leaving her house. Her shoes were red, a sexy and elegant splash of color. She looked professional, gorgeous, and...

*Scared?* Was that the faintest hint of fear he saw in her eyes?

He reached for her hand. "Are you finished up here?"

"I need to take care of some paperwork. Talk to the DA. He's going to be looking for me soon. I want to make sure Vincent sleeps at home tonight."

"And when you're done with that..." Melissa inserted smoothly. "I'd like for us to finish our earlier conversation."

Gideon glanced between the two women. "Just what conversation was that?" Aspen's hand felt chilled in his grasp.

Aspen laughed. A mocking sound. "The detective believes that I may have murdered my ex, Braden Savage, and I'm pretty sure she wants to put me in an interrogation session."

*What. The. Fuck?*

"But that's not going to happen," Aspen added, her voice even more crisp. *Prim to the extreme.* "Because I have work to do. Because Braden left years ago. Because I have no knowledge of his whereabouts. Because I know my rights." An inhale. "And just because someone has decided to play some sort of vicious game by spreading rumors about me, it doesn't mean that I have to play along, too."

"A game," Melissa repeated. "That's what you think this is?"

"I have no idea what this is, but I assure you, I am unamused by it. And if you want to question me, then do it properly. Because right now, all I see is a detective fishing for information. A detective who is biased towards me because she doesn't happen to like my clients. One client, in particular, seems to strike you the wrong way, even though you know what an amazing Good—"

"Do not start that Good Samaritan shit with me about Ramsey," Melissa groused. She pointed at Aspen. "Did you ever stop to think that maybe I was trying to help you? But I can't help if you won't be straight with me." Her voice was low, carrying only to their little group. "There have been plenty of rumors about Braden circulating at this precinct for years. Some said he was as sadistic as they came."

"Is that what they say?" No emotion was on Aspen's face.

"If something happened, if you need help...talk to me," Melissa urged her.

Aspen inclined her head. "Thank you, Detective. I will remember that kind offer. Now, if you will excuse me, there is some paperwork and quite a few loose ends that need my attention." She nodded toward Gideon. "You don't have to wait. It may take longer than I expected."

"I'm not going anywhere."

He saw the flash of relief in her eyes.

And then he watched her walk away.

Detective Melissa Wright didn't move. She also didn't speak again, not until Aspen was several feet away and leaning over the desk of a haggard-looking cop. "Hopefully, you'll be smarter than she is. If you have information to give me, do it," Melissa murmured.

"Just what sort of information could I possibly have? You'll need to spell things out for me."

She touched his arm. "Fine. How about this..."

He turned his head. Focused on her.

"Did Aspen murder Braden Savage?"

*** 

She saw it happen. Aspen glanced up, and her eyes locked on Gideon and Melissa. There was a hum of noise around her. Phones were ringing. Voices were rising and falling. Papers were fluttering. Fingers tapping on keyboards. But as she stared across at them in that one moment, she could so clearly see the movement of Melissa's mouth. Could almost hear the words...

*"Did Aspen murder Braden Savage?"*

When she'd been younger, when she'd been in so many places that she didn't belong, she'd had to amuse herself. She'd taken to watching strangers across crowded bars. Watching their mouths. Trying to understand the things they were saying.

At first, she'd just imagined silly, crazy things. She'd been so off, so wrong on the words people uttered, but...

She'd kept at her game.

She'd become so good at it that she'd been able to pick up all kinds of conversations without being close enough to hear anything. Ramsey had even used her talents for a time.

So she knew exactly what Melissa had just asked Gideon, and as Aspen stood there, feeling all the blood drain from her face, she wondered if she might actually pass out.

"Hey, Ms. Gray, you okay?" the nearby cop asked her. "You're not looking so good."

Gideon hadn't answered Melissa yet. God, what would he say? He wouldn't lie. Aspen didn't think he'd stand there and lie to a cop. And he couldn't confess. He *wouldn't*, would he?

"Ms. Gray?"

"Excuse me." She lurched away from the desk. She shouldn't have left Gideon and Melissa alone. She should have seen this coming. Melissa was a good detective, and she was so often like a shark when it came to smelling blood in the water.

Someone had tipped off Melissa. Someone had sent her charging into Aspen's life. And now...

Now Aspen couldn't get back to Melissa and Gideon quickly enough.

Because *her* life hung in the balance, and if Gideon said the wrong words...she would lose everything.

# CHAPTER FOURTEEN

People were in her way. She dodged and her heels clicked and Aspen hurried back just as—

Gideon laughed.

His warm, rich laughter stretched out to her seconds before she reached him. Aspen grabbed his arm. "Wh-what's so funny?" She hated the tremble in her voice.

"The detective," he responded easily. "She's quite amusing."

Aspen stared up at him. Could he see the pleading in her gaze? But then she forced herself to school her features and turn to Melissa. "Please, do tell me the joke."

"No joke." Melissa looked way less than amused. "Was just having a conversation with your boyfriend. Would have thought someone like him—someone who spent years protecting his country and upholding the honor of service—would understand the importance of the situation."

Her heart beat so hard Aspen feared it was going to shake her entire body. "The situation? What situation might that be?"

"She's asking me about Braden Savage," Gideon said. "She seriously just asked if you'd murdered him."

Her knees weakened. She could feel her body start to sway—

Gideon curled his arms around her and pulled Aspen against the hard warmth of his body. "As if you could murder anyone in cold blood," he continued as he held her close.

*Breathe. Breathe. You have this.* From within Gideon's strong embrace, Aspen met Melissa's watchful gaze. "I don't find the line of questioning nearly as funny as he does."

"No, I can see that."

"You get one anonymous call—a call backed with zero evidence—and now you're accusing me of being a murderer."

She felt Gideon tense. He hadn't known about the call. So Melissa hadn't gotten around to sharing that bit with him yet?

"I think this is harassment," Aspen continued briskly. "I'd hate to have to speak with the chief about it."

"It's not harassment. It's following up. I think you know the difference," Melissa returned.

"I think you do, too. I think you also know when someone is using you, and that's exactly what that call was about. Everyone knows you're not exactly overwhelmed by warm and fuzzy emotions for me. Of all the cops in this area, you'd be the one most likely to believe that crazy story."

"A story about you stabbing Braden Savage and dumping his body in the Gulf."

Her cheeks were icy. "Did you try tracing the call? Getting any information about the caller?"

Melissa's eyelashes fluttered.

"She couldn't trace him. And he probably disguised his voice," Gideon noted. "Two things that totally scream the caller was on the up and up."

Melissa's chin jerked. "Why would he lie?"

"Already told you," the prim, stiff sound of her own voice grated in Aspen's ears, "someone is just looking to send you after me. Obviously, I've made some individual angry. Sort of goes along with the job."

"So you're denying the charge?" Melissa pounced.

Gideon's embrace was so warm. He'd curled one arm over her upper chest and collarbone, and his fingers hooked over her shoulder as he kept her cradled in front of him. "Didn't realize you had charged me with something. Did I miss that part?"

Melissa's lips thinned. Before she could say more, another detective shouted for her. "This isn't finished, Aspen." She turned away.

"I'm pretty sure it is," Aspen responded.

*No, I know it isn't.*

Gideon's lips brushed over the shell of Aspen's ear. She couldn't help but shiver, both from the sensual touch and from the fear that was twisting her up. She opened her mouth to speak.

"*Trust me,*" Gideon whispered. The words were so low. Barely a breath of sound, but she heard them.

She nodded.

\*\*\*

The hospital floor gleamed as they walked toward Jake's room. Gideon had waited for Aspen to finish up at the police station, and then he'd immediately taken her to the hospital. She knew he wanted to talk to Jake. Aspen wanted to be present for that talk.

She also wanted to talk more with Gideon. There were so many things she needed to say to him, but when they'd gotten into the truck, she'd found that she couldn't say a word.

So they'd driven to the hospital in silence. The kind of super, uncomfortable silence that told you something bad was coming.

Now they were approaching Jake's room. A tall, muscled man in a thick, black coat and black pants stood outside of the door, and Aspen pegged him as Jake's protection. Only she wondered exactly where that protection had been hours before. *Where was the guard when Jake needed him?*

The guy spotted them and stiffened. "No visitors," he snapped. The door behind him was cracked open.

She didn't stop walking. Neither did Gideon. "Tell Jake that his lawyer wants to see him," she said.

The guard frowned at her.

"Send her in!" A shout from inside the room. "I want Aspen."

The guard moved to the side. Aspen wet her lips and pushed the door open fully so she could step over the threshold.

"Not you, buddy," the guard snapped to Gideon.

She looked back to see that the man had put a beefy hand on Gideon's chest.

"He said Aspen. Only Aspen."

Gideon looked at the hand on him. Then at the guard. "We're a package deal."

"What?"

"Where she goes, I go. Now move the fucking hand," a low, lethal order, "before you're the one needing medical treatment."

"Let him in!" A quick demand from Jake. "Don't cause a scene here!"

"Right. No scene," Gideon agreed with a less-than-pleasant smile. "Because who would want that?"

The guard moved his hand. Gideon followed Aspen inside, and she saw him very firmly shut the door in the guard's face.

Aspen took in the room—and Jake. He was in the hospital bed, wearing one of those horrific green gowns, and looking disgruntled as all hell. A half-eaten tray of food was beside him. His pudding appeared not to have been touched at all.

"You seem to be on the road to recovery," she noted.

He grunted. "I want out of this shithole."

"It's not a shithole, it's a hospital."

He just looked even more disgruntled. "Why are you here?"

She was there because Gideon wanted to question Jake. He'd made that very clear. Gideon was hunting for her stalker, and she wanted to be with him on the hunt. That meant she got to be in on the question-and-answer sessions.

"Did you see anything about your attacker that can help us figure out who he was?" Gideon asked.

"You sound like the cops. No, I didn't. And even if I had..." Jake's voice hardened. "I can take care of him. I don't need you stepping in."

"Serving your own justice?" Gideon came to stand at the foot of the bed, beside Aspen. "Don't know if that's the best course of action."

Jake's attention shifted to Aspen. "Sometimes, it's the only way."

Her lips parted.

"Don't do that," Gideon snapped.

Jake blinked at him. "Excuse me?"

"I thought Ramsey might be bullshitting me, just trying to rile me up, but I can see he was right."

She almost took a step back. Aspen caught herself just in time and managed to say, "Ramsey?"

"Um." Gideon didn't look her way. His focus appeared to be solely on Jake. "He told me that you used to chase after her. That you were a bit too interested in Aspen."

She could feel her jaw dropping. Aspen hurriedly snapped her mouth closed. "Ramsey is mistaken."

"I don't think so." Gideon crossed his arms over his chest. "I just saw Jake's eyes when he looked at you. It was there."

"It?" She was lost. "This had so better not be about that whole prickling nape thing of yours..."

His attention shifted toward her. "He wants you, Aspen. This whole deal has been personal to him for a very long time. *You* are personal." His head angled back toward Jake. "Let's cut through all the unnecessary chit-chat. You aren't going to have Aspen. She's with me. So don't be sending her longing-ass looks when I'm around. That shit won't fly."

This was *insane*. "Uh, Gideon, you are—"

His hand flew out. Caught hers. He'd turned toward her in an instant. "I came down here for you. Everything I do is for *you*." Emotion blazed in his eyes. "I'm not just going to stand here while some prick eye-fucks you."

*What?*

But his focus was already swinging back to a stunned Jake. "Don't make me regret saving your fool ass."

Jake pushed himself up in the bed. "You're insane. Aspen, you've done it again. You've picked another psychotic asshole to love."

"*Stop it!*" Aspen snapped. She tried to pull her hand from Gideon. He wouldn't let go. "This is ridiculous. Jake isn't interested in me. I am not interested in him. How can that be any clearer?"

Gideon smiled at Jake. "Got that?"

"Yes," Jake hissed. "I got that she's with another prick. Check. Some women have a type."

Her eyes narrowed on him. "Do not piss me off more than I already am right now." She cut a hard stare to Gideon. "Either of you."

Gideon inclined his head. Brought her hand to his lips. Kissed her knuckles. "Yes, ma'am." He let her go.

She wrapped her arms around her stomach. "We have a serious problem to deal with, and we don't have time for territorial male crap."

A muscle moved along Jake's jaw.

"Someone placed an anonymous call to Detective Melissa Wright today. You know her, of course," Aspen prompted Jake. "She's the newest homicide detective at the PD."

He swallowed. "Yes, I know her."

"A caller told her that I had stabbed Braden Savage and left him in a watery grave."

His eyes widened. His nostrils flared. *Fuck.* His lips moved to say the word, but no actual sound escaped from Jake.

"Exactly," Gideon murmured. He was walking around the room, pacing kind of like a caged tiger. "Don't know why someone would be calling with such false information." He peeked through the blinds. "Do you, Jake?"

Goosebumps rose on Aspen's arms as she held her post near the bed.

Jake shook his head.

She sidled a little closer. "You were contacted, weren't you?" Low. Barely a whisper.

His head inclined.

"Someone called you?" Aspen pushed. Because that was what had happened to her. A call. A distorted voice. *Just like the call Melissa had received?*

Jake nodded. "Couldn't trace him. Tried. The dick knows what he's doing."

Yes. Her goosebumps got worse. "What did your caller say?"

"Can your dick boyfriend be trusted?" Jake demanded.

Gideon turned from the window. Sauntered back to the bed. "How odd." His voice was low. "Sounded like he asked if—"

"Screw yourself," Jake snarled. "This shit isn't funny. I got some distorted jerk on the line telling me I'm gonna pay. I just laughed him off. Hung up on him. I mean...didn't he realize who I was? I don't get scared when some wannabe calls me. Those days are long gone. I am—" He broke off.

Gideon finished for him. "You're the one at the top of the food chain, aren't you? Frank is gone. You have everything that was his."

Jake winced. "You know what? My wound is starting to hurt again. Think it's time I call my helpful nurse and get more pain meds."

He was dismissing them. And they'd gotten *nothing* useful. Aspen's heels remained rooted to the spot. "What made you come to my office?"

"Needed a lawyer. Told you that."

No, *no*. He was not going to shut her down like this. "The caller told you something that sent you to me. We both know you've got a list of enemies a mile long."

His brow furrowed. "Come now, Aspen, you know some people like me. Once upon a time, even *you* liked me."

Gideon's arm brushed against her side. "Stop dicking around and tell us what he said."

Jake's gaze lingered on Aspen. "I *may* have received a call from some jerk telling me that I would pay...by losing the one thing I had tried to save." His lips twisted into a half-smile. "I'm not exactly big on good deeds. A family trait, if you know what I mean. But I saved something precious once, and I remembered exactly what it was."

He'd saved her. Covered her ass. Protected her from Frank and the cops.

"Yeah, I get by the way you're fucking staring at her again that you think Aspen is the thing you saved," Gideon growled. "Dumbass, he didn't come after her. The stalker came for *you* in that alley. The thing you saved back then was yourself. You saved your own sorry hide, you got the life *you* wanted, and to me, it seems like the caller was threatening to destroy *you*. Considering that you're lying in a hospital bed asking for more pain meds, I'd say he's started step one of that plan."

Jake lost his smile. "As soon as I am out of here, I will be...*assisting* the police in finding my attacker."

Yes, she understood his words were code for...*As soon as I am out of here, my people and I will be hunting down the bastard.* No way would they be turning him over to the cops.

"So you don't have to worry," Jake assured Aspen. "I will handle everything from here on out. There is no one in place who can hold me back any longer."

Because Frank was gone. If this was somehow Braden, Frank might have tried to protect him, despite everything. She exhaled and dropped her arms to her sides. "It can't be him."

But Jake's gaze cut from hers. A bad sign.

"Jake?"

He was staring toward the blinds. "A long time ago, I came home after a really...really shitty night."

"We don't need your walk down memory lane." Gideon seemed beyond annoyed.

But Aspen curled her hand around his wrist. There was something about the tone of Jake's voice...

"I walked in my back door. You remember, Aspen, I had a place back then on the water."

She remembered. A place that Frank Savage had given to him.

"The back door was unlocked when I got there."

No, no, this was not—

"And the floor was wet in spots." He kept staring toward the blinds. "You could walk out of the water, climb onto the dock, and get in the house. Wasn't far from..." He sighed. "The old house wasn't far from the beach area you used to love so much."

She couldn't speak.

"That location is how I was able to meet a friend that night so quickly when she called for me. I was close. My house was close." Finally, his gaze pulled away from the blinds. He looked at Aspen.

She shook her head. No, this couldn't be right. "You didn't...you never said..."

"The door was unlocked. Maybe because I ran out too fast and forgot to lock it. Some spots on the floor were wet. Maybe...maybe I'd spilled something."

She shook her head once more. *This can't be happening.*

"Things were chaotic. I couldn't swear to what happened. Maybe it was nothing. Why say something about nothing? Why make someone worry about nothing?"

It wasn't nothing. It could easily be a situation where Braden had gotten out of the water. He'd gone to Jake's because he thought it was a safe place—Jake was loyal to Frank Savage, after all. But then...

What?

Why vanish? Why not wait for Jake? *Why vanish*? Her temples throbbed.

"A few days later, I could have sworn..." Jake's voice was even lower. "That I found dried blood on the dock."

She swallowed. "Fish. You used to clean fish out there all the time."

He inclined his head. "Sure."

Or maybe Braden had gotten out of the water. Gotten to the dock on the inlet. Gotten inside Braden's house...

Maybe he had survived and after all this time, he was coming for them both. But *why* wait? It didn't make any sense to her. Why hold back all of this time?

Unless someone else had *held* him back. Someone who was dead now. Someone like Frank Savage.

Hadn't Jake just said no one was around to hold *him* back any longer? The same could absolutely be said for Braden. Without Frank, no one would be able to control *him*.

Provided, of course, that Braden was alive.

*Dear God, he can't be alive.* But...what if he was?

"You get any other calls, you tell us," Gideon snapped.

"If I get any more calls, I will be handling the business on my own. Count on that."

He was saying that he'd kill the caller. Jake was going to track down his attacker and end him. But it just wasn't that easy. "You're not the only one who has to worry about ghosts from the past." She bit her lower lip.

"You got the same damn calls."

Her head jerked in agreement. "There have been...attempts."

His body stiffened. "You're telling me this asshole has tried to hurt you?" His furious glare jumped to Gideon. "What? You just let that shit happen? You haven't done anything to protect her?"

Gideon's body practically vibrated with his rage. She stroked his chest in a quick effort to calm him. "The reason Gideon is here—"

"Is because I damn well don't take lightly to someone threatening the woman I love," he finished hotly.

Her mouth fell open.

"So, yes, as soon as I heard about what was happening, I insisted on coming down here. Moving in with her. Staying as close as I possibly can. Because be very sure on this, in order to get to Aspen, anyone who wants to hurt her will have to go through me." Each word was hard. Lethal. "I *will* stop the threat out there. Whatever it takes,

Aspen will be safe. I don't fucking believe in ghosts, but I do believe in shoving dangerous bastards in the ground when they come after *my* Aspen."

There was a quick knock on the door. "Time for your medication, Mr. Eros," a perky voice called out.

The door began to swing open.

Aspen pasted a fake smile on her face. Gideon, she noted, did the same. "You take care, buddy," Gideon told Jake. "I'd sure hate for anything else to happen to you."

The words were light, but Aspen could have sworn they were also a threat. Gideon took her hand and pulled her from the room as the nurse bustled inside.

*** 

Jake Eros watched the door shut behind Aspen and her asshole boyfriend. The pretty nurse smiled at him as she advanced toward the bed.

"Yeah, keep that shit. I don't want it." He had a rule about drugs—he didn't take them. Not freaking ever. He didn't care how bad the pain got, he wasn't about to surrender his control. He'd watched his mother go down that path. At first, she'd told him it was just to take the edge off. Just to give her a little happiness.

His mother hadn't ever been happy. She'd been tossed aside by the man she loved because Frank Savage hadn't thought a stripper was good enough to sit by his side. Fine enough to fuck, but not classy enough to have on his arm at all of his wannabe dinners when he went out and tried to act like he wasn't the biggest piece of trash around.

As the years passed, his mother had slipped further and further away. It would only be much later that Jake had learned Frank had been sending her monthly payments—*payments for me*—and that she'd shot those payments into her veins.

Jake had been the one to eventually find her after she'd OD'd.

"But this will help you to relax." The pretty nurse's smile was uncertain now.

"Nothing helps me do that shit. And by the way, I'll be checking out." He grabbed for the IV in his arm and yanked it out. Blood trickled across his skin.

"Sir! Don't do that, you can't—"

He swung his legs to the side of the bed.

"You're going to rip out your stitches! Stop!"

When he didn't stop, she hurried from the room, swearing she was coming back with help.

Rodney poked his head in the room. "Uh, Jake? You okay?"

He was far from fucking okay. He knew—based on the intent look in that prick Gideon's eyes—that he had a new enemy in town. "I want a tail on Aspen's new boyfriend, Gideon," he snapped. "Make it happen, *now*."

Because Aspen had very unfortunate taste in lovers. He'd watched as she'd gotten closer and closer to Braden. She'd nearly died because of that freak.

Now she had another jealous bastard crowding close to her. Jake had been able to tell when he was in that stinking alley—Aspen hadn't confided in her boyfriend. She didn't trust him enough to tell him the full truth about herself.

There was only one person Aspen truly trusted with her past...*Me*.

And he wasn't going to stand by while someone hurt her again.

# CHAPTER FIFTEEN

"Want to tell me what that was about?" Aspen asked as soon as she and Gideon were back in the truck.

He cranked the engine. Curled his fingers around the steering wheel. "Which part?"

"Oh, let me see...the part where you were acting completely over the top and saying you *loved* me." Those words wouldn't stop ringing in her ears, and her whole body felt shaky and quaky. "I mean, seriously, you don't—"

"Waving a flag." Gideon smoothly reversed the vehicle out of the parking spot. "That was the plan, wasn't it?"

She floundered. "I..." *Pretend. It was all a show.* "Of course." Her fingers were trembling so she flattened them against the top of her thighs. "But the point was to draw out my stalker, to wave the flag toward him. It was just us and Jake in that room."

He drove them through the darkened garage. "Precisely."

She was not following. "Jake was attacked by the stalker."

"Um."

"Um? There is no 'um' about it! You were there! You saved him!"

"Yes, I saved Jake. The same Jake who just admitted that he'd held back secrets from you for years."

He had a point. Jake had neglected to mention some very important things to her. The unlocked door. The wet floor. She exhaled slowly. The drumming of her heartbeat filled Aspen's ears. "Jake didn't know anything for certain. You heard him."

"I heard him. I saw him. More specifically, I saw the way he looked at you." Gideon drove out of the garage and down the road. At the red light, he stopped to spare her a glance. "How long has Jake been in love with you?"

"*What?*" Real surprise hit her. "That's—that's not the case, I assure you."

"He covered up a death for you. He came running when you called him in the middle of the night. There's not a whole lot that would make a man do that. Love would."

Gideon was wrong. "I've known Jake for a long time. Since we were kids. His mom—she had a lot of problems." And Jake had been so alone. "He would hang out with me some nights because he didn't have anywhere else to go."

"Let me guess. When he was down on his luck, you were there to pick up the pieces? Probably giving him food, passing him money, doing all kinds of saintly shit like that." A growl of disgust.

Her shoulders stiffened. "Are you making fun of me?" *The woman I love.* His words rang in her head, but this time, they mocked her. Of course, Gideon didn't love her. Of course, he'd just been playing his role. But this, saying this stuff to her *now*—

"Not making fun. Would never do that." The light changed. He didn't move. His green eyes glittered at her. "I'm pointing out a few important facts that you seem to have missed. Odd, that, considering you're such a sharp attorney."

Her own temper sparked. "You do not know everything about me—or about Jake."

"Obviously."

A horn honked behind them.

Swearing, Gideon stomped on the gas. The vehicle lurched forward, and the seatbelt pulled at her shoulder. She reached up automatically to loosen it.

Silence.

A silence she finally broke. "You're wrong." He was. "Jake isn't in love with me. He's been in my life for years, and if he loved me, don't you think he would have at least asked me out? He hasn't. Ever."

"That's because your dad told him to stay the hell away from you."

Her lips parted. "What? No. That's...no. You're wrong."

"Not wrong at all. Heard it straight from your dear buddy Ramsey. You think he lied to me?"

No, she didn't. It wouldn't make sense for Ramsey to lie about something like that. Her head turned and she gazed out of the passenger window. Her thoughts rolled round and round as she tried to sort out this new development.

"You're wondering when it happened, aren't you? Wondering when your dad delivered his message to Jake and wondering if it just so happened to be around the time when your father was killed."

She blinked quickly. "Braden admitted to hiring the hit on my father."

"Right. Sure, he did. But who did he hire for the job? Did you ever find that part out? Who was the one who actually hit your father and left him there to die? Left him to bleed and to hurt on the side of the road where you found him—"

"Stop!" She squeezed her eyes shut, but the images were still there. The memory of her father. The way he'd tried so desperately to talk to her at the end, but he hadn't been able to speak. Gurgles and pain-filled groans had been all he could manage as she held him as tightly as she could and told him over and over that she loved him. "Why are you doing this?" Aspen whispered.

"Because I think the person you need to fear is close to you. Because you are stopping me from doing my job the way it has to be done and that's putting you at risk, dammit!" He braked.

Her eyes opened. He'd pulled over to the side of the long, winding road that would take them back to her house.

"I want to protect you. I *fucking* need to do it. And I can't hold back because you don't want me looking at the people close to you. The people close to you are the biggest threats! Ramsey—"

"Ramsey didn't—" she began hotly.

"He has secrets, too. Talking to him led me back to Jake. And Jake *is* lying. Why would he keep that bit about the wet floor and the unlocked door secret from you for all this time? *Why*, Aspen?"

"Because...he didn't want me to worry."

"Bullshit. You know that." A car whizzed toward them. Darkness had fallen, and the car's bright lights filled the interior of the truck before it vanished down the road. "Try again."

"Jake was attacked! You were right there, you saw it happen, you saw—"

"I saw that the guard at his hospital door was roughly the same height and build as what you described for his attacker. I saw that the guy was still wearing black pants and a black shirt."

She couldn't pull in a breath. Yes, yes, the guard had been wearing black, but that was pretty much the standard uniform for all the guys who'd worked for Frank Savage—

*Oh. Shit.*

"Nothing vital was hit, Aspen. The wound looked bad and it bled like a sonofabitch, but I knew with one glance he wasn't dying. You handle enough battlefield wounds and you get pretty savvy when it comes to things like that. Either your boy Jake got very lucky and his attacker somehow managed to miss all vital wounds—"

"Jake *isn't* mine."

"Or maybe that attack was deliberate. Maybe it was designed to look bad but not cause serious injury. Maybe it was done to throw us off so you would think Jake was the victim, and you wouldn't look too closely at him. In fact, you'd do the exact opposite. You'd think the two of you were in this together. You'd think you could trust him. That you could lean on him. That you could turn to him. That it was the two of you against the world once more."

She'd never thought that way.

"You *can't* trust him," Gideon continued, voice strained. "You do that, and you'll be in even more danger. I am right here, Aspen. Right damn in front of you. I will stand between you and any threat, but you have to let me do it. You have to trust *me*. No rules. No blocking my investigation. I am not going to turn over evidence against you. I am not going to rush to the cops and tell them what happened all those years ago. Jesus, didn't I prove that to you today? I was *in* the police station. The detective straight-up asked me if you'd killed Braden."

Yes, Melissa had. For a heart-stopping moment, Aspen had been terrified. But he hadn't shared the truth. Only—

*I can't keep this secret any longer.* She knew it. The certainty had been growing and growing within her. She couldn't get Gideon to lie for her. Wouldn't do it. It was time for the past to come out. *One way or another.*

"You were afraid I was going to turn on you. *Because you don't trust me.* That has to end. I am in this with you. I gave you my word before, and I'm doing it again. I will *never* turn on you."

"Why?" The ragged question tore from her. "You barely know me, and what you do know isn't good." He knew she was a killer. A woman who'd lied and set a trap that had backfired horribly on her.

"I know plenty about you. Learning more every single moment, and no, everything in your life isn't good. That's not a shocker because *life* isn't always good. It's messy and it's dark and sometimes you think it will absolutely wreck you." His hand lifted. Curled under her chin. His touch was so warm. "But nothing has wrecked you. You walked through hell and barely left ash in your wake. You're smart and you're strong, and you were trying to get justice for your father. You were willing to take any risk. Willing to cross any line for someone that you loved."

"I didn't mean to kill Braden," she whispered. "I am not a killer." Yet she *had* killed.

"No, baby, you're not, but I think someone else out there is. And I think that person is screwing with you." He leaned forward and brushed his lips over hers. "Trust me." Gideon breathed the words against her mouth. "When you're scared, when you need someone to be in your corner, turn to me." Another kiss. Tender. Careful. "I will not ever let you down."

Once more, she wanted to ask...*Why?* Why was he willing to do so much for her? But before she could ask him, bright lights lit up the truck's interior once more. Except these lights were even brighter than the previous car's had been. So bright that for a moment, they blinded her as she automatically glanced through the front windshield.

"Fuck!" From Gideon.

"He's...is he coming right for us?" No, she had to be wrong. A trick of the darkness. The other car was going to curve on the road and—

Gideon shifted the vehicle into drive and the truck surged forward. As his lights hit the road, she realized that she hadn't been wrong.

The vehicle barreling toward them *was* in the wrong lane and it *was* coming right at them. "What in the hell is he doing?"

"Playing chicken," Gideon snarled. "Hold on, baby."

Hold on? *Hold on?* And chicken? What was this, some kind of insane grade school—

Gideon swung the truck hard to the right, and the other vehicle's fender scraped along the side. *His* side. The impact had Gideon's door crunching and metal screaming and Aspen screaming, too, as her hands flew out.

Then it was over. The vehicle that had hit them screeched past—after its body pummeled the side of Gideon's truck. Aspen jerked her head around and stared into the distance. The car's lights had shut off. She couldn't even see it.

"I'm calling the cops," Gideon grated. *"Now."*

She looked back at him. His side airbag had deployed. He shoved against his door—and against the airbag. The door didn't open. Hardly surprising after the impact.

"You okay?" he demanded.

It hadn't been her side of the vehicle that had taken the impact. He'd turned the truck so that he would be hit. *I will stand between you and any threat.*

But when he stood between her and danger, he was the one who got hurt.

"Aspen!"

"I'm okay."

He put his phone to his ear. Spoke curtly. "Some asshole in a Dodge Charger just tried to run me off the road!"

How did he know it had been a Charger? She'd barely seen anything.

*But Gideon had gotten the up-close view.*

Gideon barked off their location then said, "The vehicle will be busted to hell and back. Get the driver—he's a dangerous SOB! Yeah, yeah, you heard me right—he ran me off the road." He shoved down the phone.

Her ragged breathing seemed too loud in the truck's interior. "Are you hurt?" He'd taken the impact. For her.

"Scratches. That shit doesn't matter."

It mattered to her. Anger began to churn inside of her, pushing away the fear.

"My door is stuck. He dented it in too much."

He'd dented it—*when he came for Gideon.*

"We have to get out on your side. Can you open the door, baby?"

She could. She shoved it open. Jumped out. He followed behind her and climbed down to stand on the road beside her. His hands curled around her shoulders, and she saw him sweep his gaze over her body. "I'm fine," she gritted out. "You were the one who got the brunt of the hit."

Gideon's hold tightened. "He didn't come from the hospital. Opposite way." His head turned so he was staring down the road. "He came from the direction of your place."

"My place and the homes of plenty of other people." But, yes, she got what he was saying. They hadn't been followed from the hospital.

Still… "No way this was just some random event. Not with everything else happening." She wouldn't believe that. "It was someone who came to target us, and he knew we would be here."

Gideon let her go. "Maybe because someone tipped him off. Someone who knew when we were leaving the hospital and which road we'd be taking."

Someone like…"Jake."

"Yes, your good buddy Jake." Gideon walked around the truck. Moved to the driver's side and glared down at the wreckage. "Sonofabitch."

She edged closer to the road. He had his phone out again and was shining the light at the damage. The driver's side had been crushed. Glass and part of his headlight littered the pavement.

"At least it's a rental," he noted dryly.

At those words, she just exploded. "Stop it!" Aspen ran to him. Grabbed his hand and sent his phone dropping to the ground. "This isn't funny! This isn't some joke!"

"No, I didn't think it was a joke. This is exactly what we wanted to happen, remember?" His voice was low but hard. "I waved the flag. I wanted him coming for me. We both wanted this."

"*I never wanted you hurt!*" What she wanted right then was to shake the man. "That isn't a possibility! That can't happen! I will turn myself in to Melissa and just stop this because you are not going to be—"

Bright lights hit them. Blinding. For a moment, she froze. They were on the edge of the road. This…this was what it could have been like for her father. The lights coming in. Closing in. And then the impact. The bone-breaking, life-ending impact that had taken him away. *"No!"* Aspen screamed. She fisted Gideon's shirt and hauled him forward. He was already moving, though, and pretty much barreled into her as they flew around the front of the truck and to the relative safety on the other side.

Brakes squealed as the other vehicle stopped. The scent of burning rubber filled her nose.

"Stay here," Gideon whispered as he pushed her down lower beside the passenger side of the truck. "I'll take care of him."

*Him*...had their attacker come back?

She still had her hands fisted in Gideon's shirt.

He was trying to pry them off.

"OhmyGod!" A woman's sharp voice filled the night. "I almost hit you! I am so sorry! Are you— are you all right?" Footsteps clattered toward them.

Gideon and Aspen turned to see a teenager rushing to them. Under the moonlight, her face appeared utterly horrified.

"Please, please be all right," the teen begged.

Aspen swallowed. "We're good." For the moment.

*****

"Hit and run accident." The cop waved toward the wreckage. "You're both very lucky."

"It wasn't an accident," Aspen said. She'd said this twice now. Her voice was flat and cold, and her body swayed just the faintest bit.

Gideon eyed her warily. He wanted Aspen away from the scene. She wasn't in shock, but she was damn well going through something. That worried him.

"How do you know it wasn't, ma'am?" the young cop wanted to know.

"Because someone has been stalking me. There have been several other incidents and this is just the latest one." Her hands were fisted at her sides. "He didn't stop. Didn't even slow down. He came right for us."

"Uh..." The cop scratched his cheek. "Have you reported your 'incidents' to the police?"

"I'm reporting this to you right now, aren't I? And, yes, I have talked to the cops because a man was attacked right outside of my office earlier today."

Swirling blue lights lit the scene. Two police cars were on the side of the road near the wrecked truck. The scared teenager had already left. Gideon had to give the cops credit—they'd sure arrived fast enough.

"Uh, ma'am, what does that man's attack have to do with your stalker?"

"It—I...his attacker could be the same person." She seemed to stumble. Her body edged closer to Gideon.

Right. Not like she could tell the cop...*We think Jake Eros faked his attack and may have been the person who just sent someone to hit our truck.*

Only the hit had been very deliberately placed on Gideon's side of the vehicle.

"Uh, huh." The cop rocked forward. "I think we need the EMT to check you out again." The cops had arrived on scene with an ambulance in tow.

"I don't need to be checked out anymore! The EMT said I was fine the first time!" Aspen's voice shook. "Look, I just want you to understand—"

*"Make me understand."*

Great. Now it was a party.

The female voice was instantly recognizable to him. Detective Melissa Wright had joined the scene. Why was he not particularly surprised to see her?

"Aspen." She inclined her head to Gideon. "Aspen's boyfriend."

He lifted an eyebrow.

"I was on my way home." Melissa's voice was casual. "When I happened to see the flashing lights. Wanted to make sure everyone was all right." A pause. "Imagine my surprise to see you here." She flashed her badge to the uniformed cops.

"She, um, Ms. Gray thinks her stalker caused the accident," the cop on the right explained.

"You have a stalker?" Melissa's voice sharpened. "Since when?"

Gideon opened his mouth to smooth things over.

"Since a little over a month. He's been calling me. Threatening me." Aspen's words tumbled out. "He's escalating. I found a camera in my home, and he sabotaged my chandelier. It fell and shattered, narrowly missing me and Gideon when it hit the floor."

Melissa had gone silent.

"He's coming for me, and he's not going to stop." Aspen drew herself up. "It all goes back to something that happened a long time ago. I need to tell you—"

*No, you don't.* He pulled Aspen into his arms and held her tight. "I told *you*, sweetheart, everything is fine." His voice was loud, but when he put his mouth to her ear, Gideon whispered, *"What in the hell are you doing?"*

She stiffened.

*"Stop,"* he ordered, barely a breath of sound.

"Aspen?" Melissa prompted. "What is it that you need to tell me?"

He squeezed Aspen a little tighter. This was not the time to reveal all. Why the hell would she even be considering a big reveal? Aspen knew what was on the line. She knew what she had to lose.

Gideon felt her give a small nod, and he slowly released her.

"What do you need to tell me?" Melissa edged even closer. "Is this about the conversation that we had earlier today? Do you feel like there is something you need to get off your chest?"

A black SUV rolled to a stop near the scene. Elijah.

"Confession is good for the soul," Melissa added.

*Do not confess a damn thing, Aspen.*

"Gideon isn't my boyfriend. He's my bodyguard." Her voice was...*prim.* Dammit. She was locking down. The last thing he wanted her to do.

No, the *last* thing he wanted was for her to confess everything and get hauled to the police station. But he didn't want Aspen shutting down on him, either.

"I went to him because things were getting too dangerous in my life."

Melissa eyed the truck. "Things certainly seem dangerous."

"Uh, Detective, we've got an APB out on the other vehicle. It was identified as a Dodge Charger, and it's gonna have substantial damage, particularly to the front, left side." *Charger.* The same type of vehicle that had been outside Aspen's house after the chandelier incident.

Elijah climbed out of the SUV. "Someone need a ride?"

"Damn straight." Gideon curled his hand around Aspen's elbow. "Let's go."

But Melissa stepped into their path. "You're not going anywhere. I have questions—"

"They already told us everything, Detective." The uniformed cop was being extra helpful.

"They haven't told *me*." Her hands went to her hips. The movement pulled back her coat and showed her holster. "I want to know more about the stalker. I can't help if I don't know everything."

Telling her everything was not on the agenda for the night, but if he didn't get Aspen out of there, Gideon was afraid the whole story would pour out. "I'm taking care of her. You just find the driver."

"Melissa is homicide," Aspen murmured. "This isn't really her realm. Stalking isn't, either." Again, no emotion. "Sorry to trouble you with any of this, Melissa. Don't worry, I'll be sure to speak to the proper individuals soon."

Melissa still didn't move. "Aspen..." Soft. "What are you involved with?"

Not what. "She's involved with me." He wanted Aspen away from the cops. "For the record, I'm both the bodyguard *and* the boyfriend." It was time to end this scene. He guided Aspen to the waiting SUV. Opened the back door and ushered her inside, then slipped in behind her.

Moments later, Elijah was in the driver's seat, and they were driving very sedately down the road. Not like they could fly away with a squeal of tires. Nice and slow—that was the way to go.

"I stayed at the hospital after you left," Elijah said into the heavy silence that filled the SUV. "Did just as you asked in your text. You were right—Jake checked out of the place. He and his guard rushed away moments after you left."

Aspen gave a start of surprise. "You knew he'd leave?"

"I was waving the red flag." He'd expected a reaction. He'd gotten one.

"I was tailing him back to the downtown area when I got your other text," Elijah added.

He'd texted Elijah after the scared teenager arrived. Gideon had known he'd need a ride—and backup, just in case.

"So, unfortunately, I am the alibi for both Jake and his guard. They didn't run you off the road."

"No, but I'm betting Jake has plenty of other people on his payroll who could do the deed." They needed to find that damn Dodge Charger. How hard could that possibly be? Not like it was just gonna blend with that extensive front-end damage. "The cops are looking for the vehicle that hit us, but we need to be doing our own search. We should access the street cams and see if we can spot the ride."

"You can't just access street cams." Aspen cleared her throat. "That's not something you can legally do."

"Just leave it to me." Or, rather, to some very skilled techs he knew at Wilde.

"There *are* no street cams out here, and he might not have gone back to an area where there are any."

"Then I'll check in other ways." He already had his phone out and was texting War. He gave a quick description of what had gone down. Told his old buddy what car he was searching for. "I have a few more friends I can pull in on the case."

She grabbed his hand—no, his phone. "You're talking about War."

War. Odin Shaw. Even a wild card named Jinx. They were all old friends of his, and they worked at the Trouble for Hire office.

"We don't have to do this." Soft. Even next to her, Gideon had to strain in order to hear her words. "We don't need to pull in more people. It's out of control as it is."

"Aspen..."

"To end this mess, I just have to take away his power."

Hell. He knew she was going to say—

"I confess, and he can't threaten me any longer. The cops will be looking for him."

He leaned in closer. Elijah hadn't heard her words. A very good thing. Gideon pressed a kiss to her cheek. He felt the shiver that slid over her.

"It's what I-I have to do," she rasped.

He caught her chin in his hand. Held her tenderly. Stared into her eyes and said, "The hell you do."

# CHAPTER SIXTEEN

When they arrived back at her house, Gideon slammed and locked the door shut behind them. Elijah hadn't followed them inside—he was off to meet up with War and Odin Shaw as they searched for the car. Gideon figured they would find it long before the cops did. Especially since they had the combined resources of Wilde and Trouble for Hire. War also knew the best spots to dump a car in the area so that was a definite advantage.

"I can't believe you're trying to stop me." Aspen whirled toward him.

"I can't believe you are even considering this shit." Yeah, about that... "*Why* are you considering it? You're the woman who was so convinced that she had to keep all of her secrets buried deep. You're the one who didn't even trust me to—" He stiffened. "Is that it?" Gideon stalked toward her. "Is that what this is about? You still don't trust me and you think I'm going to sell you out so you are trying to cover the narrative before I can?" He stopped right in front of her.

"No! Don't be a dick!"

He blinked.

"I'm trying to protect *you!*" She heaved out a breath then swiped at her cheek.

Oh, the hell, no. Why was she *crying?*

"I was planning to use you. All along. Don't you see that? Don't you see how selfish I am?"

"Aspen..."

"I went to Wilde. I thought if you weren't someone in my life, it would be easier to handle. I could get you to sign my stupid agreement. I could keep my emotions in check. We could fake a relationship. Draw him out and then I—" A long exhale. "No one was supposed to get hurt. I made sure the agent I requested had the best possible background. You were supposed to be able to protect yourself."

Well, shit. Now she was just insulting him. "Sweetheart..." His fingers slid down her cheek. Felt the moisture on her soft skin. "I can protect myself."

"Not if you don't see him coming. Not if he's driving a damn car into you. Not if he hits you when you're not ready for him!" Her eyes gleamed. "You aren't supposed to get hurt! That was never part of the plan!"

"Tell me the plan. All of it. Because I was always a little hazy on how things would end once you unmasked the jerk playing with you."

"I thought I could buy him off. He kept saying he wanted payback, so my initial plan was to try and offer him enough money to go away."

His eyes narrowed. "Yeah, that won't work. You get that he's locked and loaded on *you*." Of course, she got that. Wasn't that the point of her trying to push the guy over the edge with jealousy?

"That was the initial plan. When I realized his, ah, personal focus, I shifted gears."

Sure, right. A gear shift. His hand fell away from her cheek. "And?"

"And I didn't plan to kill him, if that's what you're suggesting! I am *not* a killer. Dammit, I told you before—"

"Your list of requirements." His shoulders squared. "You wanted a former soldier. Someone who *had* killed."

Her lips parted.

Tension knotted in his gut. "Is that what you wanted, sweetheart? For someone to kill for you? Were you going to set the stage, draw the bastard out by making him crazy with jealousy because you were with a new lover, and when he came charging in, was I going to have no choice but to kill him? To save you, I'd have to kill him, and then all of your problems would be gone."

He waited for her to rage at him. To tell him that, hell, no, that hadn't been her plan.

But she just inhaled a soft, deep breath. Her lashes fluttered. And she took a step back. "I think it's time to end my arrangement with Wilde."

She wasn't serious. "We were just run off the road, Aspen! He's gunning for you! You need Wilde to help you find him!" *You need me.*

She walked across the foyer. Picked up her phone. Dialed quickly. She put the phone to her ear as he watched her in growing confusion.

"Hi, Eric? Yes, it's Aspen."

Gideon took a lunging step toward her before he caught himself and stopped.

"I want to thank you for the help that you've given to me, but I'm calling to officially terminate my agreement with Wilde."

The hell she was. Gideon's hand clenched and released.

"What? No, no, I don't have any problem with Gideon."

He had a big freaking problem with her. She wasn't sending him away.

"I just don't need his services. I've figured out the identity of the stalker, and I will be handling things on my own from here on out. Yes, I am sure." Her spine was ramrod straight. "I'd like for you to make certain that Gideon knows he should leave immediately. Thank you." She ended the call.

Gideon remained rooted to the spot.

His phone rang. He pulled it out of his back pocket. Brought it to his ear. Didn't bother looking at the caller ID because he knew who it was. "Eric."

"So...what the fuck is going on?"

Aspen's back was still to him.

"What have you done? Jeez, man, what part of 'VIP and handle with kid gloves' did you miss? How have you fucked this up?"

"I fucked her," he said flatly.

"*What?*" Eric's roar nearly shattered his ear drum.

Aspen spun around. Her mouth was parted in a giant O of shock.

"I got involved with the client. You know that's happened before at Wilde. Figured it would never happen to me." He kept the phone at his ear, but his eyes were on Aspen. "It did."

"I do *not* need this shit right now," Eric raged. "I told you how important Aspen was!"

"She's important. Check."

"She just *fired* you!"

Aspen had closed her mouth.

"I think there is a miscommunication."

"Miscommunication, my ass!" Eric seemed to be choking on fury. "She's in danger. She needs you, and now you've pissed her off and she wants you out of her life! What am I supposed to do? Leave her on her own when this guy is still out there? Because Elijah already told me about the hit and run tonight. I just got off the phone with him. He assured me that you were staying close to Aspen, but now I hear *this!* You can't stay close if she's kicking your ass out!"

"Don't worry. I'm not going anywhere."

Aspen crossed her arms over her chest. "When you're fired, you have to leave. That's how it works."

Eric sucked in a breath. "I will send Elijah in as primary. She's not furious at him, and I'll make sure he keeps his hands to himself."

"Elijah isn't touching her. No one else is."

"You're over the deep end. She *fired* you. That means pack your bags and get out while I try to find someone else to keep her safe. I am not leaving Aspen on her own! My family owes her too much!"

Right. Because Aspen had taken a bullet for Ben Wilde. Because she'd been willing to sacrifice herself to protect someone she cared about.

*And she's doing the same thing now.*

"Don't give her any trouble," Eric ordered. "Just...shit. I will fix this clusterfuck."

"Good luck with that." He hung up. He'd get back to Eric, later. Right now... "I wondered if you cared."

She eyed him warily. "You understand that you've just been dismissed?"

"Sure. I'm fired. Got it." He put the phone down on the nearby table. Took slow steps toward her.

Aspen stiffened, but she didn't back away. "You'll want to pack your bags and get out."

"Because I'm fired."

"Yes."

"Fine. I'm not the bodyguard any longer."

She bit her lower lip. "I...I didn't intend for you to ever kill anyone. I get that you don't exactly have a high opinion of me, but that wasn't my plan."

"I got it." *I got you.* He closed in a little more.

"Your bags are that way." She pointed over his shoulder.

"Are they?"

Her chin lifted. "You're angry."

"Don't think that quite covers it."

"Well, you don't have to worry about me making you mad any longer. Our arrangement is at an end."

"What if I don't want it to be?"

"But...you just said you weren't my bodyguard any longer."

"Yeah. I'm not. You fired me. Got it. Heard it when you told Eric. Heard it when he told me." A nod. "I'm talking about the fact that I'm still your lover."

A faint tremble of her lower lip. "You don't trust me."

"Baby, I *know* you now. I can see right through the image you have."

She shook her head.

"You were going to reveal all your secrets to the cops in order to protect me. You were fine with hiding your secrets when it was just your own life on the line, but when you thought this prick was coming to kill me, you changed your tune." She'd changed it helluva fast. He'd realized when he was on the edge of the road with her that something had shifted. "It reminded you of your dad, didn't it?"

Her lashes fluttered. "He got caught in someone else's fight."

"And you don't want me caught in your fight."

"It was different when I was getting some random agent to come in. A guy that I thought could protect himself and wouldn't be in serious danger."

He had to laugh. "Ah, sweetheart, that's just insulting." He curled his hands around her shoulders. "I *can* protect myself."

"Not if you don't see him coming. Elijah didn't see the threat. What if you *don't*?"

He wasn't Elijah. "You're trying to protect me."

She didn't respond.

"Cute. Actually, fucking adorable."

Her gaze hardened. "Asshole."

He smiled. "But I am the one who is supposed to protect *you*."

"I told you, I never wanted protection—"

"Too bad, you got it, and the fact that I am willing to put myself between you and a bullet or between you and a car—it scares the hell out of you."

She jerked out of his hold. "You don't know what you're talking about."

"I do. Because you just got me fired."

"If you don't want to pack your bags, fine. I can pack them and send them along after you." She motioned for the door. "Goodbye."

"Yeah...no."

Her shoulders rolled back. "This doesn't need to be an ugly break-up scene. I mean, you have already clearly told me about the opinion you have of me."

"I don't think you know at all how I feel about you. That's the problem."

Her delicate nostrils flared. "We agreed it would just be fucking. No feelings—"

"I'm sure I told you before that I break rules." He winced. "So I should probably tell you now that it was *never* just fucking."

"You told Eric—"

"Best for him to know where I stand."

Her hair slid over her shoulders as Aspen shook her head. "Where do you stand?"

"Isn't it obvious?" He wanted to kiss her. Wanted to pull her close. Wanted to take her and never let go. "With you." Simple.

"No." A sharp denial. "You need to leave."

"I need to stay. You need me."

"No." Just as sharp. "I need you to go." She sniffed. "Just stop making this so hard."

"Why do you want me to leave?"

She stared at him as if he had gone crazy. "Are you serious right now? Did you miss the fact that *your* side of the truck was smashed to hell and back?"

"No, pretty hard to miss that. But, apparently, there was something else equally important that I did miss. My bad. Normally, my observational skills are way better than that." He drove his hands into the front pockets of his jeans. "So I have to ask...just when was it that you fell in love with me?"

# CHAPTER SEVENTEEN

For a moment, all she could hear was the hard *thud, thud, thud* of her heartbeat as it seemed to reverberate in her ears.

"Hmm, Aspen? When was it?"

She couldn't have understood him correctly. But his slightly smug expression said...*you did.* "You're crazy."

"No, quite sane."

"I tell you to get out. I tell you that you're fired, and somehow, you twist that into me being in love with you?" Her laugh was brittle.

"I know you love me because you *are* telling me to get out. Because you *are* telling me that I'm fired. If you weren't, if you were saying, 'Hey, Gideon, let's do more red flag waving. Let's set you up as the biggest bait in the world and lure in this creep so that he can take swipes at you'—if you were telling me that stuff, then I'd just shrug and do my job."

"You're fired," she reminded him and her voice was getting all ragged at the edges. "You don't have a job any longer."

"Because you love me."

"Stop it! I have never said I loved you! I don't know why you are acting like this!"

His expression softened. "Maybe most people can't read you. Maybe they let your secrets slide, maybe they think when your voice gets all icy and proper that you're just emotionally cold, but those people are fucking idiots and that's bullshit."

Her voice wasn't cold now. It was fracturing apart—because *she* was.

"You didn't want Ramsey or Darius or anyone else that is so close to you down here knowing the truth because you were trying to protect them."

"Ram would start a war," she whispered.

"Yes. And probably get hurt in the process. And lose all that great headway he's been making to woo his lady, Whitney. War filled me in on lots of details. But, honestly, I'd already figured out so much about you by that point that I didn't even need his insight. I knew a shit-ton about you before I even got on the flight down here."

Shock rolled through her. "You researched me."

He came closer. She wanted to back away, but she forced herself to stand still even as his hand rose to press lightly against her left side. "I saw the scar when we made love."

He'd just said 'made love' but it was supposed to have just been fucking. Nothing more.

"I didn't ask about it because I already knew how you got it. Ben Wilde is one of your friends. You have a small, very exclusive circle of people that you let close. You protect those people with everything that you have. When Ben was in danger, you stepped in front of him. You took the bullet meant for him and it went into you right...here." He stared down at where his hand touched her. A faint line appeared between his brows.

She tried to ignore the way his touch sent warmth seeping through her clothing. "It wasn't a big deal. Bled a lot, but there was no serious damage."

His head lifted. The faint line was still between his eyebrows.

"Why does it matter?" she demanded to know.

"You risked your life to protect Ben Wilde because you care about him."

"Ben is my friend." The first real one that she'd had after Ramsey had sent her out of her world. And she'd been reeling at the time because of everything that had happened with Braden. "I...all of that happened so soon after the attack with Braden. I was on edge. Jumping at shadows back then. That night, a shadow jumped back at me. I wasn't just going to stand there and lose Ben." She'd already lost so much. Her father. Ramsey and Darius—yes, she'd thought she'd lost them because they had made it so clear that she didn't belong in their world. "I'd just found something good in my new life and someone wanted to take it away."

"So you protected Ben. You protect the people you care about. Like you're protecting Ramsey and Darius now." His hand slowly dropped. "Like you're protecting me. It was fine to hire a stranger. You made sure my resume was strong so that I could handle myself. You thought you'd never be in danger of getting too close to me because you were going to put up all your precious walls. You even gave me the speech that you'd given to Ben shortly after you met him."

She felt a flush stain her cheeks. She'd given that speech to a few others over the years. It was safer not to get too involved. Safer for them. For her. Because she hadn't wanted anyone to learn all her dark secrets.

Except...Gideon had.

"Things changed, though. Changed so much that you were going to tell the cops everything for me. You would have tossed away your career and possibly your freedom for me."

She sniffed. "Don't be so sure. I know a good lawyer."

The faintest hint of a smile curled his lips.

Aspen doggedly continued, "If Braden is miraculously back from the dead..." *And Jake seems to think he could be...* "Then my big confession probably won't cost nearly as much as you think." Bluffing words but the truth was...*yes, it will be a clusterfuck.* Didn't matter, though. She'd confess all if it meant taking back control from the stalker and protecting Gideon.

*Protecting Gideon.* Yes, fine, she knew exactly what she was doing.

"You were willing to reveal all to the authorities. You are trying to fire me. You want me gone from danger." His smile spread as he made his points. "Sweetheart, you're shouting that you love me."

*Thud, thud, thud.* Her loud heartbeat was back. She opened her mouth to deny his words but...

Couldn't.

"Is it so wrong," she asked him, her voice low and husky, "to want to keep you safe?"

His hand lifted again. His fingers slid into her hair. "No. I want to keep you safe. I want to take you as far away from any threat as I can. I want to make sure that you never know fear or worry again. There is nothing wrong with any of that."

She found herself pushing into his touch.

"Want to know some of my secrets?" Gideon asked her. "Sort of seems fair, doesn't it? Since I made it a point to know all of yours."

She wanted to know everything about him, and maybe, when this was all over, she could. "I'll come to Atlanta when it's safe. We can meet up then."

His head lowered. He kissed her. A sweet, tender kiss. Behind her lowered lashes, she could feel the tears wanting to fall. She wouldn't let them.

"There is no way I will leave your side. I don't care that I'm not the bodyguard. Fuck it, I'm glad that I'm not." A growl as his lips broke from hers. "Makes it easier for me to just be the man who loves you."

*What?*

Her hands flew up and pressed to his chest. She'd misheard. He'd misspoke. Both. Something.

"No more pretending." He was staring straight at her. Looking at her like she was something shiny and special and precious. He shouldn't do that.

She was a liar. She was dangerous. She was a schemer. She was...

*So in love with him.*

"I love you, Aspen Gray. If you want the full truth, I think I fell in love with you the first day. You walked into the office at Wilde and you took my breath away. It was a good thing I was sitting down because otherwise, I'm pretty sure I would have fallen on my ass. I thought you were the sexiest thing I'd ever seen, and then when you started talking and saying I was a mistake…"

"I thought that made you angry."

"Just made me want to be the best mistake you'd ever had."

Her breath came faster.

"You were smart, determined. You were scared but trying so hard to hide it. I didn't want you afraid. I wanted to fucking slay whatever dragon was in your life and prove that you could count on me."

He *was* someone she could count on. She'd learned that when he hadn't wavered from her side no matter what he'd discovered about her and her past.

"Then when I learned about Ben and the shooting…" He shook his head. His fingers skimmed over her cheek. "Couldn't believe that moron hadn't put a ring on your finger. Knew I wouldn't be such a dumbass."

"I-I didn't love Ben that way."

"Thank Christ for that. Because I like Ben, and I would have hated to kick his ass."

She could only shake her head. He wasn't serious. Was he?

"You love *me* that way," he said slowly. "Don't you?"

"I-I thought you already knew that I did."

"A man likes to hear the words."

She'd never said those words to anyone. Never said *I love you* to any person but her father and that had been so different. As she stared at Gideon, fear rose within her. She'd always been afraid of getting too close. Of having someone see her dark parts, the twisted parts inside of her. The parts that had led her to seek vengeance and risk everything in her life.

But Gideon knew. He knew everything. All of her. He *knew*.

And he wasn't leaving. Wasn't turning on her. He was standing before her, his eyes lit with what sure looked like love, and she wanted to reach out and just take what was right in front of her.

*So do it.*

"I love you." Aspen blinked. It hadn't been as hard as she thought. The words had just come out. "I love you," she said again, and Aspen meant it. With every bit of her being, she loved him.

She launched at him. Her arms flew up and curled around him as she pulled him down to her. Her lips crashed onto his, and this wasn't a tender, worshipping kiss like before. This was intensity. This was madness. This was a flood gate that had been thrust open, and there was no holding back.

She let go. For the first time in her life, she just let go with the man before her. All walls gone. All control gone.

And he responded the same way. His touch was fierce and branding. His mouth hungry with an edge of savagery.

Desire exploded in her veins. She rubbed her body against his and just wanted him. Right then. Right there. No secrets. No pretending. She wanted it all to be real because with Gideon, it finally *was*.

They were yanking at each other's clothes. Fighting to get naked. Everything was in her way when she just wanted to be with him. Her hands were rough. His hands tore more of her underwear, and Aspen didn't care.

She wanted him inside of her. She wanted to be racing toward the oblivion that he gave to her.

"Bed," he gasped. "Need you in *bed...*"

Yes, absolutely, but first...

She ran her hands down his body. Caught the heavy, hard cock that shoved toward her. Stroked him. Squeezed him. Then lowered right there in her foyer—the place where he'd saved her life the first day they'd been in town—and she took the head of his cock into her mouth.

*"Fuck. That feels so damn good..."* A growl that urged her on.

She parted her lips more. Took him in deeper. Wanted to give him just as much pleasure as he gave her every single time they touched.

But he was yanking her up. "Yeah, can't happen."

What? "Why not?"

"Can't hold on," he gritted out. "Need you *now.*"

She needed him now, too. In a blur, they made it to the guest bedroom. He took care of the condom. She grabbed for him, and when he tumbled onto the bed with her, Aspen laughed.

She couldn't believe she was laughing even as primal lust blasted through her.

*Only with him.*

She straddled his hips. Felt the head of his cock push against her core. She lifted her hips and arched down onto him.

*So good.* He stretched every single bit of her and for a moment, time seemed to stop as she just savored him. She could have sworn that he had been made for her. Crazy, of course, but...

*He's mine.*

In a way that no one had ever been before.

"Baby, you feel fucking fantastic." His hands were clamped tightly around her hips.

So did he. *Fantastic.* She pushed up on her knees. Sank back down. Over and over. The bed was rocking beneath them. Her breath panted out. His wicked fingers moved to strum her clit and when the orgasm hit her, she slammed her hands down on his chest and rode out that powerful wave that lashed through her entire body.

He held himself still. She felt the rock-hard strength of his body. She tried to catch her breath. Tried to look at him but...

*Yes, that's gonna have to wait.* She let the pleasure consume her, and it took a few moments before her head could lift. When it did, she found him staring at her.

"You are so beautiful." Rough. Low.

He was still in her. Fully erect and strong. "You...ah...didn't..."

"Wanted to watch you. But can't wait any longer." He tumbled her back onto the bed.

Hooked her legs over his shoulders and pistoned his hips against her. He took her hard. He took her deep. He took her with an undeniable possession that seemed to burn through to her very soul.

She loved it. Loved *him.*

Aspen felt a second orgasm building again. Didn't even try to hold back. She screamed his name when she came, and he plunged even faster against her.

Then he was shouting her name. Holding her as if he'd never let go. Exploding with her as everything else in the universe just seemed to stop. She was staring into his eyes. He was looking down into hers. She could see the pleasure spreading through his gaze.

Yes, she could see pleasure.

But also so much more. As he gazed at her, Aspen was pretty sure she saw love.

\*\*\*

His phone was ringing. Gideon cracked open one eye. He was in bed, Aspen was deliciously sprawled over him, and he was pretty sure he'd been having the best dream of his life.

The phone rang again.

He knew he had to answer. They'd fallen asleep after making love again. Or, twice more. He hadn't exactly been counting. He'd just been enjoying the hell out of having her in his arms. The place where he wanted her to stay.

Forever.

The phone kept ringing.

Aspen murmured something in her sleep.

"It's okay," he told her. "Be right back." Gideon pressed a kiss to her temple and dragged the covers up over her chest. There was a faint chill in the air. He'd have to adjust the temperature for her.

He hauled on a pair of sweats and made his way back to the foyer. Surprise, surprise, his phone was on the table near his discarded jeans.

And the phone was still ringing. He swiped his fingers across the screen and took the call.

"Seriously, what the fuck were you doing?" Elijah blasted.

*Sleeping with the woman I love.*

"You nearly gave me a heart attack!" Elijah added before Gideon could speak. "I thought your ass was dead. Wait...you haven't said a word yet. Gideon? Gideon, prove it's you and that some bastard hasn't stolen your phone—"

"I haven't said a word because you haven't given me time to speak," he returned. "What's going on?"

"I'm with your buddy War. We found the car."

Gideon stiffened. "Did you find the driver?"

"No, no, the car is abandoned."

There was a sound. Like pounding wind or... Waves?

"Where are you?" Gideon asked.

"Near the beach. The vehicle was left in a parking lot out here. War says it's a place locals visit, but at this time of the year, it's usually deserted."

*No, no, it won't be the same area...* "Give me a specific location."

"Uh, hold on..." Elijah's voice became a bit distorted. "Gideon wants coordinates or some shit. Does this beach have a specific name?" A pause. Then his voice cleared as Elijah began to rattle off a road name and give other landmarks.

The tension between Gideon's shoulder blades grew heavier. He knew the spot. It was the place where Aspen had taken him. The area that had once been her favorite place at the beach before she'd been attacked just a mile offshore.

The location had been deliberate. The car had been abandoned there to send a message to Aspen.

"No driver," Elijah said again. "And there is no license plate. But we *did* find something interesting inside."

"Don't leave me in fucking suspense."

"A parking tag. It was shoved into the glove box. You ever hear of a place called Shadow Pines?"

Gideon raked a hand through his hair. "No, but I'm betting you already researched it."

"War knows it. Didn't have to research it. Said it's some fancy private psychiatric clinic off the West Coast of Florida. It's on a private island there, very exclusive. Total secrecy for patients."

"How does War know about it?"

"Give me the damn phone," he heard War grouse in the background. And then...

War's voice. Loud. Clear. He'd obviously taken the phone. "Had a case once where a client's sister had been committed there. The client wanted me to prove that her sister didn't belong in that institution. Wanted me to get her out. So I got in there and took a look around. Not fucking easy, let me tell you that. Shadow Pines is like Fort Knox. Only the wealthiest get admitted and once you are in? You are there for keeps. It's where the rich and famous send their family problems. The ones they want to lock away and forget."

Gideon's hold tightened on the phone. "Did you get your client's sister out?"

"Hell, yes, I did. Her dick of a husband had put her there, and she did not belong." A pause. "There were some…violent patients in Shadow Pines. The woman was terrified when I got her out."

Gideon did not like where this was going.

"There is an employee number on this parking tag. I'm going to get a buddy I have to hack into the system at Shadow Pines and see if he can identify who the tag belongs to."

Gideon released a hard breath. "Can your buddy get us a list of patient names?"

The surf pounded in the background. "Who are we looking for?" War wanted to know.

"Braden Savage."

War cursed.

"Exactly."

# CHAPTER EIGHTEEN

"The car is stolen." They were in War's PI office above his bar, Armageddon. He sat behind the desk, Gideon and Elijah were busy prowling around the office like trapped tigers, and Aspen remained seated in the chair across from War. She'd folded her hands in her lap and kept her shoulders squared and her spine straight.

"We figured out that it belonged to an employee at Shadow Pines."

She didn't flinch at the name of the facility, though she was familiar with it. The place was one of the dirty secrets in the state. No, it wasn't just used by the rich and powerful in Florida—people all over the US would use it as a holding place for family members or loved ones who were...

Dangerous.

Shadow Pines wasn't the type of place where patients were treated for depression or anxiety. Shadow Pines was the type of place where you were sent after you became violent. After you hurt others and your wealthy family was covering up for you so that you didn't wind up in jail.

"The employee is a man named William Ray. He reported the theft, but since it was so far away, not like news of the vehicle traveled to Pensacola. Though, apparently, the driver did."

She swallowed. "There is only one way on or off the island where Shadow Pines is located." A very long, well-guarded bridge. "In order to get past the security, the driver would have needed to show ID."

"Or needed to bribe someone," Gideon said as he turned toward her. "Because that's the angle we're investigating now."

Yes, true. Bribery always had a way of smoothing things over.

"The theft happened over a month ago," War said carefully.

She would not flinch.

"William had given up on the car being located."

Aspen knew exactly where this was going. "Can we get to the point? I'm sure you checked the patient list." She didn't even touch the fact that it wouldn't be legal to access such a list. "Was Braden a patient?"

"We did find a case file on him."

She would not—

Dammit, she flinched. "I...see."

"Back when he was a teen, he was admitted. Seems he got angry with his girlfriend at the time." War's stare was on her. Unwavering. "He choked the poor girl."

Aspen's hand started to rise to her throat. She caught herself. Her hand pressed over her heart. "How terrible." *It had been terrible. His hands had tightened and the world had faded away and I was sure I was going to die—*

Gideon approached her. He put his hand on her shoulder. "War said that was the only record of Braden being at the facility. His time as a teen. He stayed there for a year and then he convinced his father that he should be released. He was."

She put both of her hands back in her lap. "Is it possible he was just admitted under another name? That happens a lot at facilities like that one." Especially when someone wanted secrecy. Privacy for the individual—and the individual's very powerful family.

"I'm going down there to find out," War told her with a roll of his powerful shoulders. "I still have contacts in there who will help me. If there aren't records that we can hack regarding Braden Savage, then I will need to talk personally with the people I know in the facility. If he was there again, I *will* find out."

"You don't work for me," she reminded him. A reminder he shouldn't need. "You don't have to do this."

"I work for him." He pointed toward Gideon. "Didn't he tell you?"

No, he hadn't. She craned her neck to peer back at Gideon. "Since when?"

Gideon merely shrugged like this was the most casual thing in the world. "Since I wanted someone else I could trust on this case. War and I go way back, and I know I can count on him."

War was already breaking the law for her. "No." Aspen stood up. Shook her head. "I don't want more people brought into this!" Involving War was the opposite of what she wanted. "*I* will go to Shadow Pines. I've been there before." With a previous client. "And I also have people who will talk to me." It chilled her to think that when she'd been there, had Braden been in the facility, too?

Was it even possible?

Her mind was spinning and analyzing...

If Jake had been telling the truth...if he'd gone home and found his house unlocked and the floor wet...

*Did Braden make it out of the Gulf?*

"War, can we have a minute?" Gideon asked quietly.

War let out a long-suffering sigh. "This is a trend. People are always trying to kick me out of my own office. It's annoying as fuck."

"I'll remember that." Gideon's response was dry. "How about you and Elijah go snag some coffee?"

"I know this good place right down the street..." Elijah began.

War pointed at Gideon. "Five minutes."

"Someone rushes his coffee," Gideon responded.

Growling, War stormed for the door.

"Don't worry," Elijah said before he followed War out, "I'll make him drink slowly." The door shut.

Aspen rubbed her chilled arms. "You're not going to change my mind."

"What makes you think I was going to try?"

Surprise rippled through her as she faced him. "You're not?"

"You want to visit this Shadow Pines place and talk to contacts you have there?" He nodded. "Great idea. We can hit the road within the hour."

*We can hit the road...* "I see what you did there."

He reached out and began lightly rubbing her arms to chase the chill away from her. "Do you?"

"You know...you know I..." She trailed away.

"That you were trying to ditch me because you have this crazy idea that I need protecting? Even though I'm a trained security agent and can handle this shit in my sleep?" He kept carefully rubbing.

Her lips thinned.

"It's not happening. I've told you that. Where you go, I go, and it doesn't have a damn thing to do with an agreement or any deal." His hands stilled even as his gaze blazed down at her. "I stay with you because the idea of something happening to you scares me more than anything else in the world. You matter to me. A whole fucking lot. And I will not let anyone hurt you."

"I don't want you getting hurt, either."

"Then we just protect each other, huh? We also do this the smart way, the *right* way. We get backup in place to help us. Backup like Elijah and War. People we can count on to be there no matter what else happens."

People who were there no matter what. For Gideon, it was friends like Elijah and War. For her...

*It's friends like Ramsey and Darius.* Friends she'd tried to shut out of her life because she'd wanted to protect them, too.

She'd wanted to keep them out of her past because she'd been trying to cover up the night that she'd killed a man. Only, what if she hadn't?

What if, for all of these years, Braden had still been out there?

"Is it even possible?" Aspen shook her head. "Could Braden have survived that attack?"

"Where did you stab him?"

She jerked.

"You may not remember. That's okay, sweetheart."

"I will never be able to forget."

Her hand lifted. She pressed to his stomach. Slid her hands over. Moved up his chest.

He looked down.

"I just grabbed the knife." Her voice sounded small. "My throat hurt so much, and I couldn't breathe and the world was spinning around me. I grabbed it and pushed it between us. I just wanted him to stop. Then I looked down and..." Blood. "I told him not to take the knife out. That I'd get on the radio and call for help, but he chased me. He took it out." She'd told him this before, hadn't she? Aspen cast a worried glance up at him.

"He took out the knife and chased you. If he'd been at death's door, seems odd that he'd have the strength for that."

"I was confused after the attack, but I know there was a ton of blood."

"Some wounds bleed like a bitch, but you still survive them."

"He could have just been fueled by adrenaline when he chased me," she murmured. Wasn't that what she'd told herself later? "Then when he hit the water..." On this, she was certain. "I *never* saw him come up."

"Maybe because he swam away from the boat, not back to it."

"*Maybe* he swam toward the lights of shore. Toward Jake's place. It was so dark that night. No moon. Hardly any stars. The main light came from the shore." *Maybe those lights called to him.*

"I want to see Jake's house on the water." He stared at her, but seemed to see *through* her.

What could they possibly find there after all of this time? "He...I don't think he stays there much any longer. He still owns it, but he doesn't live there. When Frank died, Jake inherited all of his property and holdings. He moved into the mansion that Frank had just outside of town."

"So no one will be at the house on the water?"

"Probably not."

"Then I want to see it now. Before we make the trip to Shadow Pines."

"Why?" She was more than ready to get to the facility so that she could know whether or not Braden had survived. "It's been years. It's not like you'll find anything at the house about Braden."

"Actually, I think I might."

Her eyebrows rose.

"If Braden survived that night, *why* would he go to Jake's?"

"Because...it was close by. A safe spot for him."

"Were he and Braden close?"

"No." Quite the opposite. "Braden—he and Jake made a point to avoid each other."

"Because Jake wanted what Braden had. He thought Braden had taken his life."

Braden *had* taken Jake's life. Jake had been Frank's real son, but he'd grown up with nothing. While Braden...

*He'd had everything.* Everything, and he'd still wanted to destroy the world.

"It was dark on the water." Gideon's voice was musing. "If Braden had been there, close to the boat, he would have seen when Jake came to get you."

She nodded. "Unless he'd already swam to shore by then. I was out there a while, looking for him." Aspen shifted from one foot to another. "But again, it's been years. Why go back to Jake's old home now?"

"Because if no one is using that place, then it might just be the perfect spot for our stalker to hide. It's got emotional significance for him. It was his safe spot once upon a time, and it may just be so again."

"You're doing your psych thing," she murmured. "You're pretty good at it."

"Thanks." His hand rose to slide over the nape of his neck.

Her eyes narrowed. "This is about more than it being some safe spot. Do *not* hold out on me. We're done with that, remember? I tell you my secrets. You tell me yours. That's how we work now."

His hand fell. "*If* it's Braden, then he'd be looking for a place to lay low. Jake's house gives him that spot. It has emotional significance, and it could have been a haven for him before. All of that it is true but..."

"But what?"

"But I don't fucking trust Jake Eros. I don't like the way he is with you. I don't like the fact that your father told him to stay the hell away from you and then you father ended up dying on the side of the road."

Her heart lurched. "That was Braden."

"If Jake has something to hide, maybe it's hidden in that old place because that home was *his*. Not Frank's. So, yes, I want to search it before we hit the road and go to Shadow Pines. Consider it a pitstop."

A knock sounded at the door. "I didn't go for coffee!" War called out. "And five minutes have passed." The door swung open. "So how about you two tell me what the plan is?"

She sucked in a breath. Aspen wanted to shut down. To keep War out of this. But...

She'd tried that path before. Going it alone hadn't worked out so well. Gideon was at her side, and he'd said they should do this right. That they should have backup in place.

Fair enough.

"We're doing a bit of B&E," Gideon admitted. "If you have a problem with that, you might want to hang back."

War shoved his hands into the pockets of his jeans. "Don't have a problem with that. See, I know a good lawyer." He inclined his head toward Aspen. "So where are we going?"

\*\*\*

The house was dark. Shuttered. No boat bobbed along the dock. Everything felt still.

As Aspen watched, Gideon surveyed the scene carefully. War was near the main road, keeping a lookout, and Elijah was currently standing on the dock. The place was located on a small inlet—the beach wasn't far away at all.

The sun beat down on them as Gideon and Aspen made their way up the steps that led to the house as it waited on old, wooden stilts. When they'd first arrived, they'd swept the scene nearby and hadn't seen any neighbors or tourists. The location seemed deserted.

*Seemed* being the main word. But Aspen couldn't shake the feeling that she was being watched.

*Great. Now I'm relying on instincts just as much as Gideon is.*

Gideon lifted his hand and pounded on the door. She knew the act was for show, just in case they were being observed and in case someone should happen to be inside the old house.

What would she do, Aspen wondered for one frantic moment, if Braden Savage swung open that door? If she stood face to face with the ghost from her past?

Gideon lifted his hand to knock again.

Her phone rang. She'd turned the ringer off, but she could feel the vibration in her pocket. She ignored the call.

Gideon pulled out a small, black pouch from his pocket. A lock-picking set. She peered over his shoulder to try and get a better look at the tools.

"Sweetheart," his voice was tender and low, "let's focus on looking less obvious."

Right. She turned away. Stared out at the water.

Her phone vibrated again.

Casually, she pulled it out of her pocket. This time, she'd gotten a text, not a call, and she didn't recognize the number. Her finger swiped over the screen.

One word was there. Just one.

*Boom.*

She spun back toward Gideon just as she heard the faintest of clicks. He'd gotten the door unlocked.

She could see the half-smile spreading over his lips as he began to push the door open.

"Gideon, no!" Aspen screamed.

*Boom.*

# CHAPTER NINETEEN

Someone was pounding at her door. Aspen rose slowly from her couch. Her steps were sluggish as she made her way across the den, through the foyer, and to the shaking door.

Her fingers trembled as she unlocked the door and opened it.

"Aspen!" Jake stood there, staring at her in horror. "My God! Are you all right?"

She shook her head. Felt a tear slide down her cheek.

In the next instant, Jake was stepping over the threshold. Shoving the door closed and locking it behind him. He pulled her in for a fierce hug. "I heard the news story about the explosion—heard it right before Detective Wright called me to say that my old home had become a crime scene."

Aspen shuddered.

He drew back. Studied her. "You have a cut on your cheek."

A small wound. A piece of broken glass had sliced her. Hadn't Gideon gotten a similar cut when he'd saved her from the falling chandelier?

She had to blink away tears.

"Your boyfriend...Gideon was hurt, wasn't he? I can't get specifics, but on the news, they said someone was critical and was taken away in an ambulance. At first, I feared it was you."

She pulled away from him. "I'm okay."

"Thank goodness." His hands fisted at his sides. "What about him? Is he...is Gideon going to make it, Aspen?"

Aspen turned and walked back toward her couch. "I got a text right before it happened."

"What?" He chased after her. "Wait, just back up." His hand closed around her shoulder. "Why were you even at my old home?"

"Because we were looking for Braden."

He swung her around to face him. "You're not serious. *Braden is dead.*"

"You're the one who said you found water at your house. That the door was unlocked." Her lips pressed together. "Gideon and I were hit by a driver in a Dodge Charger after we left you at the hospital—turned out the car was stolen from an employee at Shadow Pines."

"Shadow Pines? The psycho institute?"

"The residential treatment facility," she corrected woodenly.

"Braden went there." His grip tightened on her. "When he was a teen. I remember finding out that Frank had sent him to that place, and I thought—finally, he'll see that Braden is messed up. Frank will realize he doesn't need him."

She stared at him. "But Braden got out a year later."

"Yes." A hiss. His eyes flared with realization. "Shit. You think...you think after Braden attacked you, Frank found him and sent him back to Shadow Pines? That he's been there all this time?"

"It's a possibility." She wanted to wrap her arms around her body to fight the bone-numbing chill she felt. *The house on the water exploded.*

"My God, Aspen. That's...that's..."

She looked back at him. "I got a text right before the explosion. If I hadn't gotten it, I might have been inside with Gideon."

His eyes widened. "He texted you? *Jesus.* What in the hell are we going to do?"

"Go to the cops." A nod.

*"We can't!"*

"I didn't kill Braden."

His grip on her shoulder was almost bruising. "But we covered up everything! You know what a legal minefield this will be!"

"I know I need to have everyone searching for him. That's why War is on his way to Shadow Pines right now."

His brow crinkled. "War?"

"Warren Channing. He runs the Trouble for Hire PI firm in town. I was going to visit Shadow Pines myself to talk with the staff, but with the explosion and Gideon..." *Don't. Don't lose control!* She sucked in a breath. "War went instead. He's helping me. The sooner we have solid proof, the better."

"You should have come to *me*." Anger thickened his voice. "Me, not War. I'm the one who helped you before, and I will do it again." He let her go. "Call War. Tell him you have this covered. I'll handle things."

"How?"

His bright eyes glittered. "The way I should have handled them years ago. *I'll* take out Braden.

I'll make him vanish for good. Then there will be no need to tell the cops anything. There will be no need to risk losing everything that matters to you. I will protect you, and I will end this."

"Why? Why do this for me?"

"Don't you know?" Soft. "Haven't you always known? I would do anything for you."

"And anything for yourself."

He blinked at her. "What?"

"I said you'd do anything for yourself." Where his voice had been soft, hers was loud. Clear. "Anything to get what you want. I remember when we were kids, you told me that once. That you'd do whatever it took to get what you deserved. At the time, I just thought you meant working hard and never giving up. You know, that kind of inspirational BS." She wet her lower lip. "But now, I know you meant murder."

"Aspen…" A warning edge.

"You are your father's son, aren't you?"

"What is that supposed to mean?"

"It means I know."

"You know…*what?*"

"You were sloppy with that last text. Probably because you were worried that I was going to be hurt. Elijah—he's Gideon's partner, by the way, they both work for a big protection firm—he used his resources to track the number. It traced back to you."

"The hell it did."

"You have met Elijah," she added musingly. "You know, the time you snuck up and hit him from behind. Though perhaps that doesn't count as a real introduction."

"What are you talking about?"

"Let's focus on the explosion, shall we?"

"What. The. Fuck?"

"Before your old home blew, you called me and then you texted. You were frantic because I was so close to the scene and you'd rigged it to blow when someone went in the door. I'm guessing you got one of Frank's men to teach you how to set up the bomb. Maybe it was even the same guy who showed you how to trigger my chandelier to fall."

"You don't know what you're talking about."

"You weren't as careful with the text as you should have been. I could tell you all the tech info about triangulating signals and whatnot, but the simple fact is that we know *you* were the one who warned me."

His face hardened. "Why the hell would I want to blow up my own home?"

"Probably because you knew that Gideon would be going there to search it, sooner or later. Maybe you were afraid there was some evidence that you'd left behind, and you needed to be sure all of that evidence was blown to hell and back."

"Evidence..." He rocked back on his heels. "Evidence of what?"

"Maybe evidence of the time you murdered your brother."

*"He wasn't my brother."*

The rage had finally cracked through Jake's careful control. She could see it now, and she knew...

*Gideon had been right about him.*

"Braden did survive that night, didn't he?" *Get him to confess.* Wasn't that what she'd wanted Braden to do all those years ago? But she'd messed up. Been alone. He'd attacked. *I won't mess up this time.* "Braden made it to your place. When you got home, the door was unlocked. Water *was* inside. So was blood."

He glared at her. For a heart-stopping moment, Aspen thought he'd deny her words, thought that she was going to lose him—

"Yeah, the fucker survived. He came to me, ranting about you, saying that he was going to find you. Going to choke the life out of you. He'd already choked you once that night. Choked you, broken your arm. Braden thought he was going after you again. He planned to make you suffer. I couldn't let him do that." A shrug. "So I killed him."

She swayed. *"How?"*

"Well, he already had one stab wound. I figured I'd give him a few more. Funny thing, though, once I started stabbing him, I guess I got into it." He smiled at her. An utterly chilling smile. "By the time I was done, I can't remember how many times I'd stabbed him."

*OhmyGod.*

"Took him back out into the Gulf. Way out. Weighed him down. Made sure that he'd never come back from that watery grave." He paused. "You're welcome."

"You...you honestly want me to thank you?"

"I *saved* you!"

"You saved yourself. You wanted Braden out of the way, and you saw your chance. So you took it."

An inclination of his head. "Fine. That, too."

She side-stepped. It was time for this scene to end.

But he moved with her. "Where do you think you're going?"

"I want you to leave."

He shook his head. "No."

Yes, not exactly an unexpected response but...

"I've waited too fucking long for you, Aspen. I'm *done* waiting."

Her heartbeat accelerated even more. "I don't know what you're talking about."

But his smile stretched. "Yes, you do. You know I've been in love with you for years. Everyone knew. Even your dad. Couldn't believe it when he told me to stay away from you. When he said that I wasn't good enough, that I was *dangerous*."

Her pounding heartbeat filled her ears. "Please," a hoarse whisper. "Please tell me that you didn't..."

"I was driving the car." He said it proudly. Almost...with relish. "Braden paid me ten grand for the job. I was just starting with Frank's organization back then. I had to prove myself, can you believe that shit? I was his real son, but I had to prove myself by doing grunt work."

Her cheeks were prickling. Lights danced around the edge of her vision.

"They were barely paying me anything, and then Braden came along and said he'd give me ten grand for a hit. When I found out the target, hell, I was only too happy to oblige."

"You were happy to kill my dad?"

"He was in the way."

Her knees were shaking.

"Thought with him gone, you'd turn to me. I had always been there for you." His lips thinned. "Instead, fucking Ramsey swooped in and sent you out of town."

*I think Ramsey saved my life.*

"But he's not going to swoop in now, is he? Ramsey's gone all legit."

"No, he's not going to swoop in."

Jake edged even closer to her. "Ramsey sent you away, but you eventually came back. I thought you'd come back to me."

"I came back—" *To find the man who'd killed my father.*

"You came back and you hooked up with Braden. He was a monster, and you were falling for him. Hanging on to his every word."

She shook her head.

"But he turned on you, just like I knew he would. Braden always screwed up everything in his life, and when you were scared, when you were at your most desperate, you finally turned to me."

"I wasn't falling for him." Brittle. That was how the words emerged and how she felt.

"*Don't lie!* I saw you, I—"

"I was pretending. I had gotten word that he was responsible for my father's death, and I was looking for proof. For hard evidence that I could use to give to the cops." She stared straight into

Jake's bright gaze. "I never loved Braden. I never wanted him at all."

Jake began to smile once more. "Because you want me."

*No. Not even close.*

"Ramsey sent you away again after that."

"I went to law school. I wanted to help myself and to make sure that no one else ever ended up like—" She stopped. What was the point? He wouldn't understand Saul's life, and he damn sure didn't understand her.

"I followed you," Jake admitted.

She took a step back. Those words had *not* been expected. But maybe she should just get ready for the bombshells to keep dropping.

*Boom.*

"I saw you out with that prick at the bar. Laughing and talking and acting like nothing had ever happened back down here. Like your life was perfect, and I didn't exist. Like you could just move on."

"I was pretending," Aspen managed. But, oh, no...Surely, he wasn't talking about that terrible night with Ben? Except her gut said he was.

"I wasn't going to just let you go off with some rich asshole. Not when you belonged with me."

She swallowed. "So you put on a mask and you pretended to be robbing us. Only—you really just intended to shoot Ben all along, didn't you?"

"That his name? Ben?" A laugh. "Never bothered to find out. Not after you *jumped in front of him.* Dammit, Aspen! That scared the hell out of me. You could have died!"

"Because you shot me!" she shouted back. "My God, Jake, who the hell are you?"

\*\*\*

"Yeah, that's fucking enough," Gideon whispered into his comm link. "I'm going in!"

"No, dammit, stay where you are!" Elijah barked at him. "I've got eyes on her. He does not have any weapon out, and the guy is freaking spilling every secret that he has. You want this nightmare to end for her?"

Hell, yes, he did.

"Then you stay in position. If there is a threat, you can break the door down and rush inside. But I've got Jake in my sights, and this is what we needed, remember? This is the whole plan that you and Aspen created!"

Yes, but it was a plan that he didn't like, not one bit. After the house on the water had exploded, they had traced the call and text to Jake's phone. After that, it had been a matter of just putting the pieces together.

Jake's home had been blown to bits. Any evidence inside had been destroyed. Proving his guilt in an old murder would be nearly impossible. Unless...

Unless they got him to confess.

Gideon had bruises and scrapes all along his body. When Aspen had yelled for him, he'd turned and immediately thrown his body on top of hers. It had been an instinctive move. She'd been terrified, so he'd wanted to protect her. Protecting her had saved both of their asses because they'd tumbled down the stairs that led up to the house even as it had exploded.

They'd survived, but Gideon had known they had to take control of the situation. Luckily, they had just the right connections to do the job. And just the right people had been pulled into the case.

War had gotten his wife Rose to help spread the story on the news about the explosion.

Detective Melissa Wright had been used to inform Jake of the explosion. It had taken a bit of convincing to get her on board, but Ramsey had been able to use his connections to gain her cooperation, courtesy of her chief.

Then Elijah and War had wired Aspen. She was the bait inside, seemingly alone, while Gideon supposedly rested in a hospital bed far from her.

In truth, he was in the closed study just steps away from her and Jake. Gideon's gun was in his hand. He'd heard every single word that Jake had uttered and the fury and fear Gideon felt had grown.

They had more than enough to bury the bastard. There was no need to risk Aspen even a second longer.

"Gideon, calm your ass down. I get that you're not exactly rational where she's concerned, but she is fine. We need this."

He needed her. Fuck it. He reached for the doorknob—

"I'm the man who will do anything for you," Jake snarled. His voice blasted so clearly. "The only man who loves you. The only—"

Gideon yanked open the door. "Yeah, about that..."

Jake whirled toward him.

"You're not the only one who loves her. *I* love her. And guess what, asshole? She loves me, too."

Jake gaped at him. "But...but..."

*"Fuck,"* Elijah swore in Gideon's ear. *"You couldn't just wait one more minute?"*

"The little explosion missed me." Gideon aimed his weapon right at Jake. "Better luck next time."

"No!" Jake roared. All semblance of control was gone. Gideon knew he was staring straight at a very, very dangerous beast.

"Aspen, back the hell away," Gideon told her. *"Now."* He didn't want her running toward him. If she did that, Jake would grab for her.

She needed to head the opposite way. *Away* from the SOB.

And she did. Aspen shot back across the room, heading toward the fireplace.

Jake whirled toward her. "Aspen!"

"It's over!" she shouted back at him. Then she yanked out the wire from beneath her shirt. "I got everything you said. I *am* going to the cops, and you're going to be locked away. You will not hurt anyone else ever again."

Jake's shoulders rose and fell. His fingers began reaching inside the big, black coat that he wore.

Gideon took a step forward. "Don't try it. I don't know what you have in that coat, and I don't care. I will shoot you before you can even touch a weapon."

Jake spun back to him. "You think you'll take her away from me?"

"I think Aspen gets to decide who the hell she wants in her life, and, spoiler alert, it's not going to be some freak who killed her dad."

Jake's face mottled with fury. "He wanted me away from her!"

"Right. Because Saul obviously knew his shit. You weren't good enough for Aspen back then, and you damn sure aren't now."

"And you are? You think you're some prince charming?"

"No, I understand that I'm not perfect. But I will do everything I can to protect her. That's the difference between us. You want to destroy her life, and I want to make sure she is surrounded by people who love her and support her, and I want her happy. With you gone, she will be happy again."

Jake shook his head. "I'm not leaving Aspen."

"Not like you have a choice," Aspen chimed in to say.

Jake's hand was still close to the edge of his coat. "Frank wanted me away from you, too. Always said your connection to Ramsey made you too dangerous to him. Frank kept me away, and when he passed, I knew it was time to get you back."

"You mean you knew it was time you started stalking her again," Gideon summed up. "And you thought that if you used the ghost of Braden to creep her out, she'd turn to you. *Wrong*."

Jake glared at him. "You're just some asshole agent she brought in. She doesn't care about you. If you were listening, you heard her say how good she is at pretending. She *doesn't* love you."

"Cute. Nice try—"

"I can make you a wealthy man. I have more power than you can imagine. Just put down the gun and walk away. You don't have a future with Aspen. She'll dump you so fast. Take the money. Take—"

"I'll take my chances with her, thanks. Because she's worth more money than you could ever get."

Aspen sucked in a sharp breath. "Gideon, I love you."

And that was it. Those words—they shattered what was left of Jake's restraint. With a guttural yell, he launched straight at Gideon.

Gideon fired.

# CHAPTER TWENTY

The thunder of the gunshot seemed to echo in Aspen's ears. As she stared in horror, Jake's body stiffened, but he didn't stop his attack. He slammed into Gideon, and they both hit the floor in a tangle of limbs.

They were fighting for the gun. She knew if Jake got it, he would kill Gideon.

She grabbed a poker from the fireplace. "Stop!" Aspen ran forward and swung the poker at Jake's back. She hit him once.

*My dad...on the side of the road. Bleeding and staring at me with pain-filled eyes.*

Jake shouted in fury.

She hit him again.

*The chandelier falling. Broken glass all over the floor...broken, like...me?*

Jake surged off Gideon and whirled toward her. He caught the poker in one hand. "You bitch!"

She saw his fury. His hate.

He wrenched the poker from her hold. Turned the sharp end toward her. "I would have given you the whole damn world."

She backed up. Too late. He was shoving that poker toward her, and she knew he was going to impale—

*Bam. Bam.* Two fast shots. Aspen screamed and dropped to her knees.

And when she looked back up, Jake was swaying. Then falling.

"I had to do it." Gideon's grim voice. "I tried to just give him a flesh wound before, tried to slow him down, but he was going to kill you. *I had to do it.*"

She saw exactly what he meant. Blood was already pooling beneath Jake's body. He was jerking. Twitching.

Dying.

His head turned toward her. "Asp..." He reached out to her.

She stared at his hand. He would have used that hand to kill her. "It took my father over eight hours to die." She looked at the pool of blood once more. "I don't think it will take you that long."

The front door crashed in. Her head whipped up. Elijah and War burst inside.

"Call an ambulance," Gideon ordered.

"Already did it," War confirmed. He hurried in. Took in the scene. "It's not gonna do much good."

No, it wasn't.

Gideon dropped beside Jake. "Any last words?"

"She'll...leave...y-you..."

Then he didn't speak again. Gideon and War did try to help him. Aspen watched, numb, as they attempted to save the man who'd wanted to kill both her and Gideon moments before. But there truly wasn't anything to be done.

When the ambulance arrived, they were still working on Jake.

"Aspen." Elijah's careful voice. "The cops are waiting."

Yes, she was sure that they were...

\*\*\*

"Well, this is sure as shit a legal nightmare." Detective Melissa Wright sat across the interrogation room table from Aspen and glowered. "What the hell am I even supposed to charge you with?"

Aspen sat in the wobbly chair and stared back at the other woman. "I don't think you are supposed to ask me that question."

"No. Probably not. But this whole thing is a major cluster. I got the deceased on tape saying he killed Braden Savage—that he freaking stabbed him again and again—*after* Savage survived a stabbing by you. Which, by the way, the deceased also confirmed happened only *after* Savage strangled you." A huff of breath. "You should have come to the cops back then."

So she'd been told.

"Now Braden Savage's body is long gone. Probably shark food. There is no evidence that can confirm his attack on you or your attack on him—except the final words of Jake Eros, and that guy was a real piece of work." She whistled. "You know, Jake had Frank Savage's widow committed to Shadow Pines."

Aspen didn't let her expression alter. "I was not aware of that fact."

"No? Your Trouble for Hire buddies dug that up."

She'd been at the police station for hours, so whatever they'd dug up, Aspen hadn't been told, until now.

"She thought Jake had killed Frank. She was shouting it to everyone who would listen, so he shipped her off to Shadow Pines." A pause. "Kinda surprised he didn't just kill her."

Aspen was surprised, too, but she also thought...*Being in Shadow Pines may just be worse than death for a rich socialite like Virginia Savage.* Frank had married Virginia when he'd just been eighteen. Her father's cash had given him the power to build his empire. Frank had stayed with Virginia, even as he'd stepped out on her again and again. And as she'd stepped out on him. *It was because of Virginia and her family's ties that Frank always claimed Braden and not Jake.*

Melissa was still staring hard at Aspen. Aspen realized she was supposed to respond. "Maybe he thought Virginia's death would look too suspicious, especially after Frank's." The fact that she was at Shadow Pines...well, that explained why the Dodge Charger had been stolen from that location. "Something tells me Jake paid a recent visit to see Mrs. Savage."

"Guessing you're referring to the fact that a certain vehicle was stolen from that place? Yes, I heard about that, too." Melissa pointed at her. "You and your boyfriend were almost killed by that stolen car. I can't help but think that you are one lucky woman."

"That's certainly one way of looking at things." She glanced toward the one-way mirror on the right.

Melissa sighed. "No one is in there. This little talk is off the record."

Aspen arched a brow as she focused on the detective. "That's not your usual style."

"This is hardly my usual case. On top of everything else, I've got the chief having a conniption about this and even the DA is wanting this mess to all disappear." Her lips tightened. "I'm betting your buddy Ramsey is behind that, huh? We both know how much power he wields in this town, and no way is he gonna have you sitting in a cell. Must be awful nice to have such powerful friends."

"I don't know what you're talking about with regard to Ramsey. He is certainly not pressuring anyone on my behalf." She didn't *think* he was.

Melissa snorted. "Right."

"I told you everything that happened on the boat with Braden Savage. I told you everything that happened in my house with Jake Eros. Either you choose to charge me or you don't. I'm not relying on favors from friends."

Melissa leaned forward. "Did you know it would work out this way?"

"Excuse me?"

"Come on. I heard it all. Jake killed your dad. You went after Braden all those years ago because you wanted vengeance on the man who murdered your father. When you found out Jake was the one driving the car, you had to want to hurt him."

Yes, she had wanted to hurt him.

"Gideon's first shot was non-lethal. He was subduing Jake."

"After that shot, Jake kept attacking him," Aspen pointed out even as she felt sweat dampen her palms. "Jake was trying to take the gun from Gideon."

"Then *you* jumped in with the poker. Got in two solid hits from what I hear. Only then, Jake took the poker from you. He was charging at you. In order to save you, Gideon had to kill Jake. There wasn't any non-lethal firing option any longer."

"That sounds like a fair summary."

Melissa leaned forward a bit more. Dropped her voice even lower. "You knew Gideon would do anything to save you, didn't you? So when that first shot didn't kill Jake, you knew you had to get Gideon to fire again. You deliberately let that poker go, didn't you? You let Jake take it, and then you just stepped back and you waited for Gideon to kill for you."

Aspen could hear the ticking of the clock on the wall. It seemed incredibly loud.

"Not that I will ever be able to prove that," Melissa continued with a disgusted shake of her head. "But since it's just us girls in here, I thought I'd ask." She shrugged. "Jake's guard Rodney admitted he stabbed his boss in the alley near your office. And Jake had another flunky use the Charger in the attack on you and Gideon. That guy is down the hall, asking for a deal."

Aspen gazed steadily at the detective.

"Jake was a twisted bastard, and he tried to destroy you. I get why you wanted him dead. I get why you used the boyfriend to do the job. Got to say, if I had been in your shoes, I might have done the same thing."

"Just us girls." Aspen smiled as weariness swept through her. "Detective, I've always thought you had a weak interrogation game. You should work on it a bit more. Otherwise, you're solid. Great investigative skills. Strong dedication to the job. And the press even likes you."

Melissa leaned back. "It was worth a shot."

"Not really." She truly felt bone tired. "But you should know one thing. I wouldn't use Gideon Ranier. He's not some weapon. He's the man who has been there for me no matter what happened. I trust him completely, and I'm hoping to spend the rest of my life with him. Provided, of course, that I'm not behind bars."

Melissa unnecessarily shuffled some nearby papers. "Something tells me he'd wait for your crazy ass."

Maybe. She hoped.

"No charges are being filed against you. The DA sent word on that an hour ago."

Seriously?

Melissa rose. "No hard evidence, and the DA said any jury in the world would side with you. You know how to play them, and they'd feel so much sympathy for your story that they'd acquit with jury nullification or some other crap."

Aspen wouldn't let her shoulders sag in relief.

Melissa headed for the door. Stopped. "So...your buddy Ramsey is out of the game. As you keep saying, he's all legit now. Both Jake Eros *and* Frank Savage are dead." She looked back.

"Who do you think is going to take over the power vacuum in this town?"

The door swung open before Aspen could respond. Darius filled the doorway. "All right now," he snapped as he glowered at the detective and his massive shoulders brushed against the door frame. "It's been long enough. Time for you to let Asp go."

She inhaled. Rose to her feet. As she walked past Melissa, Aspen murmured. "A power vacuum, you say? I have no idea who will take over."

\*\*\*

Melissa Wright tried not to let the image of Darius Addams and Aspen Gray linger in her mind. She absolutely would *not* think about Darius right then. Or the past they shared—a past that was better off forgotten.

She swung open the door to the second interrogation room. Gideon Ranier sprawled casually in the chair near the table. No one would guess he'd been waiting there for hours.

"Do I need a lawyer?" Gideon asked. Not that he sounded concerned. More like vaguely interested.

"I'm sure you have a lawyer on retainer, but, no, you don't need her." She kept the door open. "You're free to go. Though, of course, there may be follow-up questions."

He stood. Tall and dangerous. Yes, she could see where Aspen *might* be attracted to the guy. She still didn't know if Aspen had been using him or if it was the real deal. She'd probably never know, but...

Melissa stretched out her arm to stop Gideon from leaving the room.

"Detective?"

"Have you considered that she arranged for you to kill him? That she *gave* Jake Eros that poker, knowing he'd attack with it and that you'd have to stop him?"

He stared at her.

Melissa knew he wouldn't answer her. "Just some food for thought," she murmured. "Aspen Gray is a very smart woman, and when it comes to crime, she knows how to get away with murder."

Gideon didn't blink. "Where is Aspen?"

"She left a few minutes ago...with her good friend Darius." She dropped her arm. "You know Darius, don't you? He was Ramsey's first-in-command, a man with a very long criminal past and—"

"Yes, I know Darius." Gideon strode past her. "He's not her good friend."

"No? Sure looked that way to me."

"He's her brother."

Her what? "But—"

Gideon was already gone.

*He's her brother.* Well, that was certainly news to Melissa.

\*\*\*

Gideon found her on the beach. *Her* beach. The beach she'd taken him to when she finally wanted to let him in on her secrets. She stood near the edge of the shore as the sun set, and the waves rose up to brush across her bare toes.

He approached her slowly, just wanting to take in the sight of her. So gorgeous. Everything that he'd ever wanted.

"I didn't mean for you to kill him." Quiet. She'd known he was there. She kept staring out at the water. "I don't care what the detective said—and I'm sure she ran to you with her story—but that wasn't my plan. If anything, I was ready to kill him with that poker because I was afraid he'd get the gun from you. That he'd shoot *you*."

Gideon moved to stand beside her so that they could both stare out at the waves. "I know."

Her breath expelled. "I love you."

He smiled. "I know that, too." He kept looking at the water, but he reached for her hand. His fingers threaded with hers. "You get that I love you?"

"I think you might be better off without me." Small. Quiet.

Gideon shook his head. "Nah, that shit would never happen." Now he turned toward her. Found her looking at him with those incredible eyes that had stolen his soul from the first day. "Guess what?"

Her eyebrows lifted.

"I found out where I belong."

"Gideon?"

"Told you before I was trying to figure out where I fit. I know now. It's right here. On the beach. With you." He considered it. "Screw the beach. It's just with you. I belong wherever you are."

"I'm not a good person."

"Fuck that. You are good. You're good and smart and strong. You're also the woman I love, and I *know* how special you are."

"*You* are good," she told him. "And you deserve someone like—"

He kissed her. Savored her sweet lips and her delicious taste. "Someone like you?"

"Gideon."

"We'll work out the living arrangement logistics later. Not expecting you to move to Atlanta, and I have to say, I do love the beaches here. Think I might just have to relocate, though Eric will be pissed if I leave Wilde and sign up with Trouble for Hire."

The wind tossed her hair as the waves crashed into their feet. "Are you sure you know what you're doing? What if this is a mistake?"

Gideon shook his head. "Thought we already agreed...I'm the best mistake you'll ever make."

"Gideon!"

His smile flashed. "I love you, Aspen. I loved you before I knew all of your secrets. I loved you *even more* after I learned them."

Her lower lip trembled. "I love you. I will love you for the rest of my life, and I do want to spend that life with you."

"Be careful, sweetheart, that sounds *almost* like a marriage proposal."

"I'd marry you in a heartbeat."

He froze. "Are you serious?"

A nod.

He scooped her into his arms and spun her around. "*I love you!* And we are getting married right away." Another spin. "Today, if we can. There is no way Ramsey and Darius can't make that happen."

She laughed. "Today?"

Gideon tightened his hold on her. "I want forever."

"So do I."

Then that was exactly what they were going to get.

He kissed her again. It felt so right...when you finally found where you belonged.

## THE END

# A NOTE FROM THE AUTHOR

Thank you so much for reading PRETEND YOU WANT ME! I hope you enjoyed Gideon and Aspen's story. This book was really special for me because it gave me the chance to do a cross-over with the "Wilde Ways" books and the "Trouble for Hire" series. I thought it was time for these two worlds to collide, and Aspen was just the woman to make that collision happen!

I love writing books that merge suspense, romance, and humor. And having a guaranteed happy ending at the end of the story? I like to think that is the best part.

If you'd like to stay updated on my releases and sales, please join my newsletter list.

*https://cynthiaeden.com/newsletter/*

Again, thank you for reading PRETEND YOU WANT ME.

Best,
Cynthia Eden
*cynthiaeden.com*

# ABOUT THE AUTHOR

Cynthia Eden is a *New York Times*, *USA Today*, *Digital Book World*, and *IndieReader* best-seller.

Cynthia writes sexy tales of contemporary romance, romantic suspense, and paranormal romance. Since she began writing full-time in 2005, Cynthia has written over one hundred novels and novellas.

Cynthia lives along the Alabama Gulf Coast. She loves romance novels, horror movies, and chocolate.

**For More Information**

- *cynthiaeden.com*
- *facebook.com/cynthiaedenfanpage*

# HER OTHER WORKS

**Trouble For Hire**

- No Escape From War (Book 1)
- Don't Play With Odin (Book 2)
- Jinx, You're It (Book 3)
- Remember Ramsey (Book 4)

**Death and Moonlight Mystery**

- Step Into My Web (Book 1)
- Save Me From The Dark (Book 2)

**Wilde Ways**

- Protecting Piper (Book 1)
- Guarding Gwen (Book 2)
- Before Ben (Book 3)
- The Heart You Break (Book 4)
- Fighting For Her (Book 5)
- Ghost Of A Chance (Book 6)
- Crossing The Line (Book 7)
- Counting On Cole (Book 8)
- Chase After Me (Book 9)
- Say I Do (Book 10)
- Roman Will Fall (Book 11)
- The One Who Got Away (Book 12)
- Pretend You Want Me (Book 13)

**Dark Sins**

- Don't Trust A Killer (Book 1)

- Don't Love A Liar (Book 2)

**Lazarus Rising**

- Never Let Go (Book One)
- Keep Me Close (Book Two)
- Stay With Me (Book Three)
- Run To Me (Book Four)
- Lie Close To Me (Book Five)
- Hold On Tight (Book Six)
- Lazarus Rising Volume One (Books 1 to 3)
- Lazarus Rising Volume Two (Books 4 to 6)

**Dark Obsession Series**

- Watch Me (Book 1)
- Want Me (Book 2)
- Need Me (Book 3)
- Beware Of Me (Book 4)
- Only For Me (Books 1 to 4)

**Mine Series**

- Mine To Take (Book 1)
- Mine To Keep (Book 2)
- Mine To Hold (Book 3)
- Mine To Crave (Book 4)
- Mine To Have (Book 5)
- Mine To Protect (Book 6)
- Mine Box Set Volume 1 (Books 1-3)
- Mine Box Set Volume 2 (Books 4-6)

**Bad Things**

- The Devil In Disguise (Book 1)
- On The Prowl (Book 2)

- Undead Or Alive (Book 3)
- Broken Angel (Book 4)
- Heart Of Stone (Book 5)
- Tempted By Fate (Book 6)
- Wicked And Wild (Book 7)
- Saint Or Sinner (Book 8)
- Bad Things Volume One (Books 1 to 3)
- Bad Things Volume Two (Books 4 to 6)
- Bad Things Deluxe Box Set (Books 1 to 6)

## Bite Series

- Forbidden Bite (Bite Book 1)
- Mating Bite (Bite Book 2)

## Blood and Moonlight Series

- Bite The Dust (Book 1)
- Better Off Undead (Book 2)
- Bitter Blood (Book 3)
- Blood and Moonlight (The Complete Series)

## Purgatory Series

- The Wolf Within (Book 1)
- Marked By The Vampire (Book 2)
- Charming The Beast (Book 3)
- Deal with the Devil (Book 4)
- The Beasts Inside (Books 1 to 4)

## Bound Series

- Bound By Blood (Book 1)
- Bound In Darkness (Book 2)
- Bound In Sin (Book 3)
- Bound By The Night (Book 4)

- Bound in Death (Book 5)
- Forever Bound (Books 1 to 4)

## Stand-Alone Romantic Suspense

- Never Gonna Happen
- One Hot Holiday
- Secret Admirer
- First Taste of Darkness
- Sinful Secrets
- Until Death
- Christmas With A Spy

71323632R00162